Adrian GRIGORE

RED ALERT FOR ROMANIA

RED ALERT FOR ROMANIA

Adrian GRIGORE

Translated by *Alina Maria GRIGORE*

Preface by *Prof. Ioana GRIGORE VARGA*

BOOKSIDE Press

RED ALERT FOR ROMANIA
The second edition- revised and supplemented

Copyright © 2024 by Adrian Grigore

ISBN: 978-1-77883-542-1 (Paperback)

All rights reserved. No part of this publication may be reproduced, distributed, or transmitted in any form or by any means, including photocopying, recording, or other electronic or mechanical methods, without the prior written permission of the publisher, except in the case brief quotations embodied in critical reviews and other noncommercial uses permitted by copyright law.

The views expressed in this book are solely those of the author and do not necessarily reflect the views of the publisher, and the publisher hereby disclaims any responsibility for them.

BookSide Press
877-741-8091
www.booksidepress.com
orders@booksidepress.com

In memory of the colleagues and friends from Seismology who left on the road of eternity.

"We often think that the things we have forgotten were never."
                                            Nicolae Iorga

"Those who forget the past are condemned to repeat it."
                                              George Santayana

About the Author

Adrian Grigore was born on July 8, 1956 in Humele, Argeș county, Romania, being the third of the six children of the priest Gheorghe and Floarea Grigore's family. As a child, during the summer vacations, he wandered with his friends through the legendary forests of the Teleorman River Valley, which would inspire him in his later books.

Even since childhood, he was very fond of history and wanted to become an archaeologist. Since his father was an Orthodox priest, the Romanian communist authorities forbade him to attend the Faculty of History, which was, at that time, an educational institution for the future Communist Party activists only.

He graduated the Faculty of Electronics in Bucharest and, starting from 1977, he worked for Romanian Seismic Network. The political persecution continued and he was forbidden to travel to USA for a training in the field of seismic equipment.

After the political changes in Romania in December 1989, he was finally able to move freely and participated in many expeditions of geophysical investigations of nuclear and mining sites, especially on the Scandinavian countries and Canada.

However, Adrian Grigore considers that his most outstanding professional achievement is the construction and maintenance of the Seismic ARRAY in Bucovina – Romania, in collaboration with ***Air Force Technical Application Center (AFTAC) – Patrick Air Force Base – FL, USA***. It was a good opportunity for him to travel several times to the USA, especially to Florida, where he made many friends.

Literature was and remains a wonderful world that has attracted Adrian Grigore since his childhood. His first important novel, ***Traga Şerpilor***, is a historical one, and is inspired by the adventures of outlaws from the forests of Teleorman Valley. It was published in 1998 by *Albatros Publishing House - Bucharest* and enjoyed a great appreciation of the Romanians readers and literary magazines. ***The Dragons' Trail***, the English version, will be published on 2025.

Inspired by the hard life of the Romanians under the communist regime as well as by the hidden confrontation during the Cold War, he wrote the novel ***Alertă Maximă***, which he published in 2001 by the same *Albatros Publishing House – Bucharest*. The English version called ***Red Alert for Romania*** was recently published in the USA by *iUniverse*. This second edition published by *Bookside Press* is revised and supplemented by the author.

Adrian Grigore published in 2003 the novel ***Ultima Iarnă (The Last Winter),*** which is a dramatic story about the precarious existence of a Romanian researcher, both under the Communist dictatorship of Nicolae Ceausescu and in the painful transition towards democracy and the market economy that followed the anti-communist Revolution of December 1989. This novel was very appreciated and published in English in three editions so far, having a review in ***New York Time Magazine*** *(June 18, 2023).*

In 2018 Adrian Grigore published at *ePublishers - Bucharest* the novel ***Cercetător între veacuri (Researcher Between the Ages),*** inspired by the concern of researchers to preserve properly the most important scientific and technical treasure of Humanity.

Adrian Grigore's literary mentor was and remains the distinguished **Professor Dr. Silviu ANGELESCU** from the *University of Bucharest*, to whom the author has great respect and to whom he especially thanks for his precious advice and guidance. Adrian Grigore's most demanding literary critic is his wife, the **Philologist Dr. Valerica GRIGORE**, from whom the author learned many things about the Theory of Literature and to whom he is grateful.

> For more details, please visit:
> **www.adrian-grigore.com**

PREFACE

Under the guise of a detective novel, in which the adventure occupies a generous space, Adrian Grigore's novel ***Red Alert for Romania*** brings up to date the life of Romanians in the last period of communism, namely Ceaușescu's dictatorship, a period that we tend to forget too quickly, and, unfortunately, the young people don't know it anymore. The mottos that preface the novel draw our attention to the author's intention: *"We often think that the things we have forgotten were never there."* (**Nicolae IORGA**) / *"Those who forget the past are condemned to repeat it."* (**George SANTAYANA**).

As a structure, the novel follows the scheme of a *"seductive adventure novel, built according to all the rules of the genre… But the adventure, although captivating, is only a pretext that motivates the incursion into a sick world – Romania during the last period of communist dictatorship."* (**Prof. Silviu Angelescu** – University of Bucharest**)**.

The narrative is structured into a succession of apparently independent scenes aiming, in parallel, at the technological competition, the Space Race, between the United States and the Soviet Union, in the prolongation of the Cold War. The protagonists' actions revolve around the imminent collapse of a Soviet satellite, whose atomic batteries for powering the electronic systems would have produced upon impact with the Earth, a disaster hard to imagine. The American and the Soviet estimates indicated the place of impact in Romania-the mountains in Dobrogea, near the Danube Delta. This gives the novel its detective substance; the Americans, the Soviets, and the Jews (through General Pleșca, the head of the Romanian Securitate- the communist political police) spy on each other and launch themselves into a race against the clock to recover the indestructible *code module* of this satellite, containing valuable military information.

Radioactive contamination of a large area of land that the collapse of this satellite would have produced is ignored. The focus is on the military information from the *code module,* which had to be recovered by the Soviets, respectively, captured by their rivals. Each act in their characteristic style, engaging specific forces and practices, with disaster remaining in the background. From these, defining elements for the environments in which they are produced shine through operativity, precision, rigor, suspicion, terror, degeneracy etc. An American scientist, Professor Eduard Gordon, is taken early morning by helicopter from home, against his will, and brought to a secret military base where he is asked to calculate the coordinates of the impact site as quickly as possible. He is forced to work under maximum security conditions and the strict command of General Alan King.

The staff of the Soviet Space Center is distraught by losing control of the satellite, a situation to which are added the contradictory and subversive orders of General Vladimir Ivanovici Petrovski, the special emissary of the USSR Security

Department, who wants to make an unnecessary and tendentious investigation into an alleged leakage of secret information. Igor Zapojnikov, Soviet Counterintelligence Colonel, goes through different career stages (from Senior Officer of URSS to the spy Rasputin, infiltrated into America undercover as the Jewish Soviet emigrant Alexei Leibovich), a path from ecstasy to agony.

The American espionage use students to infiltrate the universities in Eastern European Communist countries (Arab, Romanian or Bulgarian agents) and the Soviet espionage *racketzi*, who are former fighters in Afghanistan. Romanian Securitate is rounding up young people, preferably institutionalized, such as Ileana Popescu or Bebe Gold.

The sequences are assembled, like in a puzzle, giving coherence to the message. The action takes place against the background of a Romania mistreated by communism, with dictatorial sins and practices. The actors of the oppressive apparatus – the Communist Party, the Securitate, the dictator Ceaușescu - sacrifice, through starvation and deprivation, the very national being of the Romanians. Exploiting the apparent detachment towards the USSR, with aberrant ambitions of economic independence, against the backdrop of the starvation of his people, Ceaușescu dreams of becoming the leader of the Third World, using the country's resources for his purpose.

The State Securitate (General Virgil Pleșca, Major Alexe Marian etc.) is all-powerful and omnipresent: it monitors everything – listens to conversations, approves, or disapproves the *exits* of any person from the country, spies on embassies and even on its own agents. It's no wonder that General Pleșca considers himself the most powerful man in the country. The *"fight against imperialism"*, as well as *"the revolutionary vigilance"*, expressions that he often uses in his discussions with his subordinates, do not prevent him from getting drunk on Hennessy, *"the best cognac in the World, even if it comes from the imperialist system",* or from losing foreign currency in gambling at the *Stork's Nest* conspiratorial house. He does not hesitate to negotiate the possible capture of the *cod module* box for Israel, in return for some fabulous illicit pecuniary advantages, sending in action for this purpose a strong group of Securitate agents led by Bebe Gold.

Greedy for privileges, the Securitate orchestrates the *smoke screens* that envelop the messiness of people's daily lives - everyone's concern "*to put something on the family table for the children".* The permanent psychosis of Romanian citizens to find out where "*something is given*"; the queues for food are in blatant opposition to the lack of material care and the advantages of the privileged in the communist society.

The *cheese queue* is the emblematic image of the state of Romanian society in the last decade of the communist dictatorship. In the "*Citadel of Physics"*, as the official propaganda claims, different social categories coexist by party rule. It is a typical communist unfortunate social experiment, that gathered students, workers, peasants, physics researchers and valuable university professors in the same *queue*. The *communist roller* equalized people by the instinct of hunger; some were desperate to "*grab"* cheese, while others were resigned and disgusted.

The image of the two researchers who, standing in the *cheese queue,* discuss scientific problems and write formulas with chalk on the rusty board of the gate, while the peasants mock them and consider them crazy, speaks for itself about the condition of the Romanian scientist in such a society.

Rumors, waiting lists, overcrowding, shouting, unbearable heat, smoke from deliberately burning garbage, the swarm of aggressive flies swooping down on those crowding the queue, the foul-smelling brown whey spilled out in mockery by Jan, the grocer's boss, over the feet of the people, who begged him to bring for selling the hidden cheese, the swearing, roll in a grotesque uproar, like in a Hieronymus Bosch painting. Everything looks like a dark comedy, with amateur actors, in total contempt for the HUMANE.

Beyond the tensions between the confrontations of the espionage networks, the novel outlines a Romania brought to its knees by aberrant situations and decisions: lack of food, lack of fuel (even for ambulances!), the use of intellectuals (researchers) in the jobs of unskilled workers (sorting potatoes, watering crops in the field with a bucket and a mug, etc.) - all - as a tribute to the Party National Conference.

In all this whirlwind of spies, double agents, security guards and Communist Party activists, the Institute of Seismology in Romania is also automatically involved. The driver Gică and the electronics engineer George become, unwittingly, the protagonists of risky adventures. Honest characters, who do their duty professionally and seriously, facing the vicissitudes generated by the lack of technical means and the shortcomings of everyday life, physically face situations that put their lives in danger.

What stands out – and this is also the author's intention – is the absurd subordination of scientific activity to Communist Party commandments. The Director of the Institute of Seismology is obedient to the Securitate (Colonel Morar) and at the mercy of

Party activists who are people without much education, but well politically indoctrinated and rewarded with countless privileges.

The singular and feeble opposition of some researchers (the refusal to participate in the aberrant *"patriotic work"* or other stupid activities) is suffocated by political maneuvers: the refusal to grant visas for leaving the country for participation in scientific meetings, the non-granting of legitimate rights, etc. The professional competence of researchers like Stoian does not matter in front of Cătana, a turner who became an activist of the Party Branch, the technician Vasile, an undercover agent of the Securitate, who infiltrated the Institute of Seismology, the first secretary Gogea, a neighborhood communist propagandist who became the head of the Party Branch, a highly regarded political position.

The novel's epilogue takes us to Romania after the December 1989 Revolution, when the old communist customs, deeply rooted in the thinking of those who took over the leadership of the country, suffocated the fragile changes in society. The scams and contempt for the law will proliferate. Former communist activists and Securitate officers, retired or assimilated by the new Romanian secret services, are chameleonically adapting, quickly occupying the economic and political scene of society. Romania's long, painful and violent period of transition towards democracy and the market economy is borne with difficulty by the population.

In the Eastern European espionage world, the games are remade and partisan convulsions occur between former allies, where extreme means are used to eliminate inconveniences. The former head of the Securitate, General Pleșca, old and sick with cancer, is admitted to the Elias Hospital in Bucharest where attempts are being made to assassinate him. His adopted daughter Ileana, a former Securitate agent active in the USA, but self-exposed to the FBI, at her father's urging, rescues him spectacularly. She realizes that she needs a "*protective umbrella*", and decides to accept the offer of the American authorities to work for the newly established FBI office in Bucharest.

The dynamism of the action, the unadorned style, the snappy dialogue throughout the novel, make **Red Alert for Romania** an attractive and very accessible read. The author highlights the "*wooden language*" used by most characters and the stereotypes of the social actors of the times evoked. Beyond genre fiction, the novel can be considered a valuable document of the totalitarian communist era in Eastern Europe, which was an unfortunate social experiment and an accident of history, that Humanity must never repeat.

Ioana GRIGORE VARGA
Professor of Literature –
"Georg Daniel Teutsch" Gymnasium
Agnita, Sibiu county - ROMANIA

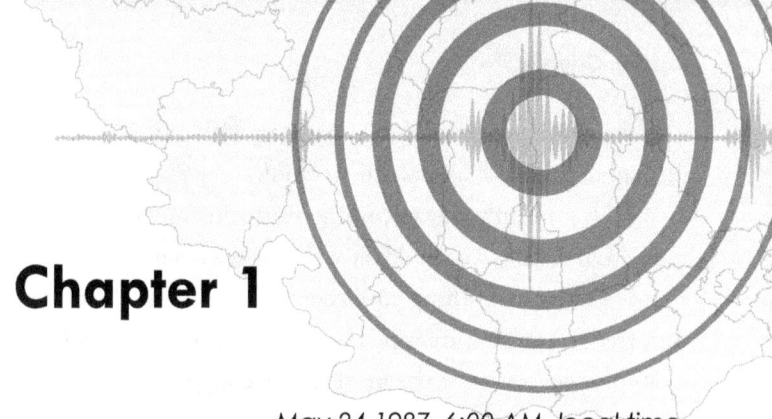

Chapter 1

May 24, 1987, 6:00 AM, local time
Somewhere on the Californian coast

The helicopter had taken off from Professor Eduard Gordon's property and was now flying like a giant dragonfly over the rocky shores of the Peninsula. Soon, the Professor saw only the Ocean's boundless expanse through the oval window, which reflected the rays of the morning sun.

Sitting next to the pilot, Captain Power motioned for Gordon to put his headphones on. The Professor did as he was encouraged to. An authoritative voice asked him to put on some goggles in transparent plastic wrap from a chair nearby. He thought they were meant for protection against ultraviolet rays, but he was wrong.

"For God's sake," he muttered, "these seem to be welding glasses. I can't see anything!"

"I'm sorry, but these are the instructions, Sir." the officer explained. "We'll fly over military bases…"

Mr. Gordon mumbled something in disapproval. The darkness he was immersed in annoyed him, so he decided to remove his headphones at least. The gesture irritated the officer who watched him through a rear-view mirror. He turned and put the Professor's headphones back on with a firm hand as if he had to deal with a disobedient child.

"It's the only way to communicate during the flight," he said. "Otherwise, we would have to yell at each other…"

"There is nothing to discuss, Captain!" the Professor retorted. "You've kidnapped and interrupted me from my scientific endeavors at the most inconvenient time. I've got a lot of work to do…"

"I understand you, Sir," the officer replied apologetically. "Indeed, time is precious. A single lost minute can lead to disaster, especially for us, soldiers. As for the alleged kidnapping… I've just carried out the orders. I'm not allowed to disclose anything. You can ask my superiors for further explanations. I've told you what I had to say."

"I will call my lawyer!" threatened Gordon. "After all, I'm a free citizen like any other."

"It's your right, Sir," the other cut him off, ending their discussion.

Professor Gordon knew that they were being tapped. Everything said in the helicopter cabin was recorded aboard and at the flight control center. He resigned with a sigh. Although he was shrouded in darkness, he could still glimpse the sunlight coming through the left window out of the corner of his eye.

He tried to figure out the direction they were flying in. Knowing the region like the palm of his hand, Gordon could guess the military base they would land at. But as the flight continued, he got worried. He had a bitter taste in his mouth. He didn't even have time to drink the glass of fresh-squeezed orange juice he had left on the desk because of his hasty departure. Soon the thirst almost obsessed him. He recalled a story once told by a geologist who boasted that he had resisted for several days in the torrid sun, on an isolated rock, with only a pair of binoculars and some fruits. It was a fabulous story because the geologist, as far as he remembered, seemed to be some Baron Munchausen of modern times.

One thing had had a great impression on him, though: if the geologist had managed to quench his thirst even for just a few hours, not to say days, that was proof of a kind of willpower he, Gordon, did not possess. The geologist's story stuck in his mind, but he wondered where and when he had heard it. Perhaps during a seismology symposium… but… where? Like a flashback, the geologist's flushed face beaming over the huge wooden casks full of wine came before Gordon's eyes.

"Vrancea… Romania!" he exclaimed, excited at remembering the wine tasting in the cellar beneath Odobeşti Hills.

"Did you say anything?" asked the officer turning to Gordon.

"Nothing," replied the Professor, a little embarrassed. His friends and close associates were used to him thinking out loud, but now he was amongst strangers.

Details from the seismology symposium after-party in Romania pierced his mind. The wine tasting hosted by a cheerful farmer from Vrancea county had taken place in a high vaulted cellar. The man told all sorts of anecdotes in a bizarre English accent about someone had ironically said is similar to the Oxford one. Gordon had also learned a few Romanian words then, which he unfortunately forgot. Yet, he still knew that *Noroc* meant *Cheers*. Whenever they raised their wine glasses and proposed a toast, the Romanians said the word *Noroc* almost in unison.

He said *Noroc!* out loud, and the officer turned his head again and asked if anything was wrong, but the Professor did not answer. He was still dwelling upon that time in Vrancea county and the story of the geologist who drank up several glasses of wine in the blinking of an eye as if he was still thirsty and needed to recover after his traumatic experience during the geophysical expedition.

Gordon let the deeper layers of his memory unfold, thus he could now see again the large framed photograph hanging on the wall behind the huge casks. It was the portrait of a smiling man. He asked if that person is the vineyard owner and he felt deeply embarrassed when he found out the man's identity in the photo: Nicolae Ceaușescu, the President of Romania. He apologized for not recognizing such an important political figure, adding wittily that the people whose leader watches them over even in their wine cellars cannot be anything but happy people.

This remark suddenly caused silence around him. His Romanian colleagues turned pale. He noticed that some were glancing anxiously at a sober, gray-haired gentleman in a blue suit, red tie, and sunglasses. The gentleman sat quietly aside and didn't seem interested in what the scientists were talking about. It was difficult to understand anything as there were simultaneous discussions in several languages, including the "*language of the wine*" as the host farmer put it.

The thirsty geologist approached him discreetly and whispered a few words into his ear. Gordon hadn't understood what the geologist said, but he suspected it was some remark about the gentleman in the red tie. The Professor had seen him listening intently to the presentations at the symposium every day, but he also noticed that the man didn't take part in any scientific discussion. Later, when everyone went out to admire the beautiful sunset from a terrace placed in the middle of the vineyard, the mysterious gentleman approached him, taking advantage of the fact that Professor Gordon was alone, far behind the others. He took off his sunglasses, carefully placing them in a leather case, then grabbed a glass of wine and said in an amiable tone:

"*Noroc*, Professor Gordon!"

"*Noroc*, Sir!" he replied, a little surprised that this gentleman didn't even care to introduce himself.

They clinked glasses like old friends, and the gentleman in the red tie asked him:

"What do you think of our wine, Professor Gordon? Do you like it?"

"Yeah, of course. It's great," Gordon replied with a smile. "The Vrancea wine is excellent. In general, Romanian wines are highly appreciated."

"I'm sure you've met many important people during your travels around the World. Do you know any businessman among your acquaintances who might be interested in buying our wine?"

Gordon apologized, saying that the wine business was not one of his preoccupations.

"We, Romanians, have many business ideas and we want to find serious partners for long-term effective collaborations," said the gentleman in a slightly reproachful tone. "We are creative and have considerable potential when it comes to natural resources: mountains, woods, hills with orchards and vineyards, plains with high agricultural production, the Danube Delta, the Black Sea. Our industry is competitive, especially the chemical industry and the steel one. Romania is the World's second-largest producer of steel per capita. We offer serious partnerships under mutually beneficial terms. Romania is the only socialist country that has an independent policy from Moscow. We didn't participate in the invasion of Czechoslovakia by the armies of the Treaty of Warsaw in August 1968. The President of Romania criticized in harsh terms this military intervention against an independent and sovereign state."

Gordon immediately understood that in front of him stood an officer from the Securitate, the Romanian political police. Perhaps he was trying to recruit him as an agent or to obtain some information.

"Indeed, I've noticed that Romanian scientists have fascinating ideas," Gordon said politely, wishing to change the subject. "The seismologists in your country presented a series of new concepts and research methods during this symposium. I think that their research and experiments will improve the prediction of earthquakes in Romania."

Hearing these words, the man looked around with professional caution. They were far from those admiring the sunset, but he still had to make sure there was no one around who could eavesdrop. He stared at Gordon with a peculiar gleam in his deep blue eyes and said in a low voice:

"You know, Professor Gordon, I am extremely interested in predicting the earthquakes occurring in Vrancea. It's my hobby. I have a kind of seismograph at home. It's rudimentary but rather sensitive. It begins to oscillate at the slightest vibration. I've made it by using a bottle of *Cico*. I suspended it from the bedroom ceiling with a piece of fishing line about one meter long."

"*Cico*? What's *Cico*?" asked Gordon puzzled.

"Well, it's a kind of… it's what *Coca-Cola* is in America!"

"Oh, I understand… It's a local soda."

"Exactly! But, you know, this one taste very good. It's made of ripe berries and it is highly recommended for children. They love it! I'm sure even you, the Americans, would enjoy *Cico*. We could export about a million bottles of *Cico* every month. If you want, we can promote together this refreshing drink on the American market. Please, note that we offer a generous bonus to the business intermediaries."

Gordon brought the discussion back to the realm of seismology.

"Well, I understand you've built an interesting device. I can say that it's quite similar to the seismic pendulums, which the Chinese made two thousand years ago for similar purposes," said Gordon a bit ironically.

By now, the man in the red tie gave up the soft drink business proposal, too, and focused on the topic of earthquakes.

"I have a parrot that senses the earthquakes before they happen," he said proudly.

"Well, that's interesting."

"Believe me, an hour before the destructive earthquake on March 4, 1977, my budgie had been very anxious. It flapped its wings madly and flew all over the cage hitting its beak against the bars. He wanted to fly out."

"Indeed, the unusual behavior of cage birds could be an important precursor to the short-term earthquake forecast," the Professor replied. He then added with a serene smile: "You have a hypersensitive budgie, sir! It does a better job than many seismologists. You have to pay close attention to it. Your budgie is a precious bird."

"However, I think we should use stray dogs to anticipate the earthquakes in Vrancea," the other continued enthusiastically. "Imagine, Professor, many hours before destructive earthquakes, they sit on their hind legs, sniffing the air and making some sinister sounds. It is a scary phenomenon, especially when it happens at night. I thought of a simple, but very effective predictive system, using a few stray dogs. We can put a bracelet with a microphone and a built-in transmitter around their neck. Then we release them in different places in the forests around the epicenter. The transmitter of each dog will be set on a certain radio channel and the radio reception will be done there, on the hill, where you can see that pole with antennas." He pointed towards the forested crests of Măgura Odobești. They could see the pole of a radio repeater against the red background of the sunset. "Imagine sinister howls being intercepted simultaneously from dogs in different places. The operator in charge of the receivers could report to us: *Pawn number one has been activated! Pawn number two has been activated!* and so on… Thus, we will be able to inform at once the state leadership to decide on the course of action needed in such a situation."

"Indeed, it's a great idea. Though it remains a matter of replacing the batteries of the emitters attached to the neck of the dogs," the Professor said with an ironical grin. "This should be done periodically. Otherwise, the dogs will most likely become wild and hard to catch"

"That wouldn't be a problem for **us**. **We** have solved more difficult cases…," he said proudly. It was easy to guess that *the red-tie man* enjoyed his job, which, most likely, consisted in monitoring of the Romanian citizens conversations, in order to investigate and punish those who had political opinions different from the official one.

"Why didn't you present this excellent idea at the earthquake prediction workshop?" Gordon asked with the typical naivety of a scientist.

"You know… I'm not a scientist… maybe next time," the other replied, slightly taken aback.

The conversation was cut short as a young man in a long leather coat and a cold, expressionless face came in a hurry. Without apologizing for interrupting them, he whispered something to the gentleman, who excused himself and walked away briskly.

The memories had absorbed Professor Gordon. He no longer cared for the direction the helicopter was flying in. He was increasingly thirsty, and recalling the Vrancea Symposium only sharpened this sensation. Soon he heard the pilot in his headphones asking for permission to land. Gordon heaved a sigh, relieved that this unpleasant journey in the dark was over, although he was still apprehensive not knowing what was to come.

* * *

May 24, 1987, 2:00 PM - local time
Moscow

Colonel Igor Vasilievich Zapojnikov was having tea while reading the Pravda newspaper in the living room. He had found something of particular interest, an eloquent article about the latest achievements of the Soviet scientists in conquering outer Space and their commitment to the future Congress of the Communist

Party of the Soviet Union. In a way, he felt like being a small part of these achievements. He had been working for the Soviet Space Center for more than ten years. He oversaw information protection and Counter- espionage. It wasn't an easy job. The Communist Party's confidence had compelled him to fulfill his duty with great conscientiousness. His moments of respite were a few.

Igor Vasilievich spent Sundays in Moscow with his family when he was not at the Space Center or investigating any leaked intelligence. Because he was rarely at home, his wife, Tania, handled all family matters. Their two daughters were teenagers now, and Igor already gave serious thought to their future. He wanted to guide them toward the exact sciences, but they were likely to follow their mother's profession, who was a dedicated piano teacher. Both girls received the grand prize at the *V.I. Lenin School Festival.* They were now preparing for an important competition organized in honor of the Communist Party Congress. Igor was proud of his daughters and tried to be with them for as long as possible whenever he got the chance.

The article in Pravda had completely absorbed him, and he hardly even noticed Tania placing a plate of cookies next to the samovar. His wife sat down in an armchair, and lit a cigarette. She stared at Igor for a long time before saying bitterly:

"Eh, Igor Vasilievich, are the news more interesting than your own wife whom you barely, see?"

Igor looked at her guiltily over the newspaper:

"I apologize, Taniucika, I have no excuse, but this is the commitment of our comrades from the Soviet Space Center. They want to launch two satellites in honor of the Congress, you know."

"Yes, interesting, very interesting," said Tania jeeringly. "This is your first Sunday with your family in more than a month, and we're finally home alone this afternoon," she added with a theatrical sigh.

"Where are the girls?" Igor asked, almost surprised.

"They are doing patriotic work ahead of the Congress. Their school decided to plant flowers in parks, and the girls won't return before seven. We could take advantage… Just the two of us alone…" she said, looking at him fondly.

Igor put the newspaper aside, removed his glasses, and stood up. He paced the room, glancing critically at his wife. She sat in the armchair in a provocative position. Her legs were bare well above the knees, and her red silk robe was intentionally unbuttoned to expose her massive breasts.

"Don't look at me like that, Igor Vasilievich," she sighed. "I know I am no longer young. I'm fat, and my boobs are larger than you prefer. I'm not comparing myself to your secretary Irina which was *planted* in your office and in the bed of your conspiratorial apartment, I'm sure."

"You have no right to talk like that, Tania," Igor cut her off. "My comrades told me all about your affair with that painter."

"We're just talking about art," she replied. "I don't know what you've been told, but nothing happened between us. When a woman speaks to a man, it doesn't mean they're having an affair."

"Yes, but you're not that kind of woman, Tania. Although you hid it, I know your past very well."

"Don't insult me, Igor Vasilievich! If you believe I'm a whore, why don't you divorce me?"

"The girls don't deserve this. Besides, it will ruin my file, and I'm comfortable enough, with or without your affairs." Nervously he lit a cigarette, pacing the room again.

The room seemed too narrow, the walls closed in on him, so he went out on the balcony. He leaned against the railing and inhaled the smoke, drawing it deep into his chest, looking down at the cars and people on the boulevard. Although it was Sunday, the city was full of life, like always. Several workers were hanging out red flags on the facades of the buildings. Preparations had already begun and the thought of the Congress made him relax. It would have been an important event for him. He hoped to be promoted to the rank of Major General. From up there, on the sixth floor, he watched everything that moved beneath him with a sense of superiority.

He took another drag on his cigarette and exhaled the smoke contemptuously. He seemed to be saying: "*What do you know? Soon I will be an even more important person. I will be General Zapojnikov.*" He looked at the walls of the Kremlin that could be seen in the distance, at the end of the boulevard. For a few moments, he imagined himself as the captain of a ship, and the walls of the Kremlin were the shore he had to sail to. He blew out the smoke in their direction, muttering:

"I have to get there one day…"

Tania joined him, shy as a cat. She hugged her husband tenderly, resting her head on his chest.

"I didn't mean to upset you," she said tearfully, "I didn't mean to upset you… Please, forgive me!"

Igor didn't seem to notice. He gazed at the Kremlin walls, still captivated.

"Forgive me!" Tania sobbed again. "Let's go in. If you don't want to make love to me, at least let me play something for you on the piano. I know you like it."

Igor snapped out of his trance and took Tania in his arms.

"Taniucika, you know what I'm thinking about?", he said suddenly changed. "The Communist Party took care of us. How many people would want to see the Kremlin from their balcony? We have this chance, this privilege. Look! Do you see how great it is? The Kremlin watch and defend the entire Soviet Union!"

Tania nodded but didn't say anything.

"Don't you see?" Igor went on in a conciliatory tone, embracing her. "We should be happy and grateful, not wasting our little time together arguing over petty matters." He looked at her gently and whispered: "Let's go into the bedroom, my dear… if we are alone…"

Tania didn't wait for another invitation. Overwhelmed with hope, she led the way, unbuttoning her robe as she went through the living room when the phone started ringing. Tania picked it up fearfully, her face going pale.

"It's for you, Igor," she said in dismay. "I believe it's an urgency again… Damn these urgencies!"

She recognized the voice at the end of the line. It was the same cold and categorical voice that always took Igor away from his family, sometimes for weeks, even in the middle of the night.

Igor put the receiver to his ear and listened intently to the given order.

"Yes, yes, comrade, I understand!" he said firmly and putt down the receiver a little nervous. He looked compassionately at his wife and gently sought to console her: "I'm sorry… I have to go… I hope to come back soon… They've already sent the car for me…"

"Damn this life!" stormed Tania. "I'm tired, Igor, I'm tired! I can't stand this kind of life anymore, believe me!"

Almost naked, she stuck her fingernails into her large breasts and burst into tears. Igor put on his military uniform, trying to ignore her. While he put on his tie, he went out on the balcony again. In the narrow parking lot in front of the building, his black Volga car had already arrived.

Before leaving, Igor stood silently in front of a framed picture in the living room for a few moments. It was the photograph of his father, an aviation officer with many decorations, who fell in the War of Liberation of his homeland. He took a martial position and saluted the portrait as he always did whenever he was called on a mission. He then hugged his wife, who was still crying and hiccupping, and dashed to the door.

Tania went out on the balcony to wave at him. After the car drove away, she rushed to the cupboard where she kept hidden her vodka bottle. She took a few sips and sat by the phone, pondering. Finally, she put the bottle aside, picked up the receiver, and dialed a number with trembling fingers.

"Hello, Tolea… Yes, he left. I'm alone again… I feel like going crazy… I'm not happy, Tolea… Yes, I understand… I promise you that… I will not refuse you… this time… I promise you…"

* * *

May 24, 1987, 6:45 AM - local time
US Space Monitoring Center

The helicopter landed, and the doors were opened only after the dust aroused by the propeller had dissipated. Finally, Professor Gordon was permitted to take off his glasses. The blinding sunlight forced him to shield his eyes with the hand as he came out of the helicopter on a small plateau bordered by rocks. The officer asked him to get on the rear seat of a convertible Jeep in which they were to continue their journey.

The driver, a red-haired guy with small, round sunglasses, was popping chewing gum and listening to music on the headphones connected to a Walkman clipped to his belt. Ignoring the two passengers in the car, he picked up a microphone from the dashboard and reported something briefly; then, he turned on the engine and spun the wheel, making more dust than the helicopter's propeller as he revved the Jeep.

The car entered a small gorge on the ridges of which was a high barbed wire fence. Gordon recognized the road. They were heading to the secret base he had worked for years ago, where every satellite in Space was monitored constantly.

When they arrived in front of a barrier, the driver hit the brakes, pulling the car with enviable precision near the video intercom. A female voice asked him to identify himself, but the driver took off his headphones and put them close to the intercom terminal for a few seconds. A cheerful *Okay* came through the speakers and the traffic light above the barrier turned green while the reflective arm rose, clearing the way. Gordon was surprised. It was for the first time when he came upon a system that used music as a passcode.

Soon, they reached the entrance to a tunnel. On the rocks above, huge satellite dishes seemed to defy the sky. The driver stopped the car and turned to the two passengers expectantly as if to say: "*Hey, you two, what are you waiting for?*"

The officer got out and shook the dust off his uniform ostentatiously. Professor Gordon, carrying his briefcase he never parted with, followed him to the gate. Two tall guys in black overalls checked them with metal detectors and looked carefully through the papers the Professor had in his briefcase.

"It's ridiculous to be checked in this primitive way," he muttered angrily. "This usually happened only at the airports in Communist countries."

Instead of answering, the officer smiled understandingly and beckoned the Professor to follow him.

"I do hope you acknowledge your contribution, Professor," he said reverently, stopping before a desk. "The access to the underground facilities is based on the digital signature program you have recommended." He asked him to sign with the pen suspended on a magnetic prop and added: "Your signature specimen is already stored in the central computer of the Security Service. Sign calmly, as any deviation of more than ten percent from the usual signature can trigger the alarm."

Once Professor Gordon gave his signature on the digital table, there was a beep, and the green light on the gate lit up as a mechanical arm opened the passage. Gordon went through a turnstile and stopped under a dome where the loud sound of ventilation could be heard. The captain followed him.

"I understand this is a security measure that has been introduced only recently," said the Professor, almost fascinated.

"Yes! Everyone with access here will soon have their signature specimen, fingerprints, and face image stored in the central computer. Establishing everyone's identity will be done automatically."

They started on a brightly lit corridor surveilled by security cameras, at the end of which they took the elevator and descended several floors.

***

May 24, 1987, 3:30 PM - local time
Military airport on the outskirts of Moscow

The Volga car carrying Colonel Zapojnikov sped onto the airport runway and stopped at the access ladder of a ready-to-fly *Antonov* military aircraft. On board, Igor found several senior officers from the Soviet Air Force Command. They were tense, their faces almost scared, and didn't look at him with too much sympathy. They were aware of his rank, of course. The Colonel greeted them and sat down in a seat at the back of the plane. One could see the activity on the runway through the portholes.

The car which had brought him was gone. Another vehicle with a blue rotating beacon stopped next to the plane. The wing covered the angle from which he was looking, so he couldn't see anything. A civilian dressed in a zipped-up anorak, with gray hair and smoky glasses, got on board. Without greeting anyone, he sat down in front of Igor.

The pilot announced the preparation for the take-off. When the aircraft started moving toward the end of the runway, Igor fastened his seat belt, still looking out the window. He tried to see the number on the car's license plate that had brought the mysterious civilian, but failed as the car had already left at high speed. Someone put their hand on his shoulder and a familiar voice whispered in his ear:

"Good day, Comrade Colonel!" It was Irina, his secretary.

"Where did you come from?!" Zapojnikov said, taken by surprise by her appearance.

"They called me. It's a special mission," Irina said and sat beside him, gracefully putting on her seat belt.

This short-haired young woman, with green eyes and an exaggeratedly short uniform, had something which invigorated the oppressive atmosphere inside the plane. Maybe his wife was right when she used to say that Irina put on airs and graces. But maybe Irina did it unconsciously due to her natural charm and naivety. Although she was only a secretary, perhaps she had a well-defined role in this mission, and Igor presumed she came together with the civilian in smoky glasses.

"Have you just got on board?" he asked.

"No. I've been in the cockpit," said Irina cheerfully. "The captain is my fiancé."

"So, you have a fiancé?!" Igor exclaimed, with a twinge of jealousy.

"Of course, I do," she chirped, batting her lashes.

They stopped talking as the noise of the engines increased. The aircraft accelerated along the runway and took off, shaking from all joints.

***

May 24, 1987, 7:00 AM - local time
US Space Monitoring Center

General Alan King, Commander of the Space Monitoring Center, was analyzing the recent information received through the network of operatives on a large color monitor covering an entire office wall. When he heard that Professor Gordon and Captain Power were already waiting in the anteroom, the General got up from the control desk and opened a safe hidden behind a fake wall. He took out a cardboard box containing a hyper-realistic silicone mask, which he put on carefully, and checked himself in a mirror. This was his *"public image"* as he used to call it. The General sat back at his desk in the black leather chair and pressed the intercom button:

"Send them in, Sergeant!" he said in an authoritative voice.

The armored door opened and Gordon came in a little shyly, almost pushed from behind by Captain Power. The officer greeted, reported the mission over, and remained in the standby position.

"Dismissed, Captain! Stay alert until further notice," the General said sternly. He held out his hand to the civilian with a cold smile saying: "Welcome to our *sweet home*, Doctor Gordon! Take a seat."

He pointed to a short-legged chair in front of his desk. Professor Gordon understood it symbolized his subordinate position as a guest so he refused to sit.

"General, it seems that you have forgotten the most basic rights of a citizen in a democratic state," he erupted, his face flushed red with indignation. "I was brought here against my will. Your agent basically kidnapped me. I've already told you and I'm telling you again: I can no longer work on military projects. My health does not allow me to work so hard, and then…" he trailed off a little confused. "I am a geophysicist; I have other concerns. I am working on a paper at the moment…"

"Doctor Gordon, my advice is not to get involved in dangerous games," the Commander warned him. "If you collaborate with *us*, you can only know the beginning. If there is an end, *we* will decide when and how that end should be."

"Is that a threat?"

"No. Just a friendly warning." He smiled coldly and added in a low tone: "***We*** are too strong, Doctor Gordon. ***We*** do not threaten scientists. Still, I don't understand one thing. Why do you refuse? By collaborating with ***us***, you could be financially secure for a long time."

"I prefer to remain what I am now: a free man with a modest income. A man who acts guided only by his conscience."

The General burst into forced laughter.

"You know you're a nice guy, Doctor Gordon. You have an arsenal of beautiful words meant to impress some naive people. Through God's grace, freedom is a gift, especially for those ignorant and poor in spirit. Things change when you are tempted to deal with many mysteries of knowledge. Both I and you know some things so we are as free as insects trapped in a jar. He typed a command on the computer keyboard and data about Gordon's family appeared on the large screen.

"I have the impression that you have been under the influence of pacifist propaganda lately," he added sternly. "You see, Professor? Information collected in recent months by our agents shows us that Janet, your wife, and your children have twice participated in demonstrations in front of our military bases. They've chained themselves with ordinary *green* activists and blocked access to military vehicles. We even have video recordings if you want to convince yourself. I hope your family does not influence you!"

"I don't understand what this has to do with my presence here. I still don't know whether you brought me here: for indoctrination or an investigation. Please, get straight to the point."

Gordon finally sat down in the short-legged chair and waited impassively. The General remained silent for a moment while typing on the computer.

"Look, Professor, I didn't bring you here because of your wife's political convictions," he said his tone friendlier. "I found the summary of a fascinating old scientific paper in one of your files. At that time, your research didn't draw too much attention, but now I believe it is the right time to bring it forth."

Gordon's face lit up. General Alan King's interest in his scientific publications was the last thing he had expected.

"What work are you referring to, Sir?" he asked, barely containing his childish excitement.

"The one about the trajectory of meteors in the lower layers of the atmosphere. We have found a remarkable contribution to the study of the motion of material points in the gravitational field."

Professor Gordon was flattered. Finally, the wind blows in the sails of his ship.

"Indeed, there are some original ideas that I cherish very much," he nodded with the typical vanity of the researcher. "I hope to find the necessary funds to experiment with my calculations in this paper."

"That's what you're here for. I'll give you the opportunity to experiment with your calculations."

"This is a delightful surprise," Gordon exclaimed, jumping to his feet. "I assure you the money will not be spent in vain."

"Money doesn't matter. Fortunately, or unfortunately, we have everything at hand, but you have to work very quickly. Soon every second will become precious. This explains your... *kidnapping*, as you said earlier. I suggest you get to work immediately. A state-of-the-art computer with priority access to our entire information network is at your disposal."

"But why the hurry? For years, this work has almost been ignored," the Professor said, quite surprised.

"We are in a special situation. The Soviets have problems with one of their satellites. It's a huge obsolete object with atomic batteries. They're trying to troubleshoot by remote controls, but I don't think they'll succeed. They might lose control of the satellite any time now. They've refused any collaboration with us. According to our data, the satellite is losing its altitude and is approaching the Earth worryingly fast. Using your theory and all our information, I want you to determine exactly where it'll collapse."

Gordon was stunned.

"For God's sake! These people are simply irresponsible. They're launching nuclear devices into Space without being able to control them. Atomic batteries could contaminate a fairly large region!"

"That's the job of the environmentalists, Professor Gordon. I'm worried about something else. I want my people to get to the crash site before our rivals and retrieve the module containing the military codes. This module is almost indestructible and will probably end up intact on Earth. Damn, it's worth a lot!"

"A few square kilometers can be radioactively contaminated. Do you understand me?"

"Ecological business, Professor, ecological business…," said the General contemptuously.

Suddenly, the shrill sound that preceded the emergency communications was heard in the room. A clear voice in a sure and confident tone came through the intercom speaker:

"Control Room for *Number One*! Control Room for *Number One*! I request priority access!"

"*Number One* is speaking! I approve priority access!" the General replied, pressing the button on the communications terminal with a mechanical gesture.

"Target adrift! It seems totally out of control! Coordinates are 241 with 16. Speed 320. We are waiting for instructions. Over!"

"It was about time," General Alan King muttered. Without hesitation, he pressed the red button on the edge of his desk and activated the alert system. He spoke in the microphone, his measured and grave voice:

"Attention, please! Attention, please! *Number One* for all: I order: *Red Alert!* This is not an exercise! I repeat: *Red alert!*" Then turning to Gordon: "Quickly, Professor! Starting this moment, time is our main enemy!"

Alarm sirens rang throughout the underground base. Professor Gordon felt their shrill sound seem to scratch his eardrums. He was a civilian scholar who was not used to such situations.

* * *

May 24, 1987, 7:00 PM - local time
Baikonur, Kazakhstan – Soviet Space Center

The minibus that had taken them from the military airport passed through all the checkpoints without stopping and brought them directly to the main entrance of the Soviet Space Center. They got off one by one and showed their work cards to an officer flanked by two armed soldiers before entering the room where they had to identify themselves and complete an access form, all except for the civilian with smoky glasses. He retired to a corner of the room and lit a cigarette casually, although he seemed to watch everyone between those walls. Igor peered at the stranger, puzzled. His position allowed him to check on anyone entering the Soviet Space Center, and he was about to approach him when Irina hissed from behind as if reading his thoughts:

"He's a big boss."

"Damn it!" Igor muttered between his teeth. "This is my territory. I'm responsible for everything that's going on here. I report directly to the Party and the Supreme Soviet."

The security officer who checked the access forms and the identity of those who entered the Soviet Space Center acted weirdly. According to the regulation, he could ask additional questions to eliminate any doubt about a person's identity. Although he knew Igor and was well aware of his role, he began to ask him a series of stupid questions, probably to prove his vigilance before the mysterious civilian. After being granted access, he went straight to the conference room, where he met the stranger in smoky glasses and General Leonid Pucinski, the Commander of the Soviet Space Center.

The meeting room door was hermetically closed, the radio jamming system was turned on, and the civilian, without mentioning his name, introduced himself as the special emissary of the USSR Security Department, with the task of conducting a special investigation.

"There is a serious leak of secret information here at the Space Center," he began in a high-pitched voice. "The Americans know everything! That means there's a *mole* in here and you are too incompetent to realize it. Make a list of all suspects, comrade Colonel. Quickly!" he ordered Zapojnikov.

"Yes, comrade," Igor replied composedly, although he couldn't help feeling a bit taken aback. "I will probably have to add the entire Space Center staff on this list, starting with Commander Pucinski and me."

"I won't allow impertinent answers, Colonel!" the emissary stormed. "Make the list as I ordered. You need to investigate the suspects immediately. If necessary, arrest them without hesitation. Comrade General, what are you doing here?" he fumed, turning to the Commander. "Do you run a horde of traitors? A cohort of spies for American imperialism?"

"If you allow me, Comrade," General Pucinski began quietly, "we had taken all the security measures here and reinforced them after the satellite didn't respond to the repositioning remotes."

"Fuck your measures and reinforcements! The American imperialists are after our satellite like a pack of hyenas as we speak!"

"My opinion is that there has been no information leakage from the Soviet Space Center I command," General Pucinski said categorically. "The Americans have a sophisticated system for tracking all our satellites. I assume they noticed the deviation immediately."

"Is there any possibility of returning the satellite to the orbit?" Igor asked, hoping to ease the discussion.

"Unfortunately, the chances are meager," the Commander replied in dismay. "Our best specialists are trying to activate the repositioning engines. If they fail, we'll lose the satellite. It will fall on Earth in a place we don't know yet."

"In this case, I think that the main task we have under regulation is linked to the *code module*," Igor stated. "We need to make sure that this module will not get into the hands of our rivals. That would be a disaster, indeed."

"We'll get to the *code module* in a moment," the emissary cut in. "My team will carry out this operation. I've summoned the best agents. They'll be here any minute now. Your task is to show them the documentation of the satellite's structure and describe the module to be recovered in detail."

"The special team of the Soviet Space Center will carry on the recovery of the module!" Igor retorted. "We have specialists trained for such situations. It's too important an operation to be handled by amateurs."

"My agents are not amateurs, comrade Colonel," the man in smoky glasses countered in the same firm tone. "They are professionals. There is no point in commenting on that. It seems I have to make myself clear: I am the leader of this operation. I receive orders directly from the General Secretary of the Communist Party of the Soviet Union. Is that understood?

He lit a cigarette, took a puff and without changing his commanding tone added:

"Now let's get back to the urgency of the moment. I want all the suspects interrogated. Who provided the service on the satellite system last night?"

"Three of the best officers I have," General Pucinski responded in a neutral tone. "They are still in the system, trying to retrieve the satellite."

"Replace them with other operators. They must be investigated immediately."

Chapter 2

May 24, 1987, 9:00 AM - local time
Bucharest-Romania – Department of the State Securitate-Central Office

General Virgil Pleşca, the head of the State Securitate, the secret service of Communist Romania, was reading the reports from the files scattered on his massive walnut desk, starting with the ones bearing the words *Top-Secret* on them. Occasionally, the phones on his desk, connected to the Operational Headquarters of the State Securitate Department, rang loudly. Each time, he interrupted his reading and responded in mono-syllabic words.

The Securitate, set up in 1949 following the KGB model - the frightening Soviet secret service - had grown even more powerful under General Pleşca. This State Force Institution could not be controlled anymore by the Communist Party, according to the laws at that time. The Securitate became increasingly independent and was already a state of its own inside the official Romanian state. However, the Securitate effectively fulfilled its main task given by the Communist Party: to prosecute and arrest all Romanian citizens with political opinions different from the official one.

Because his subordinates sometimes reported uninteresting and stupid things, General Pleşca found it appropriate to press the switch button and transfer all phone calls to his aide-de-camp, Major Alexe Marian. He was beyond the thick, soundproofed oak door, in the anteroom through which the access was made to the General's office. He had to be at the disposal of his boss at all times and, if necessary, he must defend him even at the cost of his own life. Once the calls from the operative phones were transferred to him, Major Alexe had to make sure that the General was not disturbed by anyone.

In such cases, General Pleșca answered only the "*red telephone*", through which he received calls only from Nicolae Ceaușescu himself, his Supreme Commander. He had to promptly answer every call on this phone at any time of day or night. But now he knew that Ceaușescu had just left Bucharest for bear hunting with his special guest, the President of Zaire, Mobutu Sese Seko, somewhere in the Carpathian Mountains. The chances of being called by his Supreme Commander in the next two or three hours were low.

Relieved from the stressful shrill sound of the phone calls and bored with the information in the secret files, the head of the Romanian secret police took a bottle of Hennessy cognac from under his desk and opened it. Sitting comfortably in his red Cordoba leather chair, he lit an expensive Cuban cigar. The General inhaled the smoke with avidity and drank directly from the bottle. He took three large sips at almost equal intervals then wiped the mouth of the bottle with the palm of his hand and put it on the table in front of him. It was an old proletarian ritual he used to practice as a factory worker before being recruited by the Communist Party to become an officer of the Securitate.

He closed his eyes, finding himself again among his fellows who used to pass a bottle of cheap brandy from one to the other until it was empty, before starting the working day. The rule was simple: each one had to take only three sips per round, wipe the mouth of the bottle and hand it to the next one.

That morning, the General had received a small gift from the Commercial Attaché of the Romanian Embassy in Copenhagen: a pack of six Hennessy cognac bottles. For almost two months, the diplomat had been trying to obtain a brief audience with General Pleșca to discuss some personal matter. At last, that morning, the General had decided to give the diplomat the special favor of accepting to talk to him for a few minutes. Humbly and respectfully, the diplomat had asked the General to approve a one-month voyage to the United States for his wife and his little daughter. The General had told him firmly:

"Well, I can approve this trip on one condition: you will not go to Copenhagen until your wife and daughter return. Take a leave and stay in Romania as a guarantor. You do know that the members of a diplomat's family are no longer allowed to be simultaneously outside of the Romanian borders. If they do not come back, you will be accused of betraying our country and the Socialist system. You will be convicted of forced labor and rot in the ugliest prison in Romania."

Normally, General Pleșca did not risk approving such trips that could be a real danger to Ceaușescu's politics. If the diplomat's family didn't return, the Supreme Commander would have had another reason to accuse him of incompetence. He knew, however, that the diplomat was an undercover officer with outstanding results. Although he worked as a diplomat at the Embassy of Romania in Copenhagen, being an employee of the Foreign Ministry, he was actually an active officer of the industrial espionage division. Through the years, he obtained a lot of secret technological information on the manufacture of high-performance industrial equipment.

On deciding to approve the trip to the US, the General had also taken into account another important detail: his adjutant had discreetly informed him of the cognac bottles brought by the commercial attaché and left *forgotten* under a table in the antechamber, before he entered for audience. Everyone knew that the General appreciated fine liquor, especially the Hennessy cognac. But he had taken a risk of course. Even the most trustworthy people of the Communist Party, with good political training, happened to seek asylum in different Western countries upon receiving the approval to travel there, thus betraying the great ideals of Socialism and Communism in favor of the deceptive and risky mirage of the Capitalist societies, which relied on the exploitation of the working class. This practice had become frequent lately and Ceaușescu demanded increased vigilance, especially now, ahead of the Communist Party's National Conference, to avoid any unpleasant incident that would overshadow the great political event.

Lately, General Pleșca had been increasingly worried and dissatisfied with how things were going in the Romanian espionage system. Every day, he read the *Top-Secret* reports carefully, but couldn't find any relevant information. They were simple gossip about the love affairs of some lower-rank Western politicians, compiled, outdated, or false news that perhaps his agents had read in the scandal press and believed to be valuable for the Center. Securitate was spending millions of dollars every year to fund its secret agents spread around the World and the results were pathetic. Pleșca could no longer tolerate this kind of work.

During the last working session of the State Securitate Department, Nicolae Ceaușescu pointed out the inefficiency of the Romanian espionage service and threatened General Pleșca with removing him from the position of Chief of Securitate, unless the General didn't take firm and effective measures to improve the spying activity in the Western countries, as soon as possible.

On top of everything, there was Radio Free Europe, funded by *American imperialism*, a pain in the neck for Ceaușescu. Despite all assurances that he would put an end to it, General Pleșca had not taken any serious action against this radio station. He had assured Ceaușescu that he would blow up the Radio Free Europe together with all the traitors working there. On February 21, 1981, Saturday evening, at 9:47 p.m., a powerful explosion occurred at the headquarters of the Radio Free Europe station in Munich, which was also recorded by seismographs. The bomb of almost 15 kg of Nitro Penta - a plastic explosive, of Romanian production - was, however, placed *by mistake* near the Czechoslovak Service of the radio station Free Europe. The powerful explosion did not affect the Romanian language section, which continued to broadcast uninterrupted news and commentaries that denigrated the achievements of socialism in Romania while heavily criticizing Ceaușescu's politics.

More and more Romanian citizens were listening to this radio station in secret but with great interest, which only added fuel to the fire. In the evening, they used to lock the door and sit as close as possible to the radio receiver, listening to a low-volume broadcast to avoid being heard by neighbors who might report them to the Securitate officers. It was their only way to protest against the political oppression in their country.

Drunk with power, General Pleşca had started to believe he was omnipotent, as he did whatever he wanted, without having to explain himself to anyone. He could control, watch, arrest, and torture anyone he wanted - all the people, if necessary - from ordinary citizens to those with the most important positions like renowned professors and scientists, inventors, valuable researchers, and performance athletes.

All Romanian citizens needed his approval whenever they wanted to go abroad. He could approve or reject the passport requests according to his whims. All foreign diplomats accredited in Romania were closely monitored. Their childcare staff, drivers, and maintenance staff were Securitate agents. These secret political police supervised the residences of all foreign citizens by using the latest types of equipment, and listened to and recorded all telephone and radio calls on the Romanian territory. The Securitate had everything in the country under its control and he, General Pleşca, as the head of this institution, was the only well-informed person. Having operative access to huge and correct information, made him the most powerful man in Romania, while Ceauşescu received only the reports he usually wanted to hear.

Even the top Communist Party leaders, the members of the Central Committee, feared Virgil Pleşca who knew all about their sins and weaknesses and had compromising evidence on them and their families. Many ministers' houses and cars had been bugged, so every conversation, during the day or night, was recorded. The Securitate used one of the most sophisticated and expensive electronic spying devices in the World. Purchasing them had not been easy as they were under the embargo imposed by Western states on the Communist countries where human rights were not respected. Pleșca had to use more foreign intermediaries who were allowed to buy this type of equipment. As the export agency lost track of the shipping under embargo, the equipment's price increased a lot. But it was all worth it.

The General also took pride in wrapping Ceaușescu around his little finger. To him, the Supreme Commander was nothing more than a puppy he walked on a leash and whom he had to protect from the "*dangerous dwarfs*".

Ceaușescu's own vanity made him vulnerable. He enjoyed being praised even when he was making serious political mistakes, and the flattering words of his minions were music to his ears, so he took a narcissistic pleasure in listening to the uplifting hymns composed by obedient poets and composers in his honor.

Of course, all these were part of the propaganda that had to portray Ceaușescu as a brave, relentless warrior of socialism and communism, against the imperialists who were exploiting the people. But the General knew the truth. His Supreme Commander was an anxious, suspicious man who didn't even trust his personal guards, afraid that one of them could one day put a bullet in his head. He never traveled by his presidential plane or private helicopter without his morbid fear, expecting his aircraft to be hit by a ballistic missile at any moment.

His paranoia took proportion after the assassination of the Egyptian President, Anwar Sadat, during an annual victory parade on October 6th, 1981. Since then, he had started wearing a special made bulletproof vest under the coat during his official visits around the country or at the grand rallies organized by the Communist Party propaganda services in the big cities. His anxiety could be momentarily countered only by the euphoria he felt at the sight of the thousands of Romanian citizens waving the red flags with the yellow hammer and sickle, the coat of arms of the Party, the symbol of the unflinching unity between the peasants and the workers, and holding banners with working-class slogans, as well as the large portraits of him and his wife, Elena.

The Communist ruler made uncontrollable signs with his hands in front of the crowd, as if trying to defend himself against a swarm of angry bees attacking him. It was his strange way of showing his friendship and solidarity with the working people. But when the people burst into loud cheers, shouting his name in adoration as if he were a living god, the dictator's blood ran cold. The same people who now worshiped him could easily turn against him to tear him to pieces. Nicolae Ceaușescu knew that some of those present at these grand popular gatherings could rise against him. The organizers of the rallies mobilized all factory workers and those who refused to join were severely punished. Not everyone loved him. They faked happiness out of fear of political repercussions, especially as they were constantly urged to act cheerfully by the desperate screams of the Communist agitators and Securitate agents infiltrated among them, carefully watching any movement of the demonstrators. In turn, even these political mercenaries were anxious and sought to avoid any unpleasant incident during the demonstration, because of the investigations and punishments they could get afterward.

Ceaușescu was afraid even of the hundreds of strong young men wearing red helmets and blue overalls like those who worked in construction. They were always present at such popular gatherings. Usually, they stood in the first rows, just a few yards away from the official tribune. They were vigilant and peered around cautiously all the time. They were not ordinary citizens, but well-trained soldiers of the Ministry of Interior special forces, with the task of protecting him from the crowd in case of violence. They held the red flags attached to specially made well-sharpened wooden spears that could easily become lethal weapons against the unleashed crowd. Ceaușescu couldn't trust them more than the other people. Any of those young soldiers could throw a grenade or point a gun at him. He could end up like the Egyptian president. Overwhelmed by these thoughts, the Romanian dictator instinctively reached for the bulletproof vest under his coat, with trembling fingers, and the feel of it put him at peace somehow as if it was his only chance of survival.

Thinking about all these things, General Pleșca emptied more than half of the cognac bottle. He put the cigar on a silver ashtray and stood up. He paced slowly around the room, the bottle in his hand, stepping with the soles of his well-polished shoes on the soft Persian carpet that covered the floor of his office. A pleasant numbness had fallen upon him, and although he wished to indulge himself in daydreaming, he couldn't help thinking of his Supreme Commander who seemed to watched every move of the General from his large gold-framed portrait on the wall in front of the desk. The General walked back toward the chair, feeling dizzy. When he was about to sit, he swiveled round and stared again at Ceaușescu's portrait. His vision was hazy and it seemed to him that the Ceausescu's picture is moving on the wall. Pleșca came closer and realized that the painting was not moving, but Ceaușescu seemed to look down upon him dissatisfied. Maybe he was right to be upset. As a sign of reconciliation, the General raised the bottle of cognac and babbled:

"Long live and... many happy years... Comrade Ceaușescu! I wish you... much health and many... many... many... revolutionary victories! I am here at your orders... in this position… you do not have to worry about anything. We will destroy… all the enemies of Socialism and Communism!"

He raised the bottle to his mouth and emptied it to the bottom in honor and health of his Supreme Commander. Then, with heavy, unsteady steps, he walked over and sat down in his red leather - upholstered chair. He was drunk and tired. He laid his head on the desk and fell asleep almost instantly.

* * *

May 24, 1987, 6 AM - local time
The "Citadel of Physics" Bucharest - Măgurele

Although it was Sunday, George woke up early. The Communist Party Conference was around the corner, and communists from all over the country decided to honor this important political event through patriotic work. Nicolae Ceaușescu, the General Secretary of the Communist Party of Romania, declared this Sunday a working day. The Party activists from the National Center of Physics had announced that today all employees of the research institutions in Măgurele were to take action against the prolonged drought affecting the corn crop.

George was often criticized for having a weaker political background. He had been working for the Romanian Seismic Network for several years. George was a pragmatic man, not in the least interested in watering the corn, so he had found a way to skip it by convincing his boss that it wouldn't be proper to welcome this great political event with faulty seismic stations. Thus, he had the approval to travel to Vrancea to repair two radio-telemetered seismic stations that were no longer working.

He was to leave early in the morning with the driver of the field intervention vehicle.

His wife had prepared some food for the road. She found a piece of bacon from Christmas, a strategic leftover in a corner of the fridge. She also packed half of the bread they had as a ration, but George hoped to buy another half from the province, using the documents proving he was during a delegation trip. He had this right according to the Party's instructions. However, this was possible only in some cities. Most of them could barely feed their own inhabitants.

On the way to the Institute, George stopped at the market for a bunch of radishes and green onions. The market stalls were stocked with certain vegetables, as a sign of well-being and a high standard of living described in the documents of the Communist Party, so buying them was no problem. Behind the grocery store, a group of pensioners were talking loudly. One had launched the rumor that a cheese-laden car would arrive soon.

"I know for sure," said the man. "I have a relative who works at Centrocoop, and he told me on the phone last night. They're bringing cheese to the store today. He said it is a good one, from a batch refused for export."

The others had gathered around him, listening intently. Hearing the rumor, the peasant sellers started shouting: "*Good green onions for the cheese! Buy good green onions for the cheese!*" thus, applying the capitalist principle according to which advertising is the soul of trade.

A comrade from the Union made a list of all those who hoped to buy the delicacy product. Proud of the importance of his mission, he was unyielding whenever someone asked him to write down the names of the people who were not present.

"Only one person, only one person!" he barked. "Every man for himself!"

It was, of course, a selfish principle that was not found in the Communist Party's documents and was vehemently criticized by some customers in line. After a series of negotiations, the socialist democracy came out victorious, and the names of all those who hoped to "*grab*" a piece of cheese were written down. In this way, the list had grown considerably every minute.

George got himself on the list too, but the three-digit number in front of his name was discouraging. It didn't matter anyway. He had to leave for Vrancea soon. It was almost 7 o'clock and he hurried to the Institute of Seismology. In the front yard, Gică, the driver and his fieldwork partner, fixed something on the car.

"Ready to go?" George asked impatiently. "Bring the car in front of the lab. We have to put the tool kit and the batteries inside."

"We aren't going anywhere," Gică said disappointed.

"Why? What happened?"

"My boss told me to go to the Party Branch. He got the order to give the car to comrade Cătana."

"It is not possible! This is too much!" shot George. "The car belongs to the seismic stations network, not the Party Branch. I'm going to talk to the Director."

The driver shrugged helplessly, and George, bristling with anger, went straight to the Director's office. The secretary in the anteroom barred his way.

"The comrade Director doesn't want to be disturbed! He is having his tea. What do you want from him?"

"I have to go to the epicenter in Vrancea to repair the seismic stations, and I need the car."

"The Party Branch requested that car," she retorted. "There's nothing we can do about it. Please, don't bother the comrade Director anymore."

"I want to talk to him, though. The seismic stations network is more important than the political obligations of the Institute."

"That is not true!" chided the secretary, shooting him an angry look. "How dare you say that? The Party orders are law!" She turned and looked out the window. "Why the hell is the car still here? They called for it half an hour ago! Go and tell Gică to leave at once!"

George ignored her and remained in the secretary's office, nervously moving the plastic bag with his food from one hand to the other. The situation annoyed him for it meant that he had to take part in watering the corn, after all. And he hadn't even brought a cup and a bucket from home like the rest, as he was supposed to. Not that he cared anyway.

Istrate, the Party secretary at the Institute, burst into the room, waving a sheet of paper - the list of those who were to participate in watering the corn plantation. He asked the secretary for the attendance book and began confronting it with his list.

"How dare they be absent from this? I will punish them!" he snarled, identifying several employees who were not on his list. Then he turned his bloodshot eyes to George and taunted:

"What are you doing here? The buses will leave in a few minutes. Are you waiting for a special invitation or something?"

"I'm afraid I will not be going to the corn fields, comrade. I need to travel to Vrancea. We have some problems with the seismic network."

"The seismic network can wait! We need to save the harvest first!"

George refrained from telling Istrate that their endeavor would be in vain without rain or proper irrigation systems.

"Come on, grab your bucket and go to work!" the Party secretary urged him in a true proletarian spirit.

"Still, I would like to talk to comrade Director first," replied George stubbornly.

"There's nothing to talk about if you spoke with me. Understood? Come, I'll wait for you on the bus!" Comrade Istrate shouted the last words from the threshold before quickly disappearing down the hall. As it was an important event that the Party Branch was interested in, Istrate wanted everything to go smoothly and not be criticized anymore, as it often happened.

The phone rang. The secretary swallowed the piece of pretzel she was munching and picked up the receiver. She listened for a few moments and hurried into the Director's office.

"They're calling from the Party Branch, comrade Director! Line one."

The Director's office door remained ajar and George could take a peek inside. The Director seemed a little nervous as he talked on the phone.

"Yes, comrade! We will participate with all our employees!" Then, after a short pause: "Oh… So, not all employees… Party members only… I understand!" He hung up and entered the secretary's office, muttering: "I don't understand anything anymore! It's either white or black! Comrade secretary, call comrade Istrate back quickly. No Party member will go to the fields. It's the rally of friendship between Romania and Zaire this afternoon at the Polyvalent Hall and we need to join the entire Party organization of the Institute."

The secretary opened the window and shouted:

"Comrade Istrateee! Comrade Istrateee! Come back!"

George took advantage of the Director's presence in the secretariat and cleared his voice:

"Comrade Director, please let me go to Vrancea. Two important telemetered seismic stations in the epicenter don't work."

The Director looked at him in astonishment.

"Don't you see what's going on here? I don't have time for your seismic stations. The Institute's car is now at the disposal of the Party Branch. Don't waste your time. As you are not a Party member, hurry up and catch the bus with the rest leaving for the cornfield."

The Director's attitude completely disarmed him. The intervention car was already gone. Istrate had asked the driver to leave urgently. The Institute employees holding plastic buckets had already boarded the three buses that were to take them to the cornfield from Dumitrana. The perspective of joining them was about to become a reality.

"Comrade Director, if I can't go to Vrancea," George said half-heartedly, "will you at least let me take this day off? I need to solve some personal problems."

"All right," said the Director, eager to get rid of him. "Leave your request at the secretariat and go home!"

George wrote the request right away and gave it to the secretary who commented that it should not be approved. He ignored her, cursing between his teeth and slamming the door as he went out.

There was a hubbub outside in the courtyard of the Institute. The Party members, more politically mature citizens, were getting off the buses, preparing for the rally, while the rest of the employees had to go to the field. George strode across the yard, resigned somehow at the *political discrimination.*

On his way home, he stopped at the market again. The peasants were shouting even more fiercely: *"Onions! Onions! Buy good onions for the cheese!"* Dozens of people of all ages and occupations - adults, children, retired men, and employees of the Institute - had already gathered at the back door of the grocery store, waiting breathlessly for their names to be called. Perched on a pile of crates, the trade unionist shouted the list. George remained there. Because he had the day off, he could at least wait in the queue without fear of being found by the inspectors from Human Resources Department. They had the habit of checking and penalizing, by cutting their wages, the employees they found during working hours at the food queues. Maybe, with some luck, he might get some cheese. After his name was called, he went home for some more money. When he returned, however, the marketplace was already in uproar after the arrival of the cheese car, the air filled with both excitement and the fear of not being enough food for everyone. Even the peasants had left their selling stands, to joining the long queue. Some lads climbed on a neighboring roof, trying to see how many cheese barrels were unloaded in the inner courtyard of the grocery store.

The trade unionist urged the crowd to be quiet and shouted the list again. The first twenty, thirty customers crowded into the small enclosure with metal bars, made especially at the wise indication of the local communist authorities, to ensure order in the queue for food from the grocery store. At the end of this enclosure, there was a small window cut into a rusted tin gate, similar to the firing battlement of a fortress.

All the customers in the queue, who stormed the grocery store, had the goal of arriving before that small window where the goods were sold. Exhausted, the trade unionist asked for volunteers to help him maintain order at the entrance of the barred enclosure, where it was terribly crowded. Those who managed to find themselves between the blunt bars of the enclosure could sigh in relief knowing that their chances of buying cheese were much higher. Other people pushed from behind, squeezing themselves in. There were screams and cursing. Any child or old man who didn't have enough strength to resist could be easily crushed.

There was a long tense wait after the car left and no one knew how much cheese had been brought. The store staff was silent. A salesman came out to throw some cardboard packaging stinking of rotten fish in the metal trash cans burning near the gates. He swore to his life that he didn't know anything and only his boss, Jan, could give them details. Several young people began hit the gates and to shout: *"These thieves are hiding the cheese!"*

It was getting hotter and hotter. The stifling smoke from the cardboard packaging burning in the dumpsters nearby filled the air with a heavy stench that attracted a swarm of flies. A thread of whey leaked from under the gates. Time was passing slowly. Even those in front of the queue became anxious. They pressed against each other, sweating and breathing hard, their voices louder and louder as they shouted for Jan. When the small window finally opened, a stifling silence fell over the crowd. Jan put his head out and announced that the sale of cheese was starting, in the tone of one who does a great favor to those less fortunate than him.

"Boss, give them less so that we can buy some, too!" someone shouted desperately from the back of the queue.

"I will give only one piece to each client," said Jan and the hungry crowd approved his decision.

"How much does a piece weigh?" asked a man in front.

"About… a kilogram," Jan replied. "Have the right amount of cash, I can't give any change!"

The first customers arrived at the improvised counter made of wooden crates with a scale on it placed carefully in such a way as to show the quantity desired by the seller. A group of gypsies tried to get in front of everyone else. After a short skirmish, they were pushed back and took some time for the queue to return to order. A man who had come out of the altercation with his shirt torn started shouting nervously:

"Antonescu did you a good thing by taking you to Bug, you damned bastards."

A gipsy woman in a long-flowered skirt gave him an answer that silenced everyone:

"What Antonescu did to us is nothing compared to what Ceaușescu is doing to you! He will finish all you Romanians and there will be no one to bury you! You are going to rot on the side of the road!"

One by one, the customers passed by the window where the pieces of cheese, wrapped like mummies in thick paper, were thrown onto the scale before ending up in the hands of the lucky buyers. One by one, women, men, and children, sweaty but with happy faces, took the cheese as a trophy. It didn't matter its cost or how many hours they had lost waiting. The trade unionist took his own piece of cheese and left, and a more authoritarian guy took over the list. A kind of numbness fell over the crowd. The sale was going fast.

George waited patiently in line, though he didn't believe he would get something. He felt against his back the massive breasts of a fat woman talked to her companion, boasting about how she had managed to make soup out of a single chicken for almost a week. From time to time, she interrupted her rattle to shout at those who tried to cheat and get in front.

"Hey, you idiot, go back to your place!"

Next to George, an old man was trying to cool off, using a folded cloth bag as a fan. The smoke from the burning garbage blurred their vision and the flies became more aggressive. A few people started shouting again.

"Who the hell put fire to the trash right now?"

"Well, that's mockery!"

"Of course, it's a mockery! They don't care!"

Other fellows approached the ones who managed to buy the product:

"Is the cheese good?"

"Yes, it is."

"Will you let me taste it?"

Just in front of George, in the enclosure, two researchers from the Institute talked about quasars, supernovae, and neutron stars. They defied hunger and the humiliation of waiting crammed in the crowd for a piece of cheese. They almost held a cosmology lecture. Amidst the swearing and shouting of the other people, the researchers' discussion honored the "*Citadel of Physics*", the proud nickname given to Măgurele by the Communist Party propaganda. George listened to them with pleasure.

"Imagine, sir," one explained, "the expansion of the Universe is a problem that has always fascinated me. Hubble was magnificent when he indicated the presence of relict radiation, considering it to be a remnant from Big Bang…"

"Clearly, sir, the galaxies are moving away from each other. Their spectrum turning red is a proven thing."

"I tried an original approach to determine the flux of relict radiation with double integral per unit area and triple integral per unit volume. Listen to what an interesting conclusion I came to..."

He rummaged through his pockets, took out a piece of chalk, and wrote a formula on the rusty board of the large metal gates near Jan's counter.

"They lost their minds because they read too many books!" a hoarse voice came from behind.

"Instead of paying attention to the sale of the cheese there, they scribble on the fences." someone else said mockingly.

Just then Jan announced that there was no more cheese for sale which caused a commotion.

"Thieves! Get the cheese out! Don't hide the cheese!" shouted those at the back of the queue.

The two researchers snapped out of their scientific trance and looked at Jan in dismay. Next to them, a pregnant woman stared lustfully at the crumbs of cheese stuck to Jan's hairy hands as he wiped them on a piece of paper.

"It's over, it's over!" he rattled on, avoiding the inquisitive gaze of the researchers.

"However, sir… Can you look for one more piece? At least for the lady…," one of them entreated, pointing to the pregnant woman next to him who peered disappointed through the bars at the empty cheese barrels scattered in the grocery yard.

"Oh, she's pregnant…," Jan nodded sympathetically and rummaged through the whey, gathering a handful of crumbs of cheese which he molded with his large hands into a ball. He wrapped it in a large piece of paper, added a few grams to its weight, and put it on the scale. The woman paid for it happy and relieved.

"Please, sir, can you look for more? I'm sure you can still find something. Maybe there is another barrel…," the researcher pleaded again.

"Don't you understand that I haven't got any more?!" Jan raged. "Don't you understand the Romanian language?! Where can I get it from if I don't have anymore?"

"Thieves! Get the cheese out for sale!" a hysterical woman cried. "I just saw someone from the Town Hall coming out the front door with two big bags of cheese!"

Her words stirred the crowd even more.

"Thieves! Get the cheese out!"

"Stop hiding cheese!"

"Do you want cheese? I'll give you cheese, you hungry bastards!" Jan snarled. He grabbed the barrel and discarded the whey at the feet of those in front of the counter. Surprised by his gesture, the two scientists stepped aside, as they felt their shoes getting wet. The crowd cursed and threatened, hitting the grocery store's metal doors with everything at hand, but Jan didn't care for them. He removed the improved counter and closed the window, propping an iron rod against the gates with the help of two subordinates before taking refuge inside.

George struggled to escape the crowd still waiting in front of the store. He also got his shoes stained with whey and following the example of the two researchers, he took a piece of newspaper from the trash and cleaned himself.

He started for home disappointed. As he passed by the school, he heard a choir of children singing in sad voices: "*Partiiidul… Ceauşeeescu… Româniiiia…*". They were probably rehearsing for the celebration organized in honor of the National Conference of the Communist Party.

The old ARO car, with *Seismology - Interventions* imprinted on the door, stopped abruptly right behind George, jolting him out of his thoughts. The driver greeted him laughing.

"What's the matter with you, comrade?" George asked in astonishment. "Is this your Party Branch?"

"*The Party is in all that is/ And in those that tomorrow will laugh at the sun…,*" the other recited like a diligent schoolboy.

"Indeed… Okay, okay, I see you know communist poems. What happened? Did they fire you?"

"How can they fire me, comrade? In socialism, the right to work is guaranteed. No one gets fired. In the worst case, they receive other assignments as I have now."

"What task did you get? Cultural work for porters, like Ostap Bender from *The Golden Calf*?"

"Well, not really… Cătana, a damn activist, yelled at me, saying he didn't like my car and that we were making fun of him. He called the Director and made a fuss."

"Really? And what did the Director say?"

"He said that the Institute has no other car for him. He called me back and asked me to look for you so that we can go to Vrancea as originally planned."

"Very well, let's go!" George said excitedly as he got into the car. "We shall load the instruments from the lab first, then go home, so we can get some food for the road before we leave. I have a *good onion for the cheese,* he added with a bitter smile. "But I don't have the cheese…"

"That's no problem. I saw some in my fridge. My wife queued up at Teiuș and *grabbed* a kilogram. Hey, we should get some raincoats, too. They said there are going to be thunderstorms and heavy rains."

"A rain in such a communist drought would be very good," George said with a smile. "We would cool down… and the corn would ripe…"

* * *

May 24, 1987, 8:30 AM - local time
Institute of Seismology - Bucharest - Măgurele

The telephone conversation with Party activist Cătana had annoyed the Director. He had never encountered such arrogance and impertinence before. After being accused of sending a totally inappropriate vehicle to the Party Branch, he was humiliated, having been blamed for the poor political training of the seismologists from the Institute who proved their indiscipline whenever they took part in a voluntary-patriotic action.

"Such a situation can no longer be tolerated, comrade Director!" stormed Cătana, making the phone receiver vibrate in the Director's hand. "I will report to comrade First Secretary Gogea about this and suggest punishing the guilty. You should know I haven't forgotten that serious incident from last fall at

Vârteju train station, during the potato sorting action. What sanction did you give to that undisciplined research fellow… Stoian… or… whatever his name is. Can you tell me?"

"At that time, I analyzed his case within the Disciplinary Commission of the Institute…," the Director said awkwardly.

"What analysis, comrade Director? Sanctions! That's what I want to hear! That the local Party organization gives sanctions for disobedience!"

"Stoian is not a member of the Communist Party, you see…"

"So much the worse! You should have kicked him out of the Institute! You should cancel his employment contract and mention that from now on he can only work as an unqualified worker on a construction site! He should be given as a negative example!"

"However, he is one of our best researchers…"

"What does it matter, comrade Director? I am one of the best activists in the Party Branch. I graduated from the *Ştefan Gheorghiu* political school among the first, but if comrade First Secretary Gogea wants to kick me out, he kicks me out! The Party appointed you Director of the Institute to bring order, not to protect the rebels. Kick him out!"

"I'm afraid it's not that simple," the Director tried to explain. "Stoian has a Ph.D. in Earth Physics from one of the most prestigious American universities. He is well known in the scientific community abroad."

"Ah… is that so? That's even worse! The Party trusted him, allowed him to go there and get his Ph.D., asserting himself, and now he repays our generosity by defying us. Comrade Director, I want you to reopen the case and give him a proper sanction for his acts, not mere scolding. Besides, I'll make sure he won't never see his passport. I promise he will forget what the border guards' uniform looks like! Your researchers are too fond of traveling, instead of researching here, in the country, where the Party has created all the conditions for them. They travel abroad… using the money of the working people. We will be more careful and selective when we'll have to approve the trips abroad for your researchers."

The Director knew that this warning also concerned him, as he had also made several trips abroad lately. He needed to calm down comrade Cătana, so he promised to punish Stoian.

"Comrade Cătana, as Director of the Institute, I promise you that I will do everything in my power to avoid such regrettable incidents in the future."

The telephone conversation ended abruptly, leaving the manager with his dark thoughts. The idea that the travels abroad might be severely restricted deeply unsettled him.

The incident caused by Stoian created big problems at the time, although he didn't know many details and didn't consider it too important a matter. But he couldn't neglect it anymore if comrade Cătana didn't forget that episode. He asked the secretary to call Stoian.

"Stoian is watering the corn at Dumitrana, with the rest," the secretary informed him. "He is not a Party member…"

"Yes, yes, you're right…," murmured the Director. "In this case, call comrade Vasile. Tell him to come to me as soon as possible."

Although he was employed for over a year, no one knew what comrade Vasile was doing. Many of his colleagues suspected him to be a Securitate officer working undercover as a technician at the mechanic workshop. He was also part of the leadership of the Institute's Party organization and the Director consulted him whenever he had to solve difficult matters. Vasile appeared in his usual style, knocking shyly, and coming in looking around like a ferret. He bent down and greeted servilely:

"Long live, long live, comrade Director! You wanted to see me…"

"Yes, comrade Vasile," said the Director, shaking his hand. "Are you busy?"

"Somewhat… I was preparing a banner with my comrades from the workshop. We will write on it: *Long Life to Comrade Nicolae Ceaușescu, the World Champion of Peace!* and display it this afternoon during the rally. I got approval from the Party Branch. Comrade First Secretary Gogea came up with the text."

"You spoke with comrade First Secretary?" asked the Director half-amazed and half-admiringly.

"Yes, I just called him," Vasile said in false modesty. "We've known each other from the time when he used to solve the *youth issues* in our neighborhood if you know what I mean. I gave him a call today to tell him about the banner. He said: '*You must make a beautiful banner, Vasile! You are a talented man!*' And I replied with revolutionary pathos: *Yes, Comrade First Secretary, I will do my best!*"

"Comrade Vasile, if you need extra help for the banner or any materials, we can solve it immediately. I will ask the storekeeper to provide you with everything you need."

"It's all right, comrade Director, we'll manage it. We want to make the banner from recyclable materials - the three political '**re**': *recovery, reconditioning*, and *reuse*. Miracles can emerge from apparently useless things when there is political will and guidance. For example, I found a portrait of Stalin painted on a piece of plywood and some red flags thrown in a shed at the Party Committee, the ones with the hammer and sickle in the corner…"

"Oh, those that were taken out…," the Director said, referring to the flag of the Soviet Union.

"Yes, yes," Vasile nodded. "So how did I make use of the three **'re'**? I covered the portrait of Stalin with the silk from the Soviet flags and turned it into a nice smooth surface. On it, we will stick the letters cut from pieces of the expanded polystyrene I have recovered from the packaging of those devices received from America. The boys and I invented a special installation for cutting letters for banners we'd like to patent. We use hot nickel wire for cutting the expanded polystyrene and it's quite similar to the laser cut, but without using the network's electricity. We spin a dynamo manually to produce electricity and get the nickel wire hot."

"That is… extraordinary!" uttered the Director with a forced smile. Even though Vasile was an important man, and he needed his influence within the Party Branch, he believed him to be a complete idiot.

"It was my idea and I will make it known to the other colleagues in the Party Branch who were engaged in propaganda work."

"Well done! Bravo, comrade Vasile!" the Director said. "It's good to know we have people in our Institute that we can be proud of. If only everyone were like you… I just got off the phone with comrade Cătana. Unfortunately, he is still very angry with Stoian for that incident at Vârteju train station. That's why I asked for you in my office. Were you at the potato sorting actions last year, in November?"

"Of course, comrade Director, you know I don't miss any activity organized by the Party Branch."

"Tell me, what happened? I'm afraid I didn't pay much attention to the incident then."

"It was quite serious," Vasile said, stroking his mustache. "Several train wagons had been unloaded, and Vârteju train station practically turned into a mountain of potatoes. We, the Seismologists, were tasked with unloading the wagons parked at the ramp, but our researchers - you know how they are - didn't want to unload them… Comrade Cătana, who coordinated the potato sorting action, got angry and asked the researchers to sort the potatoes, put them in baskets, and transport them to the silos. At the same time, we, the technicians, with secondary education, unloaded the wagons. It is true that the place where the researchers of our Institute had been placed was filled with rotten potatoes covered in mud, and the smell was rather unpleasant, but that's how the work in agriculture is… you get your hands dirty…"

"Yes, comrade Vasile, that's right…"

"The researchers sat around the potato stack and worked quietly. There were those from Laser, from the Reactor, and Theoretical Physics, basically all the researchers from the Institutes of the *Citadel of Physics*. Because it was too quiet, I thought of starting a competition that would cast away the boredom. Something like: *The research institute that sorted and carried the most potato baskets would win.*"

"Interesting proposal, comrade Vasile."

"Comrade Stoian didn't find my proposal interesting. He looked at me contemptuously and said: '*What, Vasile, do you think we are Stakhanovist like you?*' I didn't say anything, I went about my business, especially since the Party Committee had assigned me to make a list of those present. Because, why not admit it, we still have slackers among us."

"Unfortunately, yes," the Director shook his head. "So, what did Stoian do? I suppose he worked…"

"On the contrary, comrade Director, he didn't. He sat down on a basket and talked with some young researchers. Instead of giving them an example of how to sort the potatoes quickly, he spoke about a theory on a seismic fault or something like that. I can't tell you what he was talking about exactly. I still have some gaps in my knowledge of seismology, you know…"

"No problem, comrade Vasile," the Director nodded with understanding.

"As I was telling you", continued the other, "at one point I saw Stoian placing several potatoes on a wicker basket turned upside down. He then shook the basket, simulating an earthquake, so the potatoes were scattered on the ground. He did that only to explain some kind of theory. Comrade Cătana shouted: *'What are you doing, comrade?! Instead of sorting the potatoes, you're playing with them? Is that how you set an example for young people? Aren't you ashamed?'* Instead of remaining silent, Stoian stood up saying: *'Why should I be ashamed, sir? For teaching these young men something valuable as a scientist from the Seismological Institute?! What's your job here?' 'Take care, comrade, I'm from the Party Branch. I'm responsible for your activity here as a Party activist!'* retorted comrade Cătana. *'Party activist?! This is not a job! Tell me what you can do.' 'I'm a five-category turner,'* replied comrade Cătana proudly. *'If you're a turner, then go to your mother's lathe and leave us alone!'* shouted Stoian. That's what happened, comrade Director…"

"Very bad… I understand. And comrade Cătana?"

"Comrade Cătana left fuming, threatening to sanction the entire Institute. And if that wasn't bad enough, some colleagues even started laughing."

"Very unpleasant," murmured the Director.

"Yes, comrade Director," said Vasile, frowning. "Stoian put a stain on the face of the entire Institute, and we are now trying to clean up after him. You should do something, comrade Director!"

"Of course, I will, yes…," said the manager thoughtfully. "Although I'm afraid I can't do anything at the moment. Comrade Stoian has just been invited to a conference in Strasbourg. I have the telex here on my desk."

"Comrade Director, Stoian shouldn't be allowed to travel abroad anymore! After the potato sorting incident, I would trust him no longer."

"Of course, yes. All right, comrade Vasile! Thank you for your time and I wish you the best of luck with the banner and your - outstanding invention… We'll meet again at the rally this afternoon," said the Director, motioning Vasile to the door.

"Thank you, comrade Director! I will also let you know about the process of patenting our invention. Long live, comrade Director, long live!"

The Director returned to the desk and slapped a palm over his forehead, grunting:

"He asks his fellows to spins the dynamo manually… Incompetent lickspittle!"

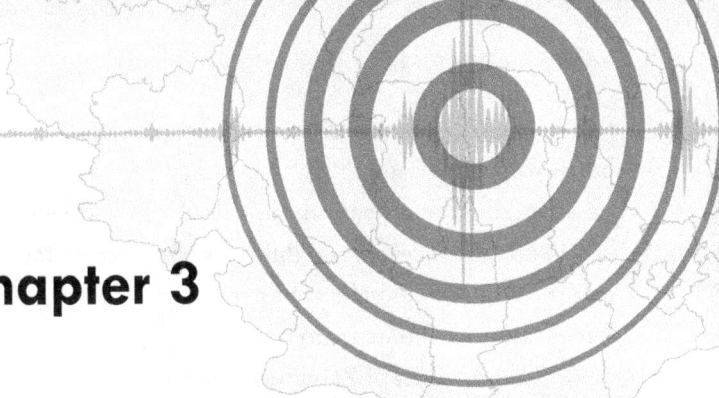

Chapter 3

May 24, 1987, 11:30 AM - local time
State Securitate - Central Office

General Virgil Pleșca was sleeping for more than two hours, his noisy snoring filling the office, when "*the red phone*" rang. He woke up suddenly and instinctively picked up the receiver, jumping to his feet and reported:

"Long live, Comrade Supreme Commander! This is General Lieutenant Pleșca Virgil, at your Excellency's disposal!"

His hoarse voice sounded like a broken barrel rolling over stones.

"You drank again, you motherfucker general! You're going to die from drinking like an idiot!" Ceaușescu shouted at him in a certain way, so that the General understood that his boss was not angry, he was even in a good mood. "Get your men ready. In three days, you'll go to Kinshasa. No more drinking on this mission, understood?"

"Yes, I fully understand, Comrade Supreme Commander!" Pleșca replied trying to make his voice clearer.

The order revived him and the hangover vanished almost instantly. His new task meant Ceaușescu had succeeded in the secret negotiations with Mobutu. The two presidents engaged in a private conversation in Russian - which both of them were fluent in - without the assistance of any translator, right after the bear hunting game. Pleșca's men had previously installed effective jamming systems in the official salon of the protocol villa in Sinaia, a quiet town at the foot of the Bucegi Mountains, to prevent the two presidents from being recorded by potential foreign agents infiltrated into the area.

The president of Zaire was very excited because he had managed to hunt a huge Carpathian bear with a magnificent trophy. To facilitate this great hunting achievement, a few days ago, Pleșca's agents had chosen the bear from the special reserve belonging to the Party's hunting farm. Before the hunt began, the bear was drugged, so the animal had no chance of escape and was shot by Mobutu, to the applause of the hunters.

Under the euphoric feeling of his achievement, he easily accepted Ceaușescu's proposals. One of these assumed that one hundred young Africans from Zaire Secret Service would become secret agents of Romania. They were to be selected by a team led by General Pleșca, brought to Romania, and trained in one of the secret camps in the Făgăraș Mountains, before being infiltrated into the African states. Ceaușescu, who considered himself a future leader of the Third World countries, wanted to establish the Communist regime in as many African territories as possible.

General Pleșca believed it to be too good news not to celebrate, so he opened another Hennessy bottle and called his adjutant. Major Alexe was used to the General being unpredictable and arrogant when drunk so he appeared before him right away and reported in the military style:

"Long live, comrade General-Lieutenant! I'm at your command."

He was a young, tall officer of an athletic build with an oval face and magnetic blue eyes. The General appreciated his ability to memorize faces, mathematical or chemical formulas, electrical diagrams, and other useful things for espionage missions.

"At ease, Major. You look as if a wooden stick has been stuck up in your ass. It's time to celebrate! Mobutu has accepted Comrade Ceaușescu's proposal. In three days, we'll travel to Kinshasa, and soon have well-trained agents in Africa. Our Supreme Commander's wish will finally come true!"

Alexe didn't seem enthusiastic and maintained the attention position.

"Let's drink together, my tough boy, our life is beautiful!" the General swung the bottle of cognac before his subordinate's eyes.

"With all due respect, comrade General, I'm on duty," Major Alexe said.

"Damn your duty and all the regulations made by some idiot military people," the General snapped. "We are always in the service of the country! Don't you see? Although it's Sunday we still work like the slaves on the American plantations. From time to time, we need to fucking relax. Now, I order you to drink this fine cognac with me."

"I understand, comrade General. As it is a special event, allow me first to go and take two crystal glasses from the officers' restaurant," Alexe asked the permission.

"Why the hell do you need glasses for? We can drink directly from the bottle," said the General upset. "In your remote village, during the fieldwork, aren't the peasants drinking water from a barrel placed in the cool shade of the trees, using the same clay pot? That's why I brought you beside me, Alexe. Because you are the son of hardworking peasants and because you have a healthy political and social background. You are not a prop of the pubs' walls, like - unfortunately for this country - many young people still are."

The General held out the bottle to Alexe who looked at it with the usual reluctance of the Romanian peasant. Pleșca asked him harshly:

"What is it, Alexe? Don't you want to share the bottle with me?"

"Of course, I do, comrade General!" the Major replied apologetically.

"Then what are you waiting for? Take the bottle and drink! Believe me, it is the best brandy in the World, even if it comes from the imperialist system. Learn how to drink properly, in the same way as our working class, not according to the decadent habits of the exploiting bourgeoisie… in crystal glasses…," the General sneered and seeing that his adjutant still pondered, he added: "Come on, my boy, don't act like a silly virgin on her wedding night, who doesn't know what she really wants. Be a man!"

To encourage him, Pleșca took three sips first and wiped the mouth of the bottle, following the proletarian ritual.

"Look, comrade Major," he said laughing, "I'm a man who cares about your health. I don't want to contaminate you with the General ranks on my shoulder. Your time will come. But now you'll have to do your job in Zaire. After completing this mission, I could write a good recommendation for the Party leadership to promote you. Your file is in order. I want to make you Colonel; do you understand me? I could very well congratulate you right now!"

"I serve my country, comrade General!" Alexe answered pleased with the news. This was the standard reply for receiving congratulations from a military superior. He grabbed the bottle and took three sips, imitating his superior's ritual.

"Allow me to report, comrade General!" he began in an official tone. "While you were busy, I received several informative notes."

"Damn it with all the informative garbage! I'm fed up with these notes," the General growled, taking another three sips of cognac.

"If you allow me, two of them could interest you," the Major went on.

"Tell me briefly, what's it all about?" ordered Pleşca, swinging the bottle as if to make sure there was still enough drink in it.

"The source *Ivan* reported that the Soviets have problems with one of their satellites. The comrades from KGB are already in *Red Alert*," Alexe said.

"Again?! To hell with the Soviet Space technology, with all their satellites and shit!", Pleşca stormed. "They lose the satellites one by one... Those fucking old iron monsters fall from the sky like boulders!"

The General was pissed off about the inefficiency of the Soviet military satellites that still were no match to the Americans' high-tech ones. He had in mind to suggest to Ceauşescu to raise this delicate matter at the upcoming meeting of the Warsaw Treaty, the military alliance of the socialist countries. A few moments later he added furiously:

"When I think of how difficult it was for me to get this fucking *Ivan* into the Soviet Embassy, I feel like putting a bullet in his brainless head. I'm bloody sure he was so reckless as to get himself discovered and the Soviets blackmailed and forced him to become a double agent. Lately, he has been sending us only the information we learn on Radio Moscow anyway."

"If you allow me, comrade General, his note says that atomic cell batteries power this satellite," Major Alexe continued.

"What's special about this? That's no longer a secret. At the time of their fabrication, the Russians didn't have solar panels, since they had not yet succeeded in stealing the technology from the Americans. They had to use atomic cell batteries and launched the satellites into Space without thinking that one day the fucking things would fall back on the Earth and contaminate our planet."

"With all due respect, comrade General, that's the main problem," Alexe insisted. "This satellite could fall anywhere, our country's territory included, thus producing radioactive contamination on a fairly large surface… It would be a real disaster if it fell into a city…"

"The World is wide enough. Its chances of falling in our country are very low. We won't receive such an expensive *gift* from the Soviets. The satellite will fall into one of the oceans, just as the others had. Don't be a panic-monger, Alexe! Be optimistic like Bulă!

The Securitate had a special service that made up jokes to distract the citizens from the daily hardships and the low standard of living. The main character of these jokes was Bulă, who represented idiocy and stupidity. Everything that Bulă was doing was wrong.

"Do you know that joke about Bulă and the atomic bomb?" the General asked in good spirits. "It is said that Bulă once heard on the radio how expensive an atomic bomb was and prayed daily to God that one would fall in his garden, so that he would get rich!" Virgil Pleşca laughed, thinking how much this joke matched Major Alexe's fear and added: "Forget about the Russian satellite. It's your turn to drink. I don't like to wait too long when I am thirsty."

Major Alexe took the bottle from his boss's hand and had another three sips, still thinking about the Soviet satellite with atomic cell batteries.

"If you allow me, comrade General," he continued. "The second important note is from our service monitoring the radio broadcasts transmitted by Radio Free Europe."

General Pleşca flinched slightly and the smile disappeared from his face.

"What the hell, you incompetent bastard!" he thundered. "This is not the *second* important note, but *the first*! That's what I'm interested in, not the Russian satellites! Tell me quickly what it says."

Without being affected by the rude rebuke of his boss or the fact that he confused the priority of the informational notes, Major Alexe continued his report with a loud and clear voice:

"Today, at 10:00 AM, Radio Free Europe broadcast news about the citizen Mihai Hohenzollern. They said the former King of Romania will soon publish a memoir that will be sold in the World's largest bookstores."

This information seriously puzzled General Pleşca. He didn't feel like drinking anymore. He put down the Hennessy bottle on his desk, and began to pace the room morosely, knowing he had to take an important decision as soon as possible. From time to time, he glanced at Ceauşescu's painting as though he wanted to make sure his Supreme Commander didn't notice his hesitation.

Whilst Mihai, the King, was a thorn in the side of the Communist leadership even now, forty years later after his abdication, Virgil Pleșca secretly admired this dignified man who held a deep respect for the Romanian people. The cousin of the Queen of the United Kingdom, with excellent connections in all the Royal families in Europe, King Mihai went through a difficult historical period. He was still a young man during the Second World War, but his remarkable contribution had shortened it by over six months, as even his opponents, including the Soviet Union, admitted at the time. On August 23, 1944, he arrested Marshal Antonescu, Hitler's ally, and ordered the Romanian Army to fight alongside the Allies' military forces, until the complete victory against Nazism. But the communists did everything in their power to overthrow the monarchic institution and send King Mihai into exile, thus illegally taking over the leadership of the Romanian State. Now he was the only state leader alive of all those who fought during World War II; a brave, faithful man who, unlike Ceaușescu, walked without fear among the people with no personal guard behind him, and who drove his own car.

Upon hearing his name, the blood usually drained from Nicolae Ceaușescu's face. The Supreme Commander's continuous endeavors to erase the memory of King Mihai from the Romanian's minds were in vain. The publication of this memoir would be a heavy blow to him and a stain on the history of the Communist Party. The timing was also unfortunate, with the upcoming National Conference of the Party in two weeks, without any doubt a strategic move of the King, his way of protesting against what was happening in Romania. If the Securitate were not able to stop the book's distribution, Ceaușescu would have one of his usual nervous breakdowns the General knew too well. Worst of all, his subordinates wouldn't have been raised in their ranks as he had promised them.

General Pleșca finally came to a decision and grabbed his cognac bottle again. He had his usual sips and invited Alexe to drink again, but his adjutant didn't dare anymore. Pleșca urged him in a friendly tone:

"Come on, my boy, have another drink. To hell with the informative notes!"

Alexe acquiesced. As he watched the young man drinking, the General thought it necessary to make a brief indoctrination and remind the Major about the attitude all Securitate officers must have against Mihai Hohenzollern. It was a precaution in case Alexe could be interrogated by the Counterintelligence Service about the General's reaction to the news about the launch of the King's book.

The job of the Counterintelligence officers was rather unpleasant. They were spying on their own colleagues, reporting on them periodically. They were, in theory, independent from the Securitate, but, basically, they worked under the same umbrella. The head of the Counterintelligence Service, Colonel Petrescu, had the duty to inform Ceaușescu directly of any illegal or suspicious action from any Securitate employee, including General Pleșca. Still, he never did that without speaking to the General first.

"The fight against imperialism requires revolutionary vigilance", he started with his stereotypical phrase that he often used in discussions with his subordinates. "I have to stop the distribution of this book at any cost," continued Pleșca, quite unconvincingly. "The former King's memoir will surely denigrate our struggles to take the power from the hands of the reactionary bourgeoisie. The Supreme Commander greatly appreciates this revolutionary stage in the history of the Communist Party of Romania, when the working class took over the country and the people's enemies were crushed. In all the Party documents, Comrade Ceaușescu called this wonderful period the time of our *Party's revolutionary romanticism*. I will not allow Mihai Hohenzollern to tarnish it with his carefully chosen, manipulative words."

As he was speaking, the General watched closely his subordinate's expression, but there was no reaction on Alexe's face. He listened to him impassively, like a statue. Pleșca knew this type of indoctrination influenced only those with weak minds. The smart ones were usually incorruptible, maintaining their own political opinions.

The General pondered a few moments, put the Hennessy bottle on the desk again, and said authoritatively:

"Major Alexe, put me on the phone with Colonel Săftoiu."

Colonel Săftoiu was the Director of *Voice of the Homeland*. This radio station had powerful transmitters that broadcast on shortwave radio. A true forest of high-technology antennas installed on the outskirts of a village in the North of Bucharest ensured the reception of radio broadcasts Worldwide. The electromagnetic field radiating in the ether within more than a kilometer radius of the antennas was so strong that locals could light up their homes using neon tubes without connecting them to the power grid. Officially, this radio station was independent and addressed to all Romanians living abroad. Its goal was to inform them correctly and objectively about the events and everyday life in Socialist Republic of Romania. It also broadcast traditional Romanian music the people listened to with tears in their eyes, thinking fondly of their distant homeland they had been forced to leave because of the oppression of the Communist regime. The Securitate took advantage of their sentimentality and patriotism, setting them diabolical traps for recruiting future agents. In time, the new agents began to believe the ideas of the xenophobe propaganda, that many enemies covet Romania because of its natural resources. They became convinced that by spying on their compatriots, friends, or neighbors who criticized Ceaușescu's regime, following the orders from the Bucharest Espionage Center, they were helping their country.

Only undercover intelligence officers worked at the *Voice of the Homeland* radio station. The technical staff and those who provided the usual services were also undercover employees of the Interior Minister. This radio station was an important strategic objective, considered by the Party as one of the best means of propaganda work carried out to put the dictatorial Communist regime established by Nicolae Ceaușescu in a good light.

The news broadcast also conveyed many coded messages to the Romanian secret agents scattered Worldwide. For this purpose, they were supplied with high-performance Blaupunkt radios, which ensured good radio reception even under difficult conditions, having the obligation to listen to the *Voice of the Homeland* at certain hours set by the Center.

General Pleșca held the receiver to his ear, waiting for Colonel Săftoiu, one of his secret poker partners, to pick up the phone. Ceaușescu had banned all gambling the State couldn't control, allowing his intelligence officers to play only *Bridge,* a smart game that stimulates the mind. But the General was a big poker fan and often lost large amounts of money when playing with prominent gamblers. Of course, it wasn't his money. The cash came from the generous budget allocated for the secret operations of the Securitate and the General didn't have to account to anyone for how he chose to spend this money.

Pleşca was losing his patience when the Colonel finally answered the call.

"What the hell are you doing, Colonel?" the General exploded half-laughing. "You made me wait an eternity, you bastard engineer turned into an officer overnight. When I call, you must answer immediately!"

"I respectfully report to you, comrade General, I have been to the toilet," replied the Colonel, his voice steady without a hint of embarrassment which only amused the General who laughed louder. He owed the Colonel a thousand dollars from the last poker game, so Virgil Pleşca replied meekly:

"Come on, Colonel, going to the toilet is our only pleasure left in this short life…"

The Director of *Voice of the Homeland* appreciated the sincerity of the General and resumed his military tone:

"Comrade General-Lieutenant, this is Colonel Săftoiu Ion and I am ready to receive your orders!"

Pleşca checked the new gold pocket watch, he had gotten as a present from the Romanian Ambassador in Berna, a few days ago. It was 12:30 PM, so he had enough time to send the instructions to the agents.

"Colonel Săftoiu, pay attention to my order!" he said determinedly. "This evening, after the 8 PM news, you will broadcast the song *Sleigh with bells* twice in a row. I repeat: *Sleigh with bells* twice in a row."

"Understood, comrade General!" he replied and added in a lower hissed voice, hoping to get extra information from his superior: "It means the situation is *blue and bloated* if I have to broadcast it twice in a row…"

"Hold your fucking tongue, Colonel!" Pleșca snapped. "This matter doesn't concern you. You know, I fuck the curious guys. Carry out my order in due time, without any comments." Then he continued more calmly: "I want us to meet tonight for a *Bridge* round. Tomorrow I won't be available. The *Big Boss* is sending me *to graze the sheep*…"

Once he ended the call, the General continued pacing around the room, still thinking over the details of the operation he wanted to launch. The song *Sleigh with bells* was a signal to all the Romanian secret agents in the Western countries, meaning they would receive a coded message regarding an important action with special political implications, in precisely one hour.

The Securitate had a long playlist of songs for similar purposes. For instance, the song *Listen, Dear Marioara*, performed by the famous Romanian folk singer Benone Sinulescu, conveyed that the Bucharest Center has received the information and everything was in order. At the same time, the song *Last Winter Was Winter* by Maria Tănase was a call to a meeting previously settled, the emissaries taking over and sending the information to the Center.

Upon deciding on the new order for his agents, General Pleșca called back his adjutant. Major Alexe returned holding a red notebook. Depending on their importance, the orders for the Securitate agents were written down in notebooks of various colors. The red one was for the most important tasks.

The General sat down comfortably at his desk and dictated:

"Warning! Warning to all of you! Follow the *Shepherd's'* special order! You must prevent the distribution of the book published by citizen Mihai by any means. Buy all the copies and destroy them! Starting from this moment, you are on *Red Alert*!"

The Shepherd was the General's code name, and although most of his agents knew that, some zealous ones still believed *The Shepherd* to be Ceaușescu. The idea that the Dictator himself sent them the orders was like a surge of adrenalin to them.

Major Alexe still waited for further orders, pen in hand hovering over the open notebook, and his superior stormed:

"Why are you still standing here like a scarecrow on the hemp field? Go and encrypt my order quickly and forward it using the usual line! Be careful, today is Sunday. You'll have to use *Little Red Riding Hood*."

"Yes, comrade General!" Alexe said and gave the regular military salute before returning to his desk in the anteroom.

On the wall behind him, several bookshelves were stacked with heavy old volumes, all of them having red covers as they belonged to the Communist political literature. The writings of Marx, Engels, and Lenin seemed forgotten on the bottom shelf. The upper one was filled with newer copies of political books. Nicolae Ceaușescu's most important work, *Romania on the Way of Building up the Multilaterally Developed Socialist Society,* had more than twenty volumes with bright red covers.

Curious enough, Major Alexe kept some children's literature books on the same shelf. He took out a copy of The

Brothers Grimm's Complete Fairy Tales and browsed through it until he found the story of *Little Red Riding Hood*.

He sat at his desk and started to work, writing down in the operative register the page number, the number of the row on which a certain word was found and the number of the selected word, counting from right to left. The rule was to use a different story from the same book every day, according to a well-established schedule. The book would be changed at the end of each month with another pre-established one. Of course, it was a tedious job demanding patience and much attention, but it was safe enough and Major Alexe did it with pleasure. He broadcast the resulting string of numbers in Russian at a certain hour set by a pirate radio station on short waves, having the transmitters close to the Eastern border of Romania. The Western secret services trying to locate its geographic coordinates were fooled into believing that the broadcast came from the territory of the Soviet Union. In this way, *The Shepherd*'s order could be safely sent to the overseas agents who decoded the numbers following the same system.

In his office, General Pleșca, hungover from drinking, took a couple of American pills that reduced the effect of alcohol on the brain. He hoped to clear his mind before the poker game that night with Colonel Săftoiu and to ease all the consequences of drunkenness the next morning when he would surely be summoned by Ceaușescu to receive the instructions on the Zaire mission. He had already made a bad impression by answering the *"red phone"* drunk and still expected serious criticism from his Supreme Commander. As he swallowed the pills, he seriously considered buying a large supply for all the

Securitate officers. He had been told that American agent always carried them in their pockets.

He put the cork back in the Hennessy bottle - so as not to lose it among the files on his desk lest they ended up in the safe where the secret documents were kept - before placing it in a cherry wood cabinet in a corner of the room. There he deposited his entire collection of drink bottles, to keep them away from the curious eyes of those who had access to his office.

This beautifully carved piece of furniture had a special history. Many years ago, the Securitate confiscated it from the house of a bourgeois writer who wrote a novel about the peasants' life in the new socialist agriculture. Because the novel hadn't been written according to the Party ideology, the Censorship Committee of the Ministry of Culture rejected it and ordered the immediate confiscation of the manuscript. The Securitate agents had found it in this elegant cabinet and they didn't resist taking as well, as a gift for the head of the service at that time, who needed to furnish his new office.

After a few moments of hesitation, General Pleşca sat back on his chair and picked up the phone connected to the Government Special Communications Service. He ordered the operator to put him through with the Romanian Ambassador in Berna using the safe encode line. He asked the Ambassador to purchase King Mihai's memoir as soon as possible and send it to him by a diplomatic courier. The General couldn't help being interested in this book, which might help him better understand the events between August 23, 1944, and December 30, 1947. He had already studied the documents in the Royal Archives, now in the custody of the Securitate. Still, he didn't find much eloquent information on the period he was interested in. Many papers with compromising evidence on the actions of the Communist Party had been falsified or destroyed by his predecessors. Pleşca had once found texts typed on a different kind of paper, probably written by an illiterate, as they had many grammar mistakes. The author of the fake pages had not used the same typewriter as the King's secretary, who edited most of the documents in the Royal Archives.

The General was particularly interested in what happened on August 23, 1944, when King Mihai ordered the Romanian Army to turn its weapons against Hitler's Germany, an act of courage which the Communist Party, with only a few hundred members at the time, took full credit for without any shame. Thus, every year on August 23, the Party celebrated the so-called: *"Anti-Fascist and Anti-Imperialist Insurgency coordinated by the Communist Party"* without mentioning King Mihai, who had a decisive role in those dramatic historical events.

Following March 6, 1945, after the Soviet troops had occupied Romania and formed a Communist government by force and blackmail, King Mihai struggled to delay the installation of Communism, through all the legal means provided by the Constitution in force. The Communist Government, Moscow's puppet, cynically called itself the *"First Democratic Government in the History of Romania"* and followed Stalin's order, destroying in fact all the democratic institutions of the State.

Prime Minister Petru Groza, whom the Romanian citizens considered a traitor to the nation and a political opportunist, forced the King to abdicate on December 30, 1947. Meanwhile, the new Government grew stronger, especially after the electoral fraud in November 1946, when all the other democratic political parties were removed and banned. The only political activity allowed on the territory of Romania remained that of the Communist Party.

Upon reading a series of papers in the Archives, General Pleșca had learned about Petru Groza's many blackmail attempts and threats against the King to coerce him to abdicate. At one point, on December 30 1947, he burst into the King's office, with a gun hidden under his coat, saying that if the King refused to abdicate, he would immediately order the police to shoot more than a thousand young students. The Communist Police had arrested the students for participating in an anti-communist demonstration a few weeks before, during the celebration of King Mihai's birthday. Finally, the monarch gave in and signed the act of abdication, taking the sad path of exile but keeping his homeland forever in his heart.

Although he did many despicable things as the head of an institution hated by most people, General Pleșca considered himself a patriotic Romanian officer. He was not indifferent to what was happening around him. He knew that the Romanian people's lives were getting worse with each day, and the dictatorial regime of Nicolae Ceaușescu strangled the country itself.

The Romanians were hungry and living in darkness and cold, in a country with fertile plains and enough oil and natural gas to meet everyone's needs. The basic food products, the fuel for heating homes during the winter, the soap, the gasoline and diesel, the electricity, and many other things necessary for a decent living were strictly rationalized under Ceaușescu's order.

After borrowing a lot of money from Western banks under unfavorable conditions and with high-interest rates to forcefully industrialize the country, he exported, at a low price, everything that could be exported, to pay all the external debts as quickly as possible, thus sacrificing the well-being of the population.

He had built many chemical plants, steel factories, and other industrial facilities, without taking into account the fact that he needed an infrastructure for such investments first. The Romanian industry was therefore a cumbersome and unprofitable one consuming a lot of energy and heavily polluting the environment because of the old technologies.

Once, at a hunting party, when he had drunk more than usual, Ceauşescu confessed to Pleşca that he would continue the high rhythm of exports even after paying off all the debts of the country. He said that the population was already accustomed to daily deprivations, and by continuing to export, he would be able to get enough money to set up a bank for the Third World. This bank, which would have been called *Banca Ceauşescu* would be willing to grant low-interest loans without asking for guarantees to all poor countries, especially the African ones, which could have even canceled their debts to the bank, if they had followed the path socialist development. These Utopian plans, which Ceauşescu wanted to fulfill by sacrificing the Romanian people, made General Pleşca think very seriously about an alternative governance of Romania.

Chapter 4

May 24, 1987, 7:30 PM - local time
Baikonur - Soviet Space Center

Colonel Zapojnikov felt he had lost control and was groping in a dark labyrinth. After the meeting with General Pucinski and the special emissary of the USSR Security Department, he went to the Operating Room to see if there were any chances for the satellite to be brought back into orbit or if any measures required in such extreme cases had to be taken. Everything was uncertain. The control desk operators were tense and hoped to find a way out.

The idea of beginning the investigation of the best officers in such a time was absurd to him. He didn't trust the emissary. His arrogance was outrageous. As an experienced officer, Igor wondered if there were no other interests behind the civilian's excessive zeal and sternness. When he got to his office, he would report the situation directly to Moscow and ask for instructions.

Being the head of Counterintelligence, he had the office, equipped with special communications technology, located in the main pavilion of the Soviet Space Center. The office door was sealed during his absence, and no one had access inside. The regulations required that the seals' integrity be checked only in the presence of a security officer before the door was reopened.

This procedure was not always followed anyway. Now Zapojnikov didn't have time for that. He went to his office alone, but, to his amazement, he found the seals broken and the door open. In the anteroom, Irina was preparing tea in a samovar. According to the rules, she would have had to wait in the Secretary's Room until she was called for.

"How did you get in here without my approval, comrade secretary?" the Colonel asked, puzzled, and rather pissed off. "You are allowed in this office only in my presence."

"The comrade in there gave his approval," Irina replied, an innocent smile, and she pointed to the red-padded door of his office. Zapojnikov could not believe his eyes. The civilian in smoky glasses sat comfortably at his desk, smoking and browsing a newspaper. The Colonel barely refrained from grabbing the intruder by the collar and dragging him out.

"You are not allowed in here. Please, leave at once!" he said firmly.

"I'm afraid you didn't understand me earlier," the emissary replied, ostentatiously blowing a cigarette smoke in Igor's face. "I am in charge now and I give the orders here."

"This is my office," the Colonel countered. "I'm going to report this situation to the Center. I receive orders only from my superiors."

He picked up the phone, but it wasn't working. Igor understood that he was being trained in dangerous game. The civilian gave a devilish smile and explained:

"I ordered the phone lines to be cut off to avoid information leakage. For now, those who want to make a phone call need my approval, but in the next few hours, I will not allow anyone to use the phones anymore. For the same security reasons, I need the keys to your safe."

He pointed to a painting of Lenin giving a speech to the crowd. Behind that painting, built into the wall, was the safe where the secret documents and the satellite communication system were kept. Zapojnikov controlled his nerves even though an arrogant civilian was sitting in his chair, giving him orders.

"This is not possible, comrade!" he said in a categorical tone. "I don't care who are you. I swore that I will hand over those keys only along with my insignia as a senior officer of the Soviet Union and my Communist Party membership card."

"Your oath means nothing to the security interests of the Soviet Union," the civilian said having a threatening undertone in his voice. "If you refuse to hand over the keys, I will arrest you on charges of high treason."

"I won't allow you to talk to me like that!" Zapojnikov warned him raising his voice and instinctively reaching for his service gun. He immediately realized he was unarmed. The holster was empty. According to the regulations, he had left his revolver in the gun rack at the entrance of the Space Center.

The civilian did not miss the Colonel's intention. He got up from the chair and, moving his wristwatch closer to his lips, whispered something that sounded like a command. Zapojnikov sensed what was to come. The next moment, two athletic young men in black uniforms and short haircuts came into the room and remained by the door, motionless like two statues. Their faces looked like they had been flattened by a jackhammer: narrow forehead, prominent cheekbones, flat nose, small green eyes. The Colonel turned to them impassively as if he had been waiting for them.

"Introduce yourself, comrades!" the civilian ordered.

"I'm Agent 236, codenamed *Petrov*, ready to serve the Soviet Union at any time!" the first said loudly, his voice echoing in the entire room.

"I'm Agent 142, codenamed *Feodor*, ready for any sacrifice in the service of the Soviet Union!" said the second in the same manner.

The civilian laughed contentedly.

"Do you see them, Colonel? They are the best elite fighters of the war in Afghanistan. They are experienced in commando battles, they are snipers, masters in martial arts, and specialists in coding information with many other qualities. It would take them less than a minute to open your safe without your keys. We can take a bet if you want."

Zapojnikov realized he was cornered. The two agents seemed unbeatable indeed. If the civilian gave a simple nod, he would have been immobilized. Triggering the alarm would have been the only solution. Igor carried a special device in his chest pocket. He only had to press a button that would alert the special forces of the Soviet Space Centre, ready to intervene in the event of a terrorist attack at any time. He coughed nervously and pretended to adjust his tie, thus trying to reach the button of the alarm device. The civilian watched him closely and understood the intention.

"Don't try for nothing!" he said, a distorted sadistic smile on his face. "The alarm system has been switched off at my order. What if the Special Brigade controlled the entire Soviet Space Center? You'd be a lost man, wouldn't you?"

* * *

RED ALERT FOR ROMANIA

May 24, 1987, 10:30 AM - local time
US Space Monitoring Center

Sitting in front of a computer terminal, Professor Gordon, assisted by General Alan King and a few other officers, compiled the data transmitted by the radar stations. After few hours of hard work, Gordon was exhausted. The excruciating thirst felt during the flight began to nag him again, so more juice, ice, and coffee were brought to him.

As he drank the cool a red orange juice breathlessly, the image of the bearded geologist came back to his mind. For a moment, he indulged in the fancy that the juice in his glass was the Romanian red wine from Vrancea.

"What's going on, Doctor Gordon?" the General asked impatiently, without giving him a minute respite.

"The fall is imminent. I estimate that impact with the ground will occur in about… 23 hours…"

"I see… But where? For God's sake, where will it fall?"

"I believe somewhere… in Eastern Europe."

"I want precise data. I want the place of impact coordinates, as accurate as possible!"

"Before the satellite enters the stratosphere, I can't give you any reliable data. I assure you I will do my best to determine the place of impact in order to prevent the population in the area. The lives of innocent people are a priority."

"Professor, I'm a military, not a charity! I don't pay you to give me lectures on humanitarianism. I want those coordinates as soon as possible!"

The General and the other officers went out, leaving Gordon alone.

In a room, specially protected against interceptors, Alan King had a brief discussion with the officers in charge. Urgent action was needed. He established a telephone connection with the Department of Foreign Affairs and requested assistance from the active agents in Eastern Europe. The news did not satisfy him for he said:

"Gentlemen, we can only rely on ourselves. The Department of Foreign Affairs doesn't want to get involved. There is a high risk of an international scandal." He looked for Captain Power. The people trained by him remained the only solution.

"Captain Power, what can you tell us about your famous *Panther* agents we've been investing in for so long?"

"They are students in Communist countries, General."

"How long do you need to put them on alert?"

Power looked at his watch.

"It's already night in Eastern Europe," he said discontentedly. "It will be difficult for me to gather fast the whole team."

"We'll need only a couple of agents, not the entire team," General Alan King explained. "Depending on the place of impact, we will decide who will take action. This is an order: all *Panther* agents must be alerted!"

"Understood, Sir! I will alert all our agents in Eastern Europe".

Captain Power greeted him, left the meeting, and went straight to the Telecommunications Room. He ordered the operators to switch on all satellite communications facilities and the shortwave transceivers utilized by radio amateurs. A few operators started immediately to send messages in ether, using the radio amateurs' specific calls:

"Calling! Calling! Calling SQ, SQ, SQ, calling SQ, and standing by!"

When he returned to the Computer Room, Alan King had a pleasant surprise. Gordon had already printed several pages showing the possible trajectory of the satellite in the lower layers of the atmosphere and the estimated coordinates of the impact site.

"General, I think this is the final result," the Professor said and pressed a key, displaying on the screen the geographic coordinates of where the impact was most likely to occur. "I tried by three different methods of calculations and the results are similar. My equations are confirmed by reality. The estimated trajectory corresponds to the real one…"

He typed again on the computer keyboard and displayed the map of Eastern Europe. A pulsating red-light dot indicated the location of the impact.

"What country is that, Professor?" the General asked, somewhat confused.

"Romania. The impact zone is near the confluence of the Danube River with the Black Sea." The Commander headed like a robot to the communication terminal nearby. He turned on the amplifier and announced:

"Attention, please! Attention, please! *Number one* for all of you! *Red alert for Romania!* I repeat! *Red alert for Romania!*"

The alarm siren echoed again, and Professor Gordon felt the same auditory discomfort he had experienced a few hours earlier in the General's office.

* * *

May 24, 1987, 7:40 PM - local time
Baikonur - Soviet Space Center

Zapojnikov wondered if what was happening to him was real. He, the vigilante Counterintelligence Colonel, so often decorated for his merits and special services to the Soviet Union, was taken prisoner in his own office by a diversionary group, and forced to hand over the keys to the safe where he kept secret documents. The door remained open. There was no movement in the anteroom. *"What is Irina doing?"* he wondered. *"Perhaps she betrayed me or they shut her up…"* Igor heard the clinking of the teacups. So, Irina was still in there. The thought that the secretary had betrayed him left him with a bad taste.

The agents of the *Special Brigade* were older *rivals*. Colonel Zapojnikov foiled their attempt to take over the Soviet Space Center some time ago. Information had been received in advance that a group of saboteurs would be parachuted into a nearby field with the mission of testing the effectiveness of the Soviet Space Center's security system. He took all the necessary precautions in such a situation and the agents trying to sneak into the Space Center were captured. Only one, well trained, managed to pass through the high-voltage fence and before being immobilized he put a label that read *mined site,* right next to a sentry post. No one was injured and the diversionary agents were handed over to their commander. After a short friendly negotiation with vodka and black caviar, the military unit guarding the objective received the qualification *very good.*

Zapojnikov tried to remain calm. If the Space Center was indeed in the hands of the *Special Brigade*, all was lost. The lack of vigilance and the inefficiency of the security services were to be recorded in the report. The consequences were serious: a possible accusation of treason, the prospect of degradation, deportation, and maybe even imprisonment.

Soon Irina came in, carrying teacups, glasses, and a bottle of vodka on a tray, an innocent smile on her face, as if everything was normal. The woman placed the tray on the desk with an elegant gesture, bending slightly. Despite his situation, Zapojnikov couldn't help gazing at her long beautiful legs. The civilian made a discreet gesture and the two agents framing the door left the room.

"The test of *revolutionary vigilance* is over." he said with a cold smile. He took off his glasses and placed them on the desk, adding in a friendly tone: "Comrade Colonel Zapojnikov, you have shown me your attachment to the cause of the Soviet Union, but you still have some shortcomings when it comes to the vigilance of a true Counterintelligence officer. The situation I have just simulated could be a real one. My current position allows me to report negatively on the status quo here. That's why I was hard on General Pucinski. He was appointed Commander of the Soviet Spatial Center on my recommendation. We have a history together and some unfinished business here, but this it is another story. Irina spoke highly of you that's why I wanted us to meet today."

Igor immediately understood that he was the subject of a dubious game that had stretched his nerves to the maximum. He fixed Irina with a reprimanding look, but she, as if nothing had happened, smiled at him so gently, that the Colonel became even more suspicious.

"Comrade Colonel, let me introduce to you my father, General Vladimir Ivanovici Petrovski," she said in a slightly subversively tone and burst out laughing.

* * *

May 24, 1987, 10:40 AM - local time
US Space Monitoring Center

Professor Gordon realized everything was pouring like an avalanche and felt it was his duty to do all he could to minimize the unwanted effects of the satellite crash.

"General, if you'll allow me, I have a suggestion," he began. "I know the impact zone."

"Do you?" the General asked in surprise.

"Yes. And I am somewhat attached to that part of the World. The impact will cause an ecological disaster! The Danube Delta, a paradise for wild birds, is quite close…"

"The fate of the Danube birds is not my business."

"I would like to warn the Romanian authorities. If you don't want to do it for military and political reasons, I will. I feel it is my moral duty."

"We disagree on that, Doctor Gordon. These are issues of huge military interest. Anyway, thank you for your cooperation." Someone gave the General a check and after he signed it, he handed it to the Professor explaining:

"This is for all your trouble. The payment also covers the hours you will have to spend here until the operation is completed."

"I think such an attitude is absurd," Gordon said, ignoring the check. "If you don't need me anymore, I want to leave. I've already told you I have a lot of work to do."

"I'm afraid that's not possible, Doctor Gordon. I regret having to change your schedule, but these are the orders. We can't risk a leak of information right now."

Professor Gordon didn't even listen to him anymore. He closed his briefcase and headed to the exit. Two athletic guys barred his way. Surprised, Gordon turned to Alan King.

"You have no right to keep me here against my will. I will sue you in Court!"

The General approached him, a cold smile on his lips.

"We take that risk, Doctor Gordon." He gave him the check and said as if he was making a toast: "For our present and future collaboration!"

Gordon looked around for a solution, both indignation and fear swelling up inside him. The two guards flanked him closely. Realizing there was no way to escape, he took the piece of paper hesitantly and put it in his pocket without even looking at it. The General frowned. He didn't like the scientist's attitude.

"Take Mister Gordon to the apartment I reserved for him," he said firmly to the guards. "He's tired and needs some rest."

Gordon left the Computers Room, taking one last look at the huge screen with the map of the Danube Delta and the pulsating red dot marking a South-West mountainous area.

Alan King called the *Telecommunications Room* and asked for Captain Power.

"Focus on the impact area!" he ordered. "Get all the details through the operating circuits and report back to me!"

"We've got some trouble in Romania," Power reported rather worriedly. "Our agent, Gilbert, cannot be activated. His paging system doesn't answer the satellite alert signal. Either the gypsies stole his pager again, or he's in a radio-shielded area."

"How is that possible?!" the General snapped. "What kind of agents do you have? This is intolerable!"

"In that part of the World, anything is possible, sir, but we have backup solutions. Gilbert has a student girlfriend. She has been checked and passed all our recruitment tests. She has recently started to do even small *services* for us. She knows where Gilbert can be found. We're trying to contact her through a radio amateur. Right now, one of our operators is chatting with one *Yankee Oscar 3* from Bucharest, an old acquaintance in the wavelength of twenty meters. He seems to be a cooperating guy."

"Hurry up and report back to me as soon as you activate agent Gilbert!"

Alan King closed the communications terminal thoughtful, speaking as for himself:

"To have the pager stolen twice! Either our agent is an idiot and needs to be withdrawn urgently, or the gypsies from Romania are experts as pickpockets and should be recruited for some of our operations."

The last thing he wanted to do was to call the US Embassy in Bucharest and ask the attaché in charge of technical equipment for agents to equip again the idiot Gilbert with another pager.

In less than fifteen minutes, Power appeared in the Commander's office and reported triumphantly:

"Agent Gilbert from Romania has been activated! His pager hasn't been stolen. As I suspected, he was in a radio-shielded area.

He has already contacted us by satellite phone and is waiting for instructions."

"Well done, Captain!" Alan King said relieved.

"I was lucky!" said Captain Power. "After all these years I've been working for the *red zone*, I've come to the conclusion that the people beyond the *Iron Curtain* have strange reactions. They are kind and ready to help you with anything, even at the cost of their own freedom. For example, this *Yankee Oscar 3* from Bucharest; I asked him to send a message as a local telephone call and he did it while he was still on the radio connection with us. He was so kind and fast…"

"Indeed, he was fast," remarked the General, busy on the computer keyboard.

"It is difficult to explain why Romanians sometimes take risks deliberately." continued Power who was in the mood to talk, despite the urgent situation in which he was. "I found the explanation for this phenomenon. Ordinary citizens in Romania suffer, above all, from isolation. It is a kind of social claustrophobia, and any contact with the Free World makes them feel free. Any communication with foreign citizens by radio or telephone gives them a feeling of euphoria, like a drug that makes them forget about the ubiquitous surveillance. Sometimes I feel sorry for them. They are like pheasants flying in the hunter's sight deliberately…"

The General, who sat at the computer, checking the flood of information coming from the database, interrupted him, eager to end Power's speech:

"I'm glad to learn you've become a philosopher, Captain! I recommend you the utmost caution, though. The Romanian secret services are quite efficient."

"I know that, but you don't have to worry. If necessary, the agents from Bulgaria *Ilf and Petrov* may also be activated. All communications are secure and double-coded. The satellite connection works perfectly. In addition, they can use ultra-fast two-meter band telegraphy on the ionized path of meteorites. My people have the necessary equipment."

These assurances did not affect Alan King, the reality immediately confirmed his pessimism. On the intercom came the voice of a radio operator who wanted to report something urgent to captain Power.

"Communicate!" he answered impatiently, not asking the Commander's permission to use the equipment on his desk.

An unpleasant message had just been received from Romania. Agent Gilbert reported that he was constantly under surveillance and his car couldn't leave Bucharest without raising suspicion.

"I just told you earlier, you must be careful!" warned the General again. "In Romania, almost all the people are monitored by the secret services, especially the foreign citizens."

With a resigned look on his face, Power said that he had considered such a possibility.

"I will ask the agent in Romania to get another car urgently. I think his girlfriend can help him. I will also activate the agents in Bulgaria. I must give the necessary instructions right now. I can't afford any more risks."

Captain Power saluted and hurried to the Radio Communications Room. At the same time, General Alan King continued to ask the operators for as much detail as possible about where the impact was to occur, authorizing their access to the National Data Center of the Defense Department.

In a short time, he was informed of something very important: several Romanian seismic stations framed the place of impact. He asked for the telephone connection to the apartment where Doctor Gordon had been kept against his will. Professor had a violent outburst. He began threatening again with the media and lawyers, invoking human rights and the freedoms guaranteed by the American Constitution.

"Doctor Gordon, let's leave this," said the Commander, trying to sound relaxed despite the current situation. "I'd like us to talk a little bit about seismology. I know you have been to Romania many times. What can you tell me about the seismologists there?"

"They're earnest scientists." came the reply.

"Interesting. So, what do you think? Do they have the necessary logistics to localize correct and fast the artificial seismic events? Such as the one we are waiting for?"

"Certainly! They are true professionals and they have a real-time seismic telemetered network and real-time localization software."

"It means they could be good partners. Thanks for the info, Doctor Gordon! Have a pleasant rest!"

The Professor wanted to add something else, but the general had already hung up. Gordon realized that he had made a big mistake by praising the Romanians. Of course, Alan King had no intention of collaborating with them, his interests were different. He wanted to warn his colleagues in Bucharest somehow, but it was impossible. He was locked in an apartment several levels underground, which was actually a nuclear war shelter. The armored door could only be opened with a code he didn't know, and the two guards who had brought him here were probably in the corridor. His only connection was a telephone, which could only make calls in the bunker. He had a short list of useful phone numbers: the first aid station, the administrative service and the restaurant. Thirst tormented him again so he went to the minibar located in a corner of the living room. He opened a can of Coke and drank it.

* * *

May 24, 1987, 8:30 PM - local time
Baikonur - Soviet Space Center

By an express order sent from Moscow, the Soviet Space Center was placed under the command of the USSR Security Department's special emissary, General Vladimir Ivanovici Petrovski. All operations from the Control Room related to the defective satellite and the calculations of the impact location coordinates were carried out in the utmost secrecy. The operators of the control desks had entered the *quarantine*, meaning they were forbidden to leave the room until further notice.

When the satellite crash became a certainty, even for the most optimistic specialists, General Pucinski convened a speed meeting with the heads of services in the presence of the special envoy of the Security Department.

"The Soviet Union is forced to officially announce the crash," he said. "As you know, according to the rules, the official statement is issued after the event and only if necessary. Now there are diplomatic pressures and we have to announce it sooner, otherwise, the Americans will compromise us."

"They dared threaten us!" General Petrovski put in. "If we don't make the announcement, they will. I received instructions from Moscow on how to write the press release. After the broadcast, the secret services around the World will go on alert."

"Our calculations show that the event will occur close to the Soviet Union, on the territory of a neighboring country," continued Pucinsky. "It is very important that we send our agents there before Radio Moscow broadcast the announcement. We have taken the necessary measures. The team that will recover the *code module* will immediately leave the Space Centre."

At the end of the meeting, Colonel Zapojnikov, upset by the entire situation, asked General Pucinski for a brief confidential discussion. "Comrade Commander, I have received the order to coordinate the *module* recovery operation personally. In a few minutes, I will be leaving the Space Center.

"Why you?" Pucinski frowned. "Usually, a counter-intelligence officer cannot be sent on such operational missions."

"The orders from Moscow are clear. The special envoy has already taken over my duties here…"

"Yeah… Their special envoy," the Commander nodded. "I've known the special envoy for too long… I know what he's capable of. According to him, we should all be arrested. How many people did he get infiltrated into the cross-border task force?"

"Only two," Zapojnikov informed. "We selected four of our best men and two Special Brigade agents. It took me a while to make him understand. He wanted to send me on this mission with his agents only."

As he was speaking, Igor took out his special notebook, opened it to a certain page, and handed it to his Commander, making a discreet sign that there was the possibility of them being heard. The General read quickly the few written words and handed back the notebook, an amazed look on his face.

"The special envoy is a very watchful fellow," Zapojnikov said as he put the notebook in his pocket. "He wants this action to take place under the best possible conditions."

The information he had just read left General Pucinski speechless, and as any pause would have been suspicious for those who probably listened to them, the Counterintelligence officer added:

"The intervention team is ready! The training required by the regulations has been completed. A special plane will take us to the border area."

The Commander didn't seem to listen to him anymore. He paced the room restlessly, his face pale. If the information was accurate, it meant that nothing was certain anymore, that everything was built on sand. He even felt that his life was in danger. The departure of the counterintelligence officer from the Space Center at such a time was dangerous. He thought about how to prevent this from happening, but he couldn't find a solution. Any action that would have delayed the mission of retrieving the *code module* could be considered treason.

He was afraid of being accused. Anyway, if Igor warned him, it meant he was not alone. He wanted to thank him in some way, so he shook the Colonel's hand firmly.

"Comrade Colonel, I wish you success in this new mission entrusted to you by the Soviet Union," he said in a loud military voice. "As your Commander, I want to give you one piece of advice before you leave: maximum revolutionary vigilance!" Looking at Igor straight in the eyes, he added in a whisper: "Thank you, take care…"

Igor nodded. Commander Pucinski relied on him even more perhaps than the Moscow chiefs.

* * *

May 24, 1987, 11:30 AM - local time
US Space Monitoring Center

General Alan King contacted the American Geophysical Union Database and searched for details about the Romanian Seismic Network. He found some well-documented works that presented the configuration of the seismic network and many other technical details. In fact, the entire seismic equipment used by the Romanians was made in the US.

The tracking systems reported the position of the drifting satellite at short intervals. Professor Gordon's estimated trajectory matched the actual one indeed. Therefore, the General's chances of grabbing the module containing the military codes from the remains of the satellite were high. He ordered that all the officers under his command be summoned to the Council Room and informed them about the details of the action:

"Gentlemen, here we are again in a difficult situation that requires determination. We need to move quickly. Our operation was approved by the Department of Defense and codenamed *Fishing in the Mountains*. It is quite suggestive if we take into account that the satellite will crash in a mountainous area, very close to the Danube River. I have summoned you to set precise tasks for each one. The *Panther* group that infiltrated the *red zone* will now carry the most important and difficult tasks. Unfortunately, at the moment, we can only rely on the agencies in Romania and Bulgaria. What's their situation, Captain Power?"

"We are constantly in contact with the agent from Romania," reported Power. "He got another car and is waiting for our instructions. Those from Bulgaria were spotted on the shores of the Black Sea, in Varna City. They have orders to cross the border to Romania. Their documents are in order and they won't face any problems."

"Very well then. We will act in two directions. The agents from Bulgaria will travel to Romania and go to the *zero point*', where the impact will occur. They will recover the *code module* from the debris. To get into the contaminated area, they need protective equipment they'll have to procure locally. If they don't manage it, we'll have to parachute the equipment. Meanwhile, the agent from Romania will try to annihilate the local seismic monitoring system. How he will do this remains to be settled. This system could jeopardize our plans. The Romanians seismologists have the necessary means to establish real-time coordinates of earthquakes, including surface explosions. The impact of the satellite on the Earth will generate seismic waves strong enough to be detected and located. The Romanian secret services could bump into our people trying to recover the *code module*. That is why the Romanian Seismic Network must be annihilated! I appoint Colonel Mc Stevenson responsible for this action."

He handed the information received from the American Geophysical Union Database, pointing out:

"Here you have all the data you need and the keywords for finding the information in our database. I want a detailed plan of action as soon as possible." He turned to the others and added: "The communication with the *Panther* agents will be made only through Captain Power who has full authorization for it. If you have any questions, I am at your disposal."

There were no questions, and everyone rushed to work.

Chapter 5

May 24, 1987, 9:00 PM - local time
Bucharest–Securitate conspiratorial house

"*Storks' Nest*", as the agents called it, the conspiratorial house of the Securitate, where the poker games usually took place, was a one-story villa located on a quiet street on the outskirts of Bucharest. Apparently, only Mrs. Maria, a retired teacher whose husband had died years ago in a car accident, lived there. She was rather withdrawn and didn't talk too much to her neighbors, but it was known that she had many relatives and friends who visited her quite often. Various cars with provincial license plates were parked in front of the high tin gates, especially in the evening. Sometimes the guests arrived by taxi and stayed until after midnight, but the neighbors had never heard loud music or other noises that would disturb them.

General Virgil Pleşca arrived in a cab when it was already dark outside. He entered the front door using his own keys and was greeted by the host in the hall.

"Welcome, comrade General! Comrade Săftoiu is already waiting for you in the living room."

Pleşca noticed a straw hat and an umbrella on the hanger.

"I see that comrade Săftoiu is hoping for the rain…

He found the colonel sitting at the table in the living room. He had a large glass of whisky with ice in front of him and was smoking a Kent cigarette.

"Long live, long live, Boss," he said standing up and waiting for the General to shake his hand.

"Good evening, Colonel!" said the General with an air of superiority. "How's your current situation with the ladies?"

"Pretty good, Boss!"

"I don't believe it anymore, Colonel. With your radio antennas spreading radiation… I don't think the women are interested in you anymore, but your money," Pleşca laughed heartily and sat down across the table.

"That may be so, Boss. If you speak from your personal experience…"

The host approached them and asked politely. "What would you like to have this evening, comrade General?"

"No alcohol this evening, comrade Maria. I've had my share today," he replied, still feeling the effects of the Hennesy cognac. "I want a large black coffee and some lemonade…"

"Very well, comrade General. I also made a cheese pie, if you'd like. It`s very good."

"Let's have some pie too, then," he nodded.

The two poker players faced each other, their eyes locked, like two roosters ready for a fight.

"I want to get my revenge tonight, Colonel," General Pleşca said firmly. He took a stack of dollar bills out of his coat, put it on the table, and lit a cigar.

Colonel Săftoiu felt the pressure of the challenge. He also placed a considerable amount of money on the table, saying:

"Okay, Boss. May the best man win!"

RED ALERT FOR ROMANIA

Comrade Maria brought them coffee, lemonade, several slices of cheese pie, and, as always, a pack of new playing cards on a tray. This way, there would be no suspicions that certain signs had been made on the back of the cards. She also put a small silver bell on the table and said:

"Whenever you need something, please ring the bell, comrades!"

"Thank you, comrade Maria, we have everything we need for now," said the General. "If someone calls and asks for me, I'm not here. We will not be disturbed even if the house is on fire, understood?"

"Yes, comrade General!" Maria nodded. "What about the calls from the Big Boss's Chancellery?"

"Don't worry. The Big Boss knows how to reach me when I don't answer the phone." He reached for his breast pocket to make sure he carried the pager in case the Supreme Commander needed him.

* * *

May 24, 1987, 12:30 AM - local time
US Space Monitoring Center

Colonel Mc Stevenson asked the General for permission to present the Romanian seismic monitoring system annihilation plan.

"There are several options, sir," he began, scattering a few photos and papers on the General's desk. "I chose the least risky one. The Romanian Seismic Network is telemetered by radio at the Institute of Seismology in Bucharest. It uses radio equipment on the 400 MHz band. It's the military version manufactured by

Monitron Corporation. Look at the configuration of the radio links on this map! As you can see, the impact site is very close to some of the most sensitive seismic stations of the network. The radio connection of these seismic stations to Bucharest is ensured by a radio repeater located at 3116 feet above sea level, on the top of Pietrosu Hill. This is where the information from the seismic network's Eastern section is concentrated and retransmitted to the Institute on two separate paths. This radio repeater is the most vulnerable node of the network and its removal would make the seismic surveillance of Eastern Romania impossible. This is where our agent must act."

"How? Taking this radio repeater out of service may raise suspicions."

"Hardly! Apparently, in the summer, lightning storms often hit the antennas and destroy the radio equipment because the lightning rods in rocky areas are less effective. Our agent has only to simulate a summer storm; for that, he needs a high-voltage source to be discharged in the Yagi antennas. In this way, the power module of the transmitter will burn, and the radio transmission will stop."

"How can he handle a high-voltage source up there in the mountains?" the General asked incredulously. "I don't know how good our agent is at electronics. We need to talk to Captain Power about this."

"It's simple. He can discharge a battery-charged photo flash into the antennas. He needs to fix the positive electrode of the flash on the tip of a fishing rod." He pointed to one of the photographs from the General's desk. "Look at the repeater here. The antennas are on fairly small masts. He can easily reach them with a fishing rod."

The General didn't look satisfied. To him, it seemed a complicated solution that required a trip to that area and sufficient technical knowledge.

"A more elegant way would be to infect their computer," said the General after carefully analyzing Mc Stevenson's plan, once more. "We have specialized viruses that can be easily transmitted through ordinary computer networks, after all."

"Impossible, sir. Their computer is isolated. It is a PDP 11 from an older generation and is not connected to any other network."

"Then I have no choice, but to approve your suggestion. I wish you good luck, Colonel!"

* * *

May 25, 1987, 1:00 AM - local time
Bucharest

The poker game ended after midnight. Both players were tired. General Pleșca was pleased. He had managed to win back the sum of one thousand dollars he owed to Colonel Săftoiu and a few hundred dollars extra. Although he lost, the Colonel was not in the least upset.

"Boss, after you return with *the sheep from the pasture*, I want us to meet again here," he said. "I wasn't in good shape tonight, but you know what they say: those who are unlucky at card games are lucky with women and… vice-versa!" He put on his straw hat, took his umbrella, and went out, in front of the gate, to wait for the taxi ordered by comrade Maria.

General Pleșca lingered for a while. During the card game, he heard the phone in the hall ringing several times. He wanted to know if it was something important concerning him.

"Comrade Alexe and comrade Ileana asked about you," Maria replied. "As you ordered me, I told them that you are not here."

"You did very well."

"Comrade Ileana seemed a bit agitated. She left a message for you. She said: *The Fox wants to come out of the den.*"

"Yes, yes, it's interesting if the *Fox* wants to come out of the den... again," the General muttered to himself.

He took out a small notebook with red covers out of the pocket and flipped through it. There he had written the new phone numbers of the undercover agents in Bucharest. Finally, he found the number he was looking for.

"What are you doing, Ileana, honey, aren't you sleeping?" he asked somewhat worried.

"I'm not sleeping, Boss. I was waiting for your call," said the young woman at the other end of the line.

"I stopped by the *Storks' Nest* and got your message. What's so urgent? This *Fox* is like any other fox. It still goes out to hunt, and still looks for *chicken coops.* We have to let it do its job. Let it have the impression that it's the most cunning *Fox*. We will catch it only when the time comes."

"Boss, this time the *Fox* seems to have a critical mission. Its masters want it eagerly. Tomorrow, it has to reach Pietrosu Hill."

"What for?" he snapped.

"It has something to do with the seismic stations…"

"Damn monkey! He's tired of archeology and now he wants seismology. I see he's interested in the Earth... The Earth will soon swallow him if he gets on my nerves."

"Boss, I need an off-road vehicle," Ileana said. "He doesn't want to use his car outside Bucharest. I said I would get one if he takes me with him."

"Very good! Don't worry about the car, honey. Go to the garage tomorrow morning and ask engineer Paraschiv to give you the new ARO car that doesn't have antennas. We don't want the *Fox* to get suspicious. Tell Paraschiv this is my order."

"Thank you, Boss!"

"Take care, dear. Be his shadow. Follow his every move. Even if he does some damage to the seismic stations, don't stop him. They can't predict the earthquakes, anyway... so fuck them!"

"Got it, Boss!"

"Let him think that you're really on their side. Just in case, take the *slingshot* with you in the purse. Who knows, maybe you might need it there in the mountains. Take care, honey, and keep me updated through Alexe."

"I fully understand, Boss!"

"Okay! Good night and have a nice trip!"

The General hung up satisfied. Lieutenant Ileana Popescu was an ambitious, efficient undercover young woman officer. Very few knew that she was actually the adopted daughter of General Pleșca. As his wife couldn't have children because of a chronic illness, they adopted Ileana from the orphanage under the maiden's name of his wife - Popescu. Ileana had graduated from the Securitate Officer School among the first and was studying at the Faculty of Electronics at the Polytechnic University of Bucharest. She managed to join the entourage of Arab students and learned many things of interest to Securitate. Lately, she became close to a Palestinian student, Yusuf Haid, whom Ileana suspected of being an American agent. It was a less common thing for a Palestinian to be in the service of the Americans, but, officially, this did not arouse any suspicions. The Securitate had assigned to Yusuf Haid the code name *Fox*. Ileana managed to gain the trust of the *Fox* agent so much that he recommended her to his superiors so as to be recruited as an agent in Romania.

When he left the conspiratorial house, the General found the taxi already waiting for him in front of the gate. He thought it was the car ordered by comrade Maria and he got in the backseat, ordering the driver:

"Take me to Calea Dorobanți!" He never said his exact home address. It was safer this way. He could walk the short distance left to his house.

"All right, Sir," the taxi driver kindly answered as he turned on the engine, driving away. After a few detours on side streets, the General realized they were going in the wrong direction.

"Hey, boy! Where do you want to take me?" General Pleșca shot. "This is not the right way! What the hell of a taxi driver are you? You don't know Bucharest, or do you want to rip me off?"

"I have the pleasure and honor to greet you, Your Excellency General Virgil Pleșca!" said the driver in a foreign-accented Romanian language. "I apologize for not introducing myself: I am Agent Amin from the Israeli Embassy and I have the mission to take you urgently to our Embassy headquarters for an important negotiation."

"Now, in the middle of the night?!" the General jumped up nervously, and taking out his service pistol he put it on the back of the driver's neck shouting: "Stop or I will blow your brains out!"

Agent Amin replied calmly, not in the least troubled by the General's reaction:

"Your Excellency, you are awaited by His Excellency Ambassador Breinstein and Mr. Colonel Villy Strauss, our military attaché, whom I think you know well. I am sure that it is a negotiation that will interest you."

"Yes, I know Colonel Strauss," said Pleşca, calming down and putting the pistol back in the holster under his arm. "I suppose this is quite a serious matter then."

They arrived on a side street and stopped next to a parked Mercedes car, with Diplomatic Corps license plates.

"We need to change the car," said agent Amin. "It's an additional security measure." He left the taxi engine running and invited the General to get into the Mercedes. Meanwhile, someone came out from the shadows and took over the taxi, disappearing into the darkness.

Amin soon reached the access road to the Israeli Embassy, which was barred by a thick metal pipe lifting gate, and guarded by several Romanian soldiers from the Securitate Forces. Agent Amin showed them his diplomatic ID and made way among the thick metal stakes planted in a zigzag along the street.

The access gate to the Embassy was flanked by Israeli soldiers armed as if for an assault. They first checked the car with bomb detectors and then asked for all the weapons and metal objects to be left in the rack at the entrance.

"We apologize, General, but the numerous attacks on our embassies in the World compel us to be more vigilant," said Agent Amin a little embarrassed.

"There's a Romanian saying: *where there's law, there's no haggling*," answered the General, although it was clear that the situation did not suit him.

Ambassador Breinstein and the military attaché Strauss were waiting for General Pleşca in a soundproof room.

"Your Excellency, General Virgil Pleşca, I have the pleasure and honor to welcome you to the Embassy of Israel!" said the Ambassador in fluent Romanian, shaking the hand of the Romanian intelligence chief heartily.

"Thank you for the invitation, Your Excellency, Mr. Ambassador, although it is a rather inappropriate time for visits," answered the General and stretched out his hand to Colonel Strauss, who, according to the protocol, could not greet a General first because of his lower rank.

A butler in a tuxedo asked for permission to bring in some refreshments. Soon he returned pushing a serving cart with various drinks, coffee, tea, and snacks. Once the butler left, closing the door firmly behind him, the jamming facilities were turned on.

"Thanks, but I'm fine." replied General Pleşca cautiously, but politely, when the Ambassador invited him to help himself to a drink. He was aware of the fact that there was also the possibility of being drugged or, even worse, poisoned. "I say we go straight to the point, he proposed firmly. Although the secret services are sleepless, I still want to know what I am doing here in the middle of the night."

Colonel Strauss agreed, smiling as he casually poured himself a glass of orange juice.

"With His Excellency's permission, I will briefly present the subject. Please, take a seat!" he said.

General Pleşca sat comfortably in an armchair.

"I'm all ears, Colonel."

"We are sure you have already learned by now about the Soviet satellite that got out of control."

"Yes, I have."

"What I don't think you know is that the satellite will fall on Romanian territory in about eighteen hours."

"Dammit! That's what we were missing…" the General growled, as if to himself, thinking of Alexe's premonition and how he had ridiculed him for his fears of this fatalistic scenario.

"We have the geographical coordinates of the place of impact, and they are confirmed by two different sources. We procured them with considerable difficulty through specific methods" continued Colonel Strauss in a confidential tone.

"I do not doubt that. Israel's secret services are perhaps the most efficient in the World," General Pleşca tried to flatter him.

"Both the Soviets and the Americans want to send their agents to the impact site to recover the *code module* from the satellite's remains. You know, it is a kind of black box containing valuable information from a military point of view and is made to be practically indestructible."

"The Israeli Embassy wants to recover this module", the Ambassador took over the discussion shortcutting to the subject. "For this, we need the Securitate permission and your help. We do not want to undermine the sovereignty of your country by deploying agents on Romanian territory, as both the Americans and the Soviets intend to do. We want to negotiate with you that two of our technicians will go to the impact site to recover the module. What do you say, Your Excellency! Can we agree on this?"

The General remained silent for a moment. High interests were involved if the Americans, the Russians, and the Jews were after that box. He asked for permission to light a cigarette, and after taking the first smoke he said:

"Things are not that simple. If the Americans, the Soviets, and perhaps other countries' agents will gather there, there is the risk of an armed conflict. I will have to take all the necessary measures so that your technicians will work safely. I can secure the area, but keeping the Romanian soldiers away will be difficult if the Army gets involved. In fact, this is a military issue of the Ministry of National Defense."

"According to our information, the Romanian Army doesn't have the means of calculation that would allow them to determine the geographic coordinates of the impact accurately", Colonel Strauss said. "The only entity that can help them is the Seismic Stations Network. Upon its crash, the satellite will produce a crater with a diameter of approximately thirty meters and generate seismic waves equivalent to a 3.5 - 4 Richter degrees magnitude earthquake. The Romanian Seismic Network uses modern technology and will accurately detect and locate the event."

"Yes, this is a real problem that must be considered," the General nodded, thinking about what Ileana had told him on the phone a while ago. "However, I have certain information that an American agent will try to turn off the Seismic Network. Probably the Soviets will try the same thing."

"Even if the Seismic Network will be functional and locate the impact zone in real-time, it will take a few hours for the Army specialists to get there, anyway. If they are not disturbed, our technicians will quickly recover the module and leave the area."

General Pleşca kept silent again as he continued to smoke his cigar thoughtfully.

"We are ready to offer a good price," said Colonel Strauss after exchanging glances with the Ambassador. "What do you think of a million dollars in cash?"

The General shook his head disapprovingly.

"There are a lot of risks as far as I'm concerned. If the Soviets discover this action, there will be diplomatic scandals," he said. "Don't forget that Romania is part of the Warsaw Pact where the Soviets make the game's rules. The Soviet Union may diplomatically request the recovery of the satellite's remains, and we can't afford to turn them down."

"They won't do it diplomatically. From what we know, they've already prepared a commando group of six special forces agents under the command of a counterintelligence officer." Strauss looked at his watch and added: "In just a few hours they will cross the border to Romania as tourists in transit to Bulgaria."

"To hell with them! If that's the case I will meet them properly, both the Soviet agents and the Americans. Do they want a confrontation on the Romanian territory? They will get one! Romania is not a village without watchdogs!" He fixed his gaze on Colonel Strauss and said, standing up: "Add another million dollars and we'll do the job."

"Isn't that too much?"

"Not at all!"

"How about a million and five hundred?"

"Gentlemen, one million and eight hundred is my last price," said the General firmly. "I will use this money to ensure your people's safe travel and work and facilitate the removal of the module from Romania. I want five hundred in advance and the rest at the end. If, for reasons beyond our control, such as the fall of the satellite on the territory of another state, the advance payment will not be refunded, as it will cover the expenses of my people's mobilization."

The Ambassador and Colonel Strauss looked at each other again. The General knew they had no choice but to accept his conditions.

"We accept the price and terms of Your Excellency!" said the Ambassador with a cold smile. "You will establish the rest of the details with Colonel Strauss."

They shook hands and the Ambassador left the room.

* * *

May 25, 1987 4:00 AM - local time
Soviet military airport in the Ukrainian SSR
- close to the border with Romania

Toward morning, after a tiring flight with many turbulences, the plane, in which Colonel Igor Zapojnikov and his intervention team were, landed on a military airdrome in *Ukrainian SSR,* near the Romanian border. At the end of the runway, a bus picked them up. The officer waiting for them gave Zapojnikov a sealed envelope. These were the last instructions from Moscow. The original plan had been changed. Igor was to remain in the Soviet territory and monitor everything from afar. This got him thinking. His early suspicions were now confirmed. Someone wanted to sabotage the mission, someone influential who pulled the strings from the shadow. His hands were tied. At least he had done his duty and even managed to warn Commander Pucinski before he left the Soviet Space Center.

During the flight, he reflected upon the situation he had left behind. The Moscow chiefs had given him no explanation. He did not understand why he, a Counterintelligence officer, had been sent on this mission. These were questions to which he had no answers but assumptions.

The agents intended to enter Romania with three Lada cars, so they were taken to a hangar near the airport to get them. The vehicles were fueled up, but each had an extra gasoline supply in two canisters in the trunks above. The fuel crisis in Romania was well known; lately, it has given a lot of trouble to all those sent on missions. Measures have been taken to ensure the autonomy of the cars, but increased vigilance has been strongly recommended as the natives could steal the gasoline.

Once the agents signed the papers for the cars, the civilian clothing, and equipment, Colonel Zapojnikov felt compelled to give the final instructions.

"Comrades, you have the honor of being chosen to carry out an action of the utmost importance for the security of the Soviet Union. Be careful! You may encounter hostile forces on the foreign territory. Put all your knowledge and experience into practice, so as not to create any incidents or suspicions. You know that the Romanians do not look at us very kindly."

As he spoke, he noticed that the two *Special Brigade* agents were not listening to him. They looked around as if they didn't care about what he said, and Igor felt frustration. He was sure they had other instructions. Nevertheless, Zapojnikov continued his speech:

"You have all the necessary equipment, including specialized weapons. You will find them in the specially arranged places inside the cars. We will keep in touch by radio in our frequency range. Report immediately to me any unforeseen situation. Don't do anything that would provoke diplomatic conflicts. And remember: The Soviet Union is the promoter of World Peace and understanding between nations. Do not respond to provocations without carefully analyzing them first. The ultimate goal is clear: to recover the *code module* at any cost. I'm sure our rivals will try the same thing and send well-trained commando groups to the area. Use the fighting technique only if necessary! You will act in two directions, as planned: the agents of the *Special Brigade* will travel to Bucharest and deal with the Seismological Institute, and the agents of the Space Center will go to the impact area. I wish you good luck, comrades!"

The six agents replied in unison: *"We serve the Soviet Union!"* and they hurriedly got into the cars. They crossed a section of several kilometers through the Soviet Socialist Republic of Moldova and reached the border between the USSR and Romania. Zapojnikov accompanied them in a separate car.

The head of the border checkpoint was waiting for them. Because an important delegation had been announced, all the border agents were on alert. Someone from border police staff discreetly placed a box of vodka bottles in one of the cars. The Soviet agents had been advised to offer some liquor to the Romanian customs officers as a sign of friendship in the hope of avoiding any unpleasant incidents, such as the thorough checking of the cars. Passports were stamped and the barrier was lifted. The cars crossed the bridge over the Prut River, separating the two countries. It was still dark. No light could be seen in the distance. Everything seemed camouflaged in Socialist Republic of Romania and that gave a sense of insecurity.

* * *

May 25, 1987, 6:00 AM - local time
Bucharest - Dorobanți district

General Pleşca lived alone in a villa on Calea Dorobanți after his wife had died three years ago from cancer that had progressed rapidly. His house was guarded non-stop by two soldiers from the Securitate forces.

The Securitate car came every day at 7:00 am to pick him up. Sometimes, however, the General asked his most trusted man, Captain Gheorghe Stănescu, known as Bebe Gold, to come and take him to the office, especially when they had to talk about secret matters. The captain's nickname originated from the fact that he was born into a gypsy family that processed gold. He was a solid and brutal guy, swarthy with long curly hair and strong muscles. He was a former champion in Greco-Roman wrestling. The General had hired him in the Securitate to recruit a group of bullies, especially among recidivist gypsies, to use them as shock troops if necessary. Bebe followed only the General's direct orders and enjoyed the complete obedience of his subordinates. His car was an old Dacia that didn't attract attention but had a particular quality: it was free of *bugs* because the Counterintelligence people didn't look for trouble with Bebe. Thus, the General could talk in his car without the fear of being listened to by Colonel Petrescu's men.

The General hadn't slept more than a few hours. After he woke up at 6:00 am, he made himself a coffee, called Bebe Gold to come and pick him up, and phoned Ileana to give her one last piece of advice:

"Honey, your *Fox* wants to damage those seismic devices in Pietrosu Hill. Let him do his job! Don't try to stop him. On the contrary, try and help him. Make he believe you're on their side. And don't forget to take the *slingshot* with you. You might need it.

"Yes, Boss! I understand," Ileana replied.

On the way to the office, the General briefly presented the details of the mission to Bebe Gold:

"Gather up your gang quickly, take as many cars as you need, and go to the Dobrogea Mountains".

"Three cars are enough. When we get to Tulcea County, we'll use local registration plates so they'll think we are local gypsies."

"Good! Go via Urziceni. Two *tourists* from the Israeli Embassy are waiting for you at the gas station in Afumați. You can't miss them. They will be wearing straw hats, sunglasses, and backpacks. To make sure, ask them: '*Would you like to go fishing?*' They will answer: '*No, we want to go hunting.*' They both speak Romanian fluently, so don't worry. Take them with you and protect them with your life. They will lead you close to where that damn satellite will fall. After the event, they'll search the remains and take what they need. You bring them back to Bucharest safe and sound and leave them at the same gas station, where a taxi will be waiting for them. It's simple."

"Boss, it's not that simple! I'm sure the Russian and American agents will swarm the area like flies around honey. What do we do if they bother us? Do we arrest them?"

"Do you want to start a war, you idiot?! You are professional bullies! Do I have to teach you what to do?"

"I understand, Boss, I know what I have to do," Bebe Gold assured him. "I'll borrow a cart from the local gypsies, get a few boys in it and slowly approach any uninvited guests. We ask them if they have anything to sell or if they want to exchange currency… and other things like that. Then, we suddenly get angry and rush at them with cudgels. We cut their tires with knives, break their windshields and make them wish they were home, in their countries, instead of stealing in Romania without telling us."

"That's my boy!" said the General satisfied. "If everything goes well, I'll give you a substantial bonus."

"I serve the country, Boss!" answered Bebe, winking like a trickster.

Chapter 6

May 25, 1987, 8:30 AM - local time
Buzău-Bucharest national road

It was raining heavily. The windshield wipers proved ineffective. Gică, the driver, jerked the wheel to avoid the large puddles, his eyes strained as he tried to see ahead.

"We should have taken a boat instead," he muttered.

"It hasn't rained like that in a long time," commented George thoughtfully.

"Have you got a smoke?"

George searched through his pockets and took out his last cigarette from a crumpled package.

"Here, you deserve it. Now, where is that matchbox?"

"Take a look in the glove compartment," the driver said and swore between his teeth: "Who the hell patched this damned road?"

"There's no matchbox in here," replied George frustrated. "If I remember well, there was once a lighter in this car."

"It was, yeah, about two hundred thousand kilometers ago, when this car wasn't running on our socialist roads full of potholes yet."

A dumb truck coming from the opposite direction splashed them with mud which infuriated Gică even more. He once kept a matchbox in the glove compartment, but he remembered giving it to a shepherd who watched him changing a flat tire by the side road. The man complained there were no matches in his village shop, so Gică gave him his last box.

"The nickel wire!" the driver exclaimed. "Look for the nickel wire!"

"Good idea!"

George found the nickel spiral, unscrewed the fuse panel's cover, and connected the two ends of the wire to the battery until it was warmed up enough to light the cigarette. The driver watched him out of the corner of his eye. A single short-circuits and they would catch fire.

Just then, a voice came out of the loudspeaker on the dashboard. George set the reception level until they could better hear the duty operator from the Seismological Command who called them insistently. He picked up the microphone from the stand and answered a little grumpily:

"Yes, *Vrancea One*! I'm *Vrancea Two*! I hear you intermittently! Communicate!"

Gică kept swearing loudly at the other drivers on the road and George begged him to be quiet, so he could make the radio connection. Since the Command's operator did not seem to hear them well, they stopped in a parking lot. The operator was angry:

"Attention, *Vrancea Two*! Attention, *Vrancea Two*! Where are you? Come in!"

"*Vrancea One*! *Vrancea One!* This is *Vrancea Two*!" George shouted into the microphone. "We're on our way back. It's a storm here! We fixed the damage in the epicenter area! What's the matter? Over!"

The operator's voice sounded somewhat ironic:

"This is *Vrancea One*! Let me make you happy, *Vrancea Two*! We have problems on Pietrosu Hill. I think there was a thunderstorm and the lightning struck the radio relay equipment again! The Eastern section of the seismic network is completely out of service. The boss said you must go up there and solve the problem! Confirm!"

Upon hearing this, the driver burst out:

"Listen, guys! I can't do this! There is no way I can get to the top of the mountain with this car! The brakes are barely holding! The steering gear is fucked up! The floor is like a sieve! It's like Fred and Barney's car! I lost the exhaust pipe today! Do you hear the engine screeching like a chainsaw? Let's be clear! I won't go up there in Pietrosu with this car!"

George waited for Gică to calm down before confirming to the operator on duty that they had received the message and were heading to the lightning-damaged radio relay.

* * *

May 25, 1987, 8:00 AM - local time
Bucharest – Măgurele Faculty of Physics

Relieved that his parking space was free, Professor Dumitriu turned off the engine, got out, and locked his car, carefully checking the other doors, too, as usual. He was about to walk away when he turned round. He forgot to take the windshield wipers from their holders and put them in the car. He has done that ever since someone stole them.

It was still drizzling, and the thunders could be heard somewhere far away, over the Argeş River valley. He hurried the short distance to the entrance to the Faculty of Physics, head bowed and almost tripped over the umbrella a student was trying to open. Embarrassed, the young woman took a step back, blushing.

"Good morning, Professor! Excuse me!" she babbled.

"Good morning, young lady." He stopped and raised his hand to his temple. "Good to meet you. Are you by any chance one of the students doing the internship at the Department of Earth Physics?"

"Yes, I am," the student replied a little surprised.

A large group crammed in front of the entrance. The young woman stepped aside to continue the conversation with the professor who seemed stuck in the doorway, with his hand still raised in a gesture almost identical to Detective Colombo's. With his hunched shoulders, disheveled hair, and beige coat, Professor Dumitriu looked like the famous policeman. He looked at the student in a trance while she waited politely for him to say something.

"Oh, yes! I remember," he said. "Tell your colleagues who want to do the practice in my department, that today, after classes, I want to talk with everyone. You will have to do a project at the end of the practice session."

He was about to leave, but swiveled round and added:

"By the way, we have class today and I will let you all know this personally. Good-bye!"

Inside, the doorkeeper greeted him in a military style:

"Long live, Professor!"

The students in the lobby greeted him in chorus with a long *"Hello!"*

"Good day, good day, my young colleagues!" Dumitriu answered with a smile as he walked along the hallway. He hurried up the staircase to the second floor and quickly entered his office. He looked at his watch. The class would begin in a few minutes, so he didn't have time to stop by the secretariat, as he intended. He hastily removed his sweatshirt, put it on the tree hanger by the door, and ran his fingers through his wet hair, peering at a piece of paper in the receipt spindle on the desk. He recognized Silvia's small calligraphic handwriting. His assistant informed him that he had been called on by Mircea Achim, one of his former students who worked at the Institute of Seismology. Dumitriu checked his watch again. He should have been in the amphitheater already. He rushed to the phone, called the Institute, and asked for Achim.

"What happened, Mircea? I was told you looked for me."

"Could you visit us today, Professor? We had a very interesting *swarm* of earthquakes and would like to analyze the data together."

"With the greatest pleasure! I'll be there in a moment!" Then, with an almost sadistic start: "Of course it's coming, I told you! At what depth were the most important shocks?"

"About a hundred kilometers."

"It's coming, it's coming, it's ready... I feel it!"

The Professor didn't even notice his assistant entering the office. She stood by the door, waiting for him to finish the conversation. After hanging up, Dumitriu rubbed his hands with satisfaction.

"That's it! It's coming! I told them it's coming!"

"What, Professor?" the assistant asked puzzled.

"The one of 7-magnitude!"

Realizing that this was the earthquake the Professor had predicted, Silvia had a start. She was used to Dumitriu talking about earthquakes as if they were guests who sometimes were late, or popped up without any notice in advance. The Professor was pleased whenever his predictions, no matter how small, became true. He recently wrote a number of articles the specialists frowned upon. The gloomiest prediction was that soon, at the end of May, a 7-magnitude earthquake would occur in Vrancea. Silvia had been one of the few who encouraged him to publish these articles, although she dreaded whenever she looked at the calendar on the wall and saw that May was drawing close. No matter how much she appreciated and respected him, she secretly wished he was wrong. Dumitriu's own pride so blinded him, he would have even enjoyed a catastrophe.

"Did the seismologists tell you anything interesting?" she asked.

"A *swarm* of earthquakes, my dear. The phenomenon can be a precursor. I'm going to see what is going on. Carry out the lecture in my place, please!"

He put on his sweatshirt, grabbed the briefcase from the desk, and hurried out. Downstairs he realized that he forgot his car keys in the office. As the Institute of Seismology was only a few hundred yards away, he walked briskly under flowering chestnut trees lining the pavement, trying to shelter himself from the light rain.

Immersed in his thoughts, he walked past the gatekeeper's lodge and someone shouted:

"Hello, comrade! Where are you going?"

"I'm Professor Dumitriu from the Faculty of Physics," he said, slightly confused, as if awoken from a trance.

"Okay, okay, but you can't go in like that. I want to see your ID."

Dumitriu rummaged through his pockets, then, putting his hand to the temple as usual, thought for a moment, and said:

"I don't have it! I don't know where the hell I put it, but I'm sure you know me! I come here often!"

"Long live, Professor! I know you, but you can't enter the Institute without an ID card. That's the order."

"Come on, comrade! Are you keeping me in the rain? I'm expected inside!"

"I'm sorry, Sir, but that's the order!" the gatekeeper shrugged.

A loud knocking coming from the building next door, where the Seismotheque was kept, made them turn their heads. From the upper window, engineer Apolzan, the head of the Seismic Network, was making signs to the gatekeeper to let the Professor pass. The man understood, put the right hand to his cap, and said politely:

"Long live, Professor! You can go in! Welcome!" Then he muttered to himself: "If the boss allowed it…"

* * *

May 25, 1987, 9:30 AM - local time
Pitrosu Hiil

The road to the Pietrosu radio relay was narrow and difficult: boulders and rocky ridges as far as the eye could see. The car was running rough and the engine was making an infernal noise.

The driver was tense and more focused. Any wrong maneuvering would cause him trouble.

"That's our fate with the lightning strikes," he sighed for the tenth time. The car got on a better stretch of road and he relaxed a bit. "The storms season is a nuisance for us. Let's hope we get away safely…"

"Nonsense!" George retorted. "In winter, the antennas get covered with ice and the transmitters become powerless."

"Yes, but the ice doesn't damage the equipment. It melts in the end while this lightning destroys everything! Damn it! Can't you do something about it? A better lightning rod perhaps?"

"A lot could be done with money, but, you see, money is the engine of corrupt capitalist societies," George replied ironically. "Here, persuasion takes the first place. I persuaded you to get us on the mountain because society needs us to fearlessly face nature's elements, as the General Secretary teaches us… We must defeat nature!"

"Damn!" the driver growled. "You have been contaminated by Communist political education. We need better lightning protection, not empty talk."

"Well, it's not like that! Political work must be completed first, thus the level of socialist consciousness raised," George explained equally ironically. "Suppose we make perfect lightning rods. It is not enough."

"Why?" asked the other puzzled.

"Because those with weaker political training steal everything! They tear, pluck, dig up, cut, and take home everything they find unguarded, as no one lowered to their level of understanding to explain why this is not a good thing to do. If they were aware that piece of cable, from which they make an extension cord, or a handmade lamp, interrupts the operation of a system of national importance, maybe they would steal more selectively."

* * *

May 25, 1987, 8:30 AM - local time
Institute of Seismology

In the Seismotheque room, Professor Dumitriu found a group of senior researchers studying the seismograms with magnifying glasses and rulers. They measured the length of seismic events and filled in tables.

"Well, what do you think, gentlemen? Will the big one come?" Dumitriu asked as he entered the door, without even greeting them.

The researchers ignored him, making it clear that his presence was unwelcome. Mircea Achim approached him and whispered:

"Let's go to the Computer Room, Professor. We have very good digital recordings."

"Great!" Dumitriu's face lit up. "The processing of analog recordings, which our colleagues are doing here, is already outdated and cannot provide accurate information… I often say this to my students."

Mircea was holding a seismogram on which a part of the *swarm* of earthquakes was recorded. Dumitriu analyzed it for a few moments and said:

"Look at this, gentlemen! It's like a squadron of fighter jets coming from the epicenter."

The comparison was suggestive, because the recording of each seismic event, with the primary waves distinctly separated from the secondary ones, somewhat resembled the fuselage of a fighter jet.

In the Computer Room, Mircea Achim and his colleague, Eugen, had printed all the events recorded during the night. After a brief discussion, they all agreed that each seismic event had to be accurately located to get a picture of the breakage mechanism in the seismic focus.

"All seismic stations must work perfectly in the next period," the Professor told them. "Although many will contradict me, I argue that this *swarm* of earthquakes is a clear precursor of a major seismic event that could occur in the next few hours."

Professor Dumitriu's statement silenced everyone. They went into the Analog Recordings Room where the electric motors spinning the paper drums of the helicorders buzzed like a beehive. A row of red lights blinked frantically. The seismic alarm made a sharp sound and the computer printed the preliminary data of the seismic event.

"Yeah, another one…," Eugen murmured. He sat down at the computer console and began to move his fingers on the keyboard with enviable skill, as if he had entered a trance, like a pianist during a concert. All the others circled him and almost held their breath as they silently waited for the result. After a short analysis, the young researcher affirmed:

"This is the seismic event with the highest magnitude of this *swarm*: 4.8 Richter degrees, 118 km deep. The epicenter is located in the Vrancea region. Normally, we can expect a gradual decrease in magnitudes until the earthquakes *swarm* will end."

"My dear, I have a different opinion," Professor Dumitriu said. "I think we have a warning shock in front of us. I told you: the big seismic event could come in a few hours."

Engineer Florian Ionică, the head of the Technical Service Department, was a little nervous. He told them that the intervention crew had repaired the damage in the epicenter area, but there were still problems due to a thunderstorm that affected the radio relay in Pietrosu Hill.

"Our boys are on their way there. I just talked to them by radio," the duty operator put in.

"My dear fellows, it's crucial that everything goes perfectly," the Professor said. "We don't want to miss an event that happens only once every few decades. Not to mention that any earthquake is a unique physical phenomenon in its own way. The mechanism in the seismic outbreak is never the same."

"Alas, Professor, you speak so categorically you frighten me!" said the duty operator in disbelief. "Do you really think there will be a big earthquake today or tomorrow?"

"Definitely, my dear! Maybe I should have you as a witness that I made the prediction right now and here! A Vrancea earthquake with a magnitude over 7 Richter degrees is likely to occur in no more than… let's say… ten hours! But who should I tell? Who will listen to me? Everyone would say I'm crazy!"

"I understand, but something should be done," engineer Apolzan said. "Lives could be saved. The population should be warned in some way. Maybe you should talk to… the Government…"

"Do you want to see me locked up? A seismic alarm would drive everyone crazy. People would run desperately everywhere… starting with… we know who…"

He clasped a hand over his mouth, looking around intently. It was clear that he said the *wrong things* again. He forgot he was in a place with many ears and many microphones. The Professor went from one recorder to another, carefully examining the seismic noise drawn by the pens on the paper. He fixed his gaze on the digital clock installed in the console of the seismic recorders which indicated Greenwich Mean Time, the universal time used in seismology. After a few moments, he turned with a triumphant smile, and said almost shouting:

"I know! I'll call Professor Gordon. It's night in California right now, but that doesn't matter. I will tell him everything and perhaps he'll also believe I'm crazy. But tomorrow, when everyone will comment on the event, Gordon will be able to confirm that I foresaw it. At the next International Symposium on Earthquake Prediction, I will subclass all the seismologists involved in the prediction. Gordon is a great personality, and everyone will believe him."

He looked at the handful of phones on the operator's desk, with the expression of a man who wants to challenge the whole World, and asked:

"Which of these phones can get an international connection?"

"None," the operator replied dryly. "Where do you think you are? In America?"

"It's a pity." Dumitriu shook his head. "Seismology should be able to make phone calls quickly anywhere in the World."

"We have not yet received the approval from the Ministry of Internal Affairs for automatic access to international telephone links," explained the head of the Technical Service.

"However, we can speak by command at the International Telephone Exchange of the Ministry of Communications," Mircea intervened. "But we need written approval from comrade Director. I will write the request."

"Don't mention my name, please," Dumitriu said. "You know how he is… Especially if he hears what I want to say…"

"Don't worry, Professor. I will ask permission to talk to Professor Gordon about a scholarship. I have to give him a telex, anyway.

"Thank you, Mircea! I don't want to cause you any problems."

"Well, Professor, we, the young ones, are brave enough." Mircea said confidently and went to write the application.

Engineer Florian Ionică invited Dumitriu for a coffee in the office next door while he waited for the Director's approval. The Professor sat on a hard chair and watched the duty operator preparing the coffee in a kettle, using an improvised electric stove strategically hidden between some bricks behind the door. In this way, the rudimentary *coffeemaker* was protected by the prying eyes of the Party activists who controlled how the employees of the Institute saved electricity.

"Do you realize? If my calculations will be confirmed, seismological research will take a new course!" Professor began to support his scientific arguments, enthusiastically. "The Americans spent millions of dollars on prediction and got nothing out of it. So far, in February 1975, the Chinese had some success in Haicheng, Liaoning Province. They managed to predict a 7.3-magnitude earthquake, but then they also had the Tangshan disaster in July 1976, when a 7.8-magnitude earthquake destroyed an entire city of nearly a million inhabitants."

"Officially, they didn't announce more than about two hundred thousand dead," Eugen said, remembering that he had recently read about this devastating earthquake in a publication.

"Unofficially, there were over eight hundred thousand dead," the Professor explained. "Can you imagine what that means? I visited the situ five years after the event, and everything looked like the massive ruin of an ancient graveyard. The epicenter had been just below the city. A great disaster and a failure of Chinese prediction."

"But was the earthquake from Haicheng really predicted, or was it just sheer luck?" Ionică debated.

"That is a completely different story," said Professor Dumitriu in the tone of a *grandfather* who is about to tell his *grandchildren* a story full of teachings. "It was a Chinese-style prediction that only the Chinese could make. They relied more on studying the abnormal behavior of living things. They also had the advantage of supervising an area where surface earthquakes occurred, unlike in our country, where they have intermediate depth. The Chinese authorities had trained more than two thousand people in Liaoning Province to monitor various living things. Everyone had been assigned a certain place to observe: the fields, the woods, or their own households. Hens, geese, piglets, cattle, and wild animals were kept under strict surveillance, and whenever they observed something unusual, they wrote it down in a special notebook. All results were reported to a Center."

"Sounds like a menagerie…" a young researcher laughed. "Didn't they hear of a science called geophysics?"

"On the contrary. The geophysicists didn't want to be outshined by common citizens," Dumitriu countered. "They installed everything they considered helpful in recording the precursor phenomenon of the earthquake. They measured the changes in the level of the Earth's surface, telluric currents, the radon concentration in the water, and all the things that came to mind. It was a real competition supervised by the Communist Party."

"Of course," Ionică said mockingly. "The Communist Party is the same everywhere. If they asked to change the landform of the Earth, someone would try their best to do it."

"Well, in China, some things are different," the Professor replied. "The Chinese people go to work every morning singing as they walk lined up with the Communist Party flag in front of them. I have seen them with my own eyes. This is not something you'd expect to see here, in Romania, or any other Communist country in Europe."

"It is true, but we aren't far from that moment. Soon, the Party will put a cattle bell under our windows to wake us up at sunrise so that we all go to the construction sites of our homeland dressed in overalls."

"Boss, stop talking like that! You don't know who's listening!" one of Ionică's subordinates chimed in. "Let the Professor say how the Chinese predicted the earthquake…"

Professor Dumitriu became aware of his audience. Several young researchers gathered around him and listened intently.

"About a month before the earthquake," he continued, "the birds started behaving strangely, and the rats came out of the dumps. The Chinese were convinced the earthquake was coming. The Party ordered the set-up of a real city of tents with street numbers and everything. The population was evacuated. They kept the people in tents for a while, but the earthquake didn't come. A whole scandal broke out! Why doesn't the earthquake come? Opinions were divided. Party meetings were held, and sanctions were imposed. The population was brought back to the city. At the end of February, a few days before the earthquake, thousands of reports on the unusual behavior of the creatures began to flow."

The memory of something funny made him smile before he went on:

"I had the opportunity to read the translation of such a report written by a Chinese peasant two days before the earthquake. It was hilarious! He described the behavior of his two piglets, who got along well. He said he had managed to educate the piglets by showing them daily a picture of the Great Leader Mao visiting a pig farm. One day, his obedient piglets suddenly became naughty. They started fighting and tried to break the shelter. The peasant was troubled. He showed them Mao's picture but without any effect."

Some burst out laughing. Dumitriu continued undisturbed:

"At the end of February, the geophysicists also noticed some anomalies in their measurements. When the snakes came out in the snow, they realized something unusual would happen and raised the alarm, thus managing to evacuate the population again just a few hours before the earthquake. Only a single old Buddhist didn't want to leave his home and died under the rubble because the entire city was destroyed."

"A spectacular result, indeed," said Apolzan.

"Spectacular, but without perspective," the Professor pointed out. "The Chinese believed they found a way to predict earthquakes and boasted about it in massive propaganda. If the devastating Tangshan earthquake, which they couldn't foresee, hadn't come a year and a half later, they would have kept bragging for a long time. What happened in Haicheng was just a mere coincidence. They relied on measurements and empirical observations while I trust the rigorous scientific calculations and statistics regarding the Vrancea seismic events from the last thousand years."

Caught up in conversation, the Professor didn't even notice the cup of steaming coffee in front of him.

"Please, drink, Professor!" the operator urged him. "The coffee is getting cold."

Dumitriu took a sip. It was chickpea coffee or *horse coffee*, as they called it, the only one they could find in the socialist market.

"It's delicious, my dear," the teacher smiled politely at her, even though he absolutely hated this fake coffee.

In the analog recordings room, a phone rang shrilly.

"The International call, Professor!" Someone shouted so loudly, his voice echoed in the entire corridor.

Dumitriu got up in a hurry and everyone else followed him, some out of curiosity, while others had their own interests, especially to inform the Securitate officer in charge of controlling the Institute's activity about this phone call.

At the same time, the field crew *Vrancea Two* was trying to contact them on the radiotelephone. Slightly nervous, the duty operator pressed the transmitter switch and said firmly:

"Be patient, *Vrancea Two*! I'll come back to you later! We're talking to the Americans right now. Over!

"I wouldn't care if you talked to the President of the United States himself! We have big problems here!" George hollered. "The road is blocked by…"

The operator swiftly turned down the speaker's volume, because Professor Dumitriu waited for the connection with the phone receiver close to his ear. When he finally heard Gordon's phone ringing, he shouted:

"Hello!... Hello!... Hello!"

Gordon's prerecorded voice explained something in a noisy background and then came a long beep.

"I got the answering machine. He's probably sleeping or he's not at home," Dumitriu said knowingly to those around him, covering the receiver of the phone with his palm. He cleared his throat and said in a didactic tone:

"Dear Doctor Gordon, this is Professor Dumitriu from Bucharest. My colleagues here and I consider that, in ten hours at most, we will have a major seismic event in Vrancea area. Last night it was a very interesting *swarm* of earthquakes. In our opinion, this is a precursor factor. We, therefore, consider an event of magnitude above 7 Richter degrees to be imminent. Please, confirm this prediction publicly. Thank you, and best wishes to you and your family! This was Professor Dumitriu from Romania. Good-bye!"

* * *

May 25, 1987, a few minutes later after the end of the telephone conversation with America

Doctor Ion Gonea, the Director of the Institute of Seismology, was carefully analyzing the case of a researcher who had been invited abroad to a Symposium. The Party Branch had refused to approve his travel visa upon being indicted by an anonymous. It was common for seismologists who intended to travel abroad were complained about through anonymous letters to the Communist Party and Securitate.

However, the novelty of this anonymous letter was that it was not written with the left hand, or in crooked, cramped letters, as usual, as if its author was a schoolboy eager to finish his task and go to play. This one had a special graphic appearance because it was composed of words carefully cut from the pages of a newspaper. The same words and expressions used, in an article glorifying the achievements of Socialist Romania, were now rearranged in another succession and pasted on a sheet of paper and expressed much hatred and envy. The researcher was accused of having a hostile attitude toward the Socialist achievements and want to take advantage of the trip to the West to betray his homeland and never return.

The Director was puzzled. He did not know how to react. The invitation was made by the prestigious University of Karlsruhe, and the researcher involved was well-known and appreciated in the international scientific community. There was no other choice but to ask for the researcher to politely reject the invitation, through an official letter, citing that he has serious health problems. This was the most common excuse when the Communist Party and the Securitate did not approve the exit visa of the scientists from Romania.

The secretary interrupted his whirlwind of thoughts to tell him Colonel Morar waited on the special line. He jumped up and picked up the phone immediately. Colonel Morar was an influential person in the Securitate. He was the one who granted visas for the researchers who traveled abroad. The Director believed he wanted details on the latest seismic events and was about to give him the most important information from the list on his desk, but the Colonel began in an irritated tone:

"Comrade Director, what the hell is going on in your Institute? A few minutes ago, an alarming message was sent abroad from one of the telephone stations!"

"Yes, yes, I know that Mircea Achim called abroad," the Director replied slightly taken aback. "I gave my approval, but I don't know anything about an alarming message. There was talk of a scholarship…"

"You are totally misinformed, comrade Director!" the other replied sharply. "Professor Dumitriu, from the Faculty of Physics, contacted an academic from the United States and left him a message, saying that in a few hours, there will be a catastrophic earthquake in Vrancea. This is outrageous and offensive. We, the State Securitate, are supposed to know about all such things first!"

"Yes, comrade Colonel, of course, of course," Ion Gonea stammered, loosening his necktie. "I gave the approval to one of my employees, Mircea Achim, in a matter related to a scholarship, not to Dumitriu. I don't even know what he's doing here in my Institute, but I'll find out right away!"

"See what this is all about and report back to me as soon as possible! I don't want this information to get to the upper leadership of the Party and the State!"

"I'm going to investigate, comrade Colonel, don't worry! And I will punish the gatekeeper for letting Dumitriu in, and all the researchers affiliated with him!" the Director ranted.

"Do it quickly and clarify the issue of the earthquake. Is it really coming or is it a false alarm?" Morar hung up before the Director had the chance to say: *"Long live, comrade Colonel!"* He was still holding the phone receiver to his ear, like an obedient soldier reporting to the influential Securitate Colonel. The situation was very serious.

He stormed into the secretariat and raged:

"Achim! Call Achim! I want him in my office right this instant!"

He paced the room nervously while his secretary tried to reach Mircea Achim. After a few moments of thought, the Director decided it would be wiser to go easy on the young researcher. As for the matter of the earthquake, it was risky to make a decision alone.

"Convene the Scientific Council! Everything must be discussed in the Council," he said more calmly, and went back into his office, leaving the door half-open.

* * *

May 25, 1987, 10 AM - local time
Pietrosu Hill

Collapsed boulders from the slope blocked the road. George and Gică made a kind of lever out of a fir-tree trunk and scarcely managed to move one of the giant rocks, but despite their efforts, they couldn't make a passageway for the car. They were still a few miles away from the damaged radio repeater. After reporting the situation to the Institute, they packed the tool kit and measuring instruments, locked the car, and started going up.

Streams of murky water flowed from the mountain through ditches that furrowed the road. The sky had cleared, but dark gray clouds loomed on the horizon. The blowing wind made the roar of the pine forest sound like a pipe organ. The thunders were louder and more menacing as they got closer. The rain was about to start again. Arriving on a small plateau, the two men stopped to rest for a while and exchanged luggage. The driver took the backpack with tools and George got the travel bag with the raincoats and food: a piece of bacon wrapped in newspaper, bread, green onions, and two cans with rusty edges.

"I'm a little hungry. We'd better stop and eat," George suggested, looking for a spot where they could sit down.

"Don't bother. It's wet everywhere," Gică said. "Anyway, it's going to rain soon. We will stop at the Bear Grotto. We'll find shelter there and a spring with good drinking water."

"You're right, my friend," George nodded. "If we walk briskly, I think we'll get there in half an hour."

They set out again on the road that passed under the dark vaults of the forest.

"Our job sometimes resembles that of the Sherpas from Nepal," George said grumpily after a while, shaking his feet to remove the thick mud stuck on the soles of his shoes.

"If only we were paid a tenth of what a Sherpa earns," replied the driver, quickening his pace. After a while, he stopped and, turning to his colleague left behind, urged him:

"Come on, boy, we've got work to do!"

Chapter 7

May 25, 1987, 11:00 AM - local time
Institute of Seismology

Mircea Achim was subjected to a relentless interrogation during the Scientific Council meeting. He was blamed for many things, especially for misinforming the Director, taking advantage of his trust, and using the Institute's phone for the wrong purpose. A member of the leadership of the Communist Party Organization had even used the expression "*hostile provocation*" and reproached him for his poor political training. The young researcher countered that he did not understand what politics had to do with seismology.

"They are strongly connected, comrade researcher!" said the Director sharply. "Seismic events have often been taken advantage of for political purposes. Let's not forget that the Islamic Revolution broke out in Iran after the devastating earthquake in 1979. The population was instigated against the Shah, being told that the earthquake was Allah's rebuke for the sins of the sovereign."

"I don't see what that has to do with our country," retorted the young man in wonder.

"You don't see many things, comrade Achim!" the Director fumed. "You should pay more attention to what we are doing and not let Dumitriu influence you. Everyone knows he's a lunatic. If that's how he prepares his students, it's dangerous! Think about the situation he's created. He gave the seismic alarm without even consulting us! The country's top management found out and now we are held responsible for everything! Do you realize what you did, Achim?"

"Comrade Director," the young man was trying to defend himself, "first, we must separate things. I admit my guilt, and I am ready to bear the consequences. As for Professor Dumitriu's alarm, I have nothing to do with it, although, from a scientific point of view, he might be right. The *swarm* of earthquakes from last night can be considered a precursor…"

"Dear young colleague, the prediction of earthquakes doesn't work like that," a senior researcher intervened. "Many others have worked hard before us and failed. Dumitriu has become a kind of fortune teller for earthquakes overnight. His prediction is scientifically unfounded and should not be taken into consideration. What he did is very dangerous and immoral, I should say."

"For some time now, we've been coming across guys like him more and more often," said another senior researcher. "An acquaintance of mine from Vrancea called me this morning to tell me that his dog had been restless all night and there was going to be an earthquake. *Feed him well and he'll calm down.*, I urged him." He laughed and added: "I know he's stingy, and probably doesn't feed the dog properly."

"There was also that citizen walking in the field with a hazelnut stick, claiming he predict earthquakes," chimed in comrade Istrate, the Secretary of the Communist Party Organization in the Institute. "He used to call the responsible factors of the Government in the middle of the night to tell them there was going to be an earthquake soon. He was a troublesome fellow. It's a good thing he left the country, and our society got rid of him. I heard he tried to make the same predictions in the USA but failed."

"Such predictions must be seriously considered from all points of view," explained the Director gravely. "Think about the major social implications. In my opinion, the absurd attempt to evacuate an entire city before an earthquake would lead to a greater loss of lives than if the population was taken by surprise. Experiments and polls have been conducted in this regard by disciplined people like the Japanese…"

The Council members barely noticed the secretary who entered the office holding a piece of paper.

"Comrade Director, a telex from Strasbourg. Looks like it's urgent."

The Director frowned at the paper and burst out: "Look at this, comrades! The European Seismological Centre in Strasbourg asks if we need help. Apparently, Dumitriu sent them a telex as well. This man has got out of his mind completely!" He turned to the secretary who was still waiting behind his chair: "You can go, comrade… You can go!"

"There is something else", she dares. "The colleagues from the Seismic Network couldn't reach the Pietrosu repeater by car. Rocks fell from the slopes and blocked the road, so they had to leave the car in the forest and go up there on foot."

"Very well, very well," the Director muttered, waving his hand dismissively as he reread the telex to be sure it wasn't a farce. He used to receive fake telexes in which he was invited abroad to give lectures at universities that did not even exist.

"They need you to phone the authorities in the area and ask them to remove the boulders from the road," insisted the secretary.

"Okay, okay, remind me to call them later. Now we have more important issues."

After the secretary left the room, the Director got up and said solemnly like a commander of a battleship:

"Comrades! Given the current situation and the responsibility weighing our shoulders, we should draft an official statement. Once we get the approval of the higher forums, we will broadcast it on the radio and television to disprove the rumors about a possible earthquake."

The proposal was voted unanimously and two members of the Scientific Council received the task of drafting the official statement. Also, by a unanimous vote, Mircea Achim received a written reprimand, subject to a commitment that he will respect the internal regulation of the Institute in the future.

* * *

May 25, 1987, 3:30 PM - local time
Forest road on Pietrosu Hill

The car slowly descended the narrow mountain road. The driver was whistling a cheerful song.

"We solved it this time, too!" said George with professional satisfaction. "We had to walk a little, but it wasn't that bad. We breathed fresh air and cleansed our lungs." He looked at his watch and added optimistically: "With a little luck, we'll be home early. What do you say?"

"Yes, I hope we get home before dark," said Gică. "I need some rest, too. I have to queue tonight. Rumor has it they'll bring meat to the grocery store tomorrow morning. There are spider webs inside our fridge. My wife and I can manage it, but we must put something on the family table for the children."

"My wife warned me that our refrigerator is empty as well," George said thoughtfully. "I think I'll be queuing too. I heard they will make a list this evening and check clients' presence at every hour all night. Worse than in prison."

"Soon we'll envy those in prison," the driver replied bitterly. "We will be more humiliated. Did you see the welded metal bars behind the grocery store? It looks like an enclosure for milking the sheep."

"I already had the honor to experience it yesterday, while I was queuing for cheese," George boasted ironically. "It is wonderful! Indeed, it seems to be a kind of sheep's milking enclosure, a fascinating combination between the ancient tradition of our people and the effervescent requirements of this *glorious present*. Sometimes, when it's crowded, it can even test the physical endurance of our ribs. Still, it fully rewards you with the feeling of discipline, the golden dream of any client who aligns himself with the *Communist Party policy of rational feeding*". He shook his head and, changing his tone, added with a sigh: "Only bad things are on the minds of our leaders! Instead of bringing enough food on the market, they find all sorts of methods to organize the queues."

"I heard they started to sell through the back door all over Bucharest. At the Party Branch, the bosses' drivers still talk to each other. I eavesdrop often and hear a lot. Ceaușescu doesn't want foreign journalists to see the queues in front of the stores. It is said that *Țața Leana*, his wife, nicknamed us: *hungry grasshoppers that spoil the image of the country*".

"This is an old truth. Those in power never cared about the wellbeing of common people."

"Sellers are benefiting a lot from this food crisis. For example, Jan, the head of the grocery store, was a loser, and now he has a new Mercedes. He cheats on the scale, he does nothing but tricks, and no one punish him."

"Well, who's to punish him? You're a driver with distributed attention. Didn't you notice in the evening the cars loading food packages behind the grocery store? All activists from the Party Branch and Miliția chiefs in the district get supplies from him."

Gică shook his head with a biter sentiment:

"These queues make you feel no longer human. Soon we'll be like a herd of cattle…"

"That's their goal, my friend!", emphasized strongly George. "Abolishing the individual's thinking is the first step in creating a *new type of man,* brainwashed, who asks for nothing and does not eat too much. He would work day and night and procreate only with the approval of the Party for the *rejuvenation of the nation and the flourishing of the socialist homeland*."

"This is no laughing matter," said the driver, a deep frown on his face. "Our generation can hardly be brainwashed, but the children are indoctrinated from kindergarten and taught to recite only poems glorifying the Communist Party."

George exclaimed in disapproval:

"This is a mental illness, to organize politically from the age of three, as *Homeland Falcons.* A stupid nickname generated by a diabolical thought!"

"The children of our days lose their childhood while queuing with their parents. It's sad to see them suddenly ending their play when a food truck arrives at the grocery store."

"Yes, I know. Some run to sit in line, others run round the block, shouting in despair: *Mom! They brought something to the food store!* or *Grandma! Come on, I held your place in line!* Sometimes it's only a false alarm."

"I noticed that these children have mature, bold, determined faces as if they are going to a battle," George said. "Armed with bags and crumpled money dampened by the sweat of their hands, they wait in line somewhat desperately. Adults often argue with them and push them aside. This reminds me of something that haunted me as a child: when my grandmother fed the chickens, I was always pitying the chicks nibbled and chased away by the old hens. As a basic instinct, the hunger manifests itself in the same way, no matter the species."

"Hunger is a damn thing. It turns people into beasts!"

They were crossing a narrow plateau from where they could see the villages scattered down in the valley, under the huge rainbow arch. The sun shone through the clouds and the sky gradually became clear. The earth was steaming and a light mist was floating above the plains.

"It's a pity this beautiful country has such bad rulers," George said in deep regret.

"It's a pity that we were born here in these hard times and have this cursed fate," replied the driver.

"Let's thank God that we were not born in forced labor camps in Siberia, as our colleague Ion Ilieş, the seismologist from Chişinău, or in other much worse places on the World." added the other.

After a short break in which the both tried to get rid of the dark thoughts, George proposed:

"Let's leave to hell the troubles and have a laugh! Do you know the *Homeland Falcons' oath*?"

"Of course, I do," replied the driver rolling his eyes. "Do you think I have poor political training?" He began to recite in a thin voice like a child: "*I, the falcon from kindergarten, / Swear with my hand on the bow, / and with my ass on the potty/ To grow big and strong/ Without eating anymore!*"

They both laughed out loud.

Upon arriving at the well whose dip bucket swayed in the wind, they made their usual stop for a few minutes. It was a great pleasure for George to drink fresh water straight from the mossy green wooden bucket, a kind of ritual, a merging with the life-giving sap of the Earth. Gică filled a large plastic jerry can and poured the water into the car's radiator to cool down the engine after the rough mountain drive. Then they decided to wash the taillights and license plates. The emblem that read *Seismology - Interventions* was completely lost under a crust of mud, and George, in a fit of professional pride, found it appropriate to bring it to the light.

An engine rumble echoed down the valley.

"I think it's the bulldozer," George said, slightly surprised. It hadn't been long since he notified the Seismology Command about the boulders on the road.

"I don't think so," the driver said knowingly. "It sounds like an ARO SUV, but the driver lacks experience with such roads. Can't you hear him forcing the engine?"

Indeed, a white ARO SUV with nickel-plated bars appeared from behind a rock spur. The two men were dumbfounded. Next to the driver was a young blonde lady with sunglasses, a rather unusual appearance on the roads of Pietrosu Hill. Gică rushed over and moved his car out of the way, closer to the fountain so they could pass. However, the car stopped beside them, and the young lady got off energetically and addressed them in a friendly tone:

"Hello, gentlemen! Could you give us some directions?"

"With great pleasure!" jumped the driver. "It's not every day that we have the chance to help a distinguish young lady like you, you know!"

Flattered, the woman smiled, showing her white teeth, and asked:

"Does this road lead to the ruins of the Roman Fort in Valea Mare?"

George felt somewhat challenged. Archeology was an old passion of his, and only an unfortunate situation led him to choose another profession.

"I don't believe you're on the right path," he began didactically. "It's a circuitous route. You have to get to the other side of the mountain. Wait a minute, I think have a map."

He rushed to the car and rummaged through the glove compartment, throwing around papers, dirty rags, and screwdrivers until he finally found a crumpled tourist map at the bottom. To his disappointment, the part which the young woman was interested in was stained with oil. Smiling with understanding, the blonde took a much more attractive map out of her jacket pocket and unfolded it on the slabs near the fountain.

"We were told we were going to pass a seismic station. Is this the way?" she asked, running her index finger along a squiggly red line on the map.

"Yes, that's the one," George agreed, his eyes drawn to the blonde's perfectly manicured hands. "Now we're right here at the fountain," he pointed on the map, gently touching her hand. "The seismic station is somewhere on the hill. We come from there," he added, proudly showing to the emblem on the car's door, which read *Seismology - Interventions.*

"Oh, you're seismologists?!" The young woman blinked in surprise. "It must be an interesting job."

"Yes, quite interesting and a bit tiring sometimes." George measured her from head to toe and asked with a tinge of envy: "Are you an archaeologist?"

"Yes, in a way, yes," she replied uncertainly.

Meanwhile, Gică and the other driver, a young, dark-skinned man, were caught up in a lively discussion about Diesel engines. The blonde's companion spoke Romanian poorly and the woman felt obliged to explain:

"My friend came to Romania recently. He wants to study Roman art in Dacia."

"Is that so?" George looked at him suspiciously.

He could hardly believe that the guy in front of him was a lover of ancient art who came to Romania to study Roman art right at the foot of Pietrosu Hill.

"I love Romania. Beautiful country, beautiful girls!" the young man said, a sly smile distorting his mouth. He pulled out a packet of Kent cigarettes and invited the other two to help themselves.

Excited, Gică rubbed his dirty hands and grabbed a cigarette, using only two fingers in an attempt to be graceful and to not get dirty the white filter. He put it to his nose, sniffed it, and said:

"Now that's real life! Thank you, sir!" He instinctively began searching his pockets for the matchbox, but, before he could remember he no longer had one, the foreigner came to his help with a nickel-plated lighter that caught George's attention.

"Is that an electronic lighter?" he asked as he watched a bluish flame appear when the other pressed the ignition button. Behind him, the blonde was making desperate signs to her companion to hide the lighter quickly from the prying eyes. But it was too late, for the lighter began to make long beeps. With a sudden gesture, the foreigner stopped it and put it back in his pocket.

"Yes, it is an electronic lighter...," the young woman replied drily. Because the two men were amazed, she added hastily: "It's an electronic cigarette lighter with an alarm that's triggered if it stays on too long."

George didn't find the explanation plausible, but before he could say anything, the woman turned to the foreigner and said:

"Let's go, honey, it's getting late."

She got into the car a little nervous, slamming the door, but still smiling. The car started in a hurry over the ditches in the middle of the road and began the climb to the top.

Savoring the aroma of the cigarette, Gică watched them for a while as they drove away, then got in his driver's seat and turned on the engine reluctantly.

"Come on, buddy, we're missing the queue for meat!" urged George. "Or are you thinking of the *blonde woodpecker*?"

"Some are more fortunate than others," Gică sighed, shaking his head in resignation.

"They have a very interesting lighter."

"Damn the lighter..."

"Anyway, these guys seemed rather peculiar. He can barely speak Romanian and came here to study Roman art while I climb the hills to send seismic signals to Bucharest. It's not that I don't like my job, but something doesn't feel right."

"Why didn't you become an archaeologist?"

"I thought you know. The *communist comrades* didn't allow me to enroll at the Faculty of History because I don't have *healthy origin*. I am the son of an Orthodox priest…," he trailed off, his gaze lost in the distance, but the driver snapped him out of his melancholy:

"Damn! We forgot to tell her about the rocks on the road!"

"Yeah, well, they'll be fine, don't worry," George said with a laugh. "They'll get to the first village and that guy can bribe a bulldozer driver with Kent cigarettes. He'll say: *I give Kent to you; you help… the bulldozer to me!* and the *blonde woodpecker* will wink…" They both burst out laughing.

Above the fields, somewhere far away, storm clouds were swirling on the dark blue sky.

* * *

May 25, 1987, 3:35 AM- local time
US - Space Monitoring Center

In the Telecommunications Room, sitting in front of state-of-the-art radio equipment, Captain Power carefully supervised the radio connections with the agents engaged in the *Fishing in the Mountains* operation. The subordinate operators sent coded instructions at certain intervals. Upon analyzing the latest received messages, he decided it was time to inform his superior. He asked for permission and reported:

"The agent from Romania, codenamed *Gilbert*, is about to annihilate the seismic surveillance. The team from Bulgaria, codenamed *Ilf and Petrov*, has crossed the border without any problems, but does not see any possibility to procure the equipment and dosimeters necessary to enter the radioactive area. We'll contact them again in a few minutes. They wait for our instructions."

"I think this can be solved relatively easily," General Alan King said confidently. "The Foreign Department didn't approve the idea of parachuting the necessary items because is risky. Instead, we've been offered the collaboration of one of their agents from a Panamanian ship in Constanța harbor. His radio code is *Hotel Lima 3*. He's waiting to be contacted on the backup radio frequency. I authorize the operation!"

The captain received the news with relief and returned to the Telecommunications Room. He set a transceiver to a certain frequency, and sent in ether a typical ham call:

"Attention, *Hotel Lima 3*! This is *Yokohama Honolulu*. Attention, *Hotel Lima 3*, this is *Yokohama Honolulu*' Radio check. Come in!"

"This is *Hotel Lima 3*. I read you loud and clear, *Yokohama Honolulu*. I copy you with 5.9. I'm waiting for details about your *antenna*. Go ahead." The agent's voice echoed through the speaker.

"Copy, *Hotel Lima 3*! Glad to hear you, my friend! It's a rough, windy day here, and since you're interested in my *antenna*, please notice that it has only two North-East-facing elements. Over!"

"Roger that! You probably need to protect the two elements from the *wind*. I think I could help you with that. I'll remain on the same frequency and wait for the offer. Over!"

"Thank you, *Hotel Lima 3*! Out!"

Captain Power rose abruptly from his desk and turned quickly to one of the operators:

"Urgent connection with *Ilf and Petrov* team! Tell them to contact *Hotel Lima 3* on the backup frequency. He's our agent from Constanța harbor and will provide them with the protective equipment and everything else they need."

* * *

1987, May 25, 2:30 PM - local time
Black Sea shore - Constanța Harbor

A couple of fishermen were perched on the rocks, waiting for the fish to bite. The wind was blowing heavily from the sea, breaking the waves in the seawall, and noisy seagulls circled above the water ready to pounce on the fish. Far away, in the port roadstead, the silhouettes of the ships waiting at anchor stood out against the grey sky.

Two athletic-looking foreign tourists parked their car in front of the Doina Hotel. They took the fishing gear out of the trunk, put on their boots and raincoats, and hurried to the pier, looking for a safer place to fish, hidden among the rocks.

A local man walked by, admired their rods and asked if they had anything for sale. They were kind enough to offer him a cigarette and made large gestures with their hands to explain they had nothing to sell. The local man got the idea but sat down next to them anyway, setting up his fishing pole. He soon caught a fish and yelled proudly at the tourists that he was ready to compete with them. The foreigners didn't understand what he was saying and tried to make the same vague hand signs.

A few moments later, one of them took out his binoculars and peered at the ships anchored offshore while his colleague opened a device that looked like a telescopic rod. Hiding behind a cliff where the local man could not see him, he turned on the *rod* and launched a radio call for *Hotel Lima 3*. The answer came immediately, followed by a brief conversation in which some details were established.

"We need to get rid of the neighbor," he said turning off the transmitter and making a discreet gesture with his head toward the local.

"I don't know how. He's a nuisance," the other hissed.

The local man with a shabby hat was laughing as he pulled another fish out of the foamy waves and kept challenging them to a competition.

"He must leave at once! We decided to *fish* the package here. It's too late to change the plan," his colleague countered.

To their dismay, two other fishermen came toward them along the seawall.

"I'll take care of them," the first one said curtly, hastily packing his fishing tools which he put back in the cylindrical leather box, and approached the local man who didn't notice him. The two fishermen arrived.

"What are you doing, Uncle Marin? Got any luck?"

"Lots of it!" Marin replied excitedly. "What about you? Did you catch anything?"

"Just a few pounds. If you say this is a good spot, we'll stay here for a while. Want some brandy?"

"What do you have? *Two plums*?"

"Yes. Don't you like it?"

"I do, I do. Give me a sip! Come here, there's enough room!"

The fishermen sat on the rocks, flanking Marin, while the foreign tourist watched them in dismay, without understanding what they were doing. This situation could sabotage the entire mission. The physical annihilation of the three men seemed to be the only solution. He looked around him for a suitable place to abandon them when one of the fishermen handed him the brandy bottle.

"Have a drink, sir! It's good!"

"He's a foreigner, he doesn't understand what you're saying," Marin clarified.

"Polski, Polski?"

"*Niet, bŭlgarski*," the stranger replied, trying to be polite. Then he said *Miliția* and explained through gestures that he couldn't drink because he was driving.

"Oh, maybe you don't like it," one of the fishermen shrugged, unable to understand the foreigner's hand signs. "You, Bulgarians, have such good brandies. Cognac, *ima* cognac?" The fisherman put his hand to his mouth, suggesting the need to drink.

"*Ima, ima*," the stranger replied happy to have finally found the solution and motioned for them to follow him. He was to take them to his car, in the parking area of the hotel, and give them a bottle of drink.

"*Scolko?*" the fishermen asked with interest.

The tourist showed such a small amount of money on his fingers that all three men accepted his proposal, didn't waste any more time, and followed the foreigner to the hotel nearby.

The other tourist remained on the seawall, sheltered from the sharp wind between two rocks. He looked through the binoculars over the crests of the waves, in the direction of the ships anchored offshore. The seagulls circled him, screaming shrilly. The man checked his watch impatiently. The minutes passed slowly. From time to time, he glanced around to make sure he was alone. He could see only a group of fishermen a few hundred yards away.

Finally, a diver came out of the waves. He crept through the slippery rocks and handed him a package wrapped in a waterproof material. The diver gave him the thumbs-up, the sign that he has fulfilled successful his mission and disappeared back into the restless sea.

* * *

May 25, 1987, 4:30 PM - local time
Parking on the Buzău-Bucharest highway

Arriving on the National highway, the Seismology Intervention vehicle stopped in the first parking lot. Gică got out and cut off the front wheel drive. It was one of the many disadvantages of this type of car. Coupling and uncoupling the wheels for double traction was done only from the outside.

A little further, three Lada cars with Soviet Union license plates were parked and each of them had two gas canisters anchored to their trunks. Their occupants, some athletic young men, had their lunch on an improvised concrete table nearby, dropping the waste on the ground around them. They talked rather loudly and divergently, at least that's what George thought. One of them, a tall, freckled man, approached him with a map in his hand and asked in broken Romanian if he could help them find their way. George replied in English, hoping they could understand each other better, but the stranger shook his head and said he preferred to get the explanations in Romanian.

"Here in Romania, it's so hard to drive…," he complained. "You drive on bad road and… not know where you go. You get lost! Everywhere it is written: *Long Live Ceauşescu! Long Live Socialism*, but don't write which city and how many kilometers you're going…

"Well, in Romania, the spies have a hard life," said Gică, laughing. "They need a local guide. Even we, Romanians, can barely manage though if we know the places. So, you have no chance! Where do you want to go?"

The freckled man hesitated for a moment before pointed to the Dobrogea Mountains on the map. The driver looked at him in astonishment and asked:

"What the hell are you doing there? If you want to get to your fellow Russian Lipovans, you should go further east, to the Danube Delta."

"Yes, we go to the Delta, we fish," another *tourist* chimed in.

Gică knew all the routes and showed them the best one on the map. The tourist thanked him and shook his hand, but the driver made sure to charge him with a cigarette.

"This is the real Russian tobacco that makes you cough until your eyes pop out," he said with a laugh, taking better notice of the cigarette he had received. "Do you have a light, boy?"

The man gave him a lighter that barely worked. The other *Russian tourists* remained sat around the concrete table, talking in whispers as they threw surreptitious glances at the Seismology Intervention car. George didn't miss this and became suspicious when another young man with short hair and a flattened pugilist's nose, approached them.

"Bucharest?"

"Yes, we're going to Bucharest," replied George.

"Me too!"

"So, we're heading in the same direction," Gică said in a friendly tone. "You can follow us."

George didn't like the invitation. When they were alone, he said reproachfully:

"What are you doing? It's unsafe to get dubious strangers tag along with us."

"Why do you think they're dubious? They're only *tourists*."

"It depends on what kind of *tourists*. When a man goes on holiday, he takes his wife and children with him. As far as I know, all these *Soviet tourists* are single, healthy, and good fighters. They can shoot from any position. Don't you see? They all seem cut from the same cloth."

"Poor lads. They're just like us: they sleep in the parking lots, eat canned food… and smoke these things," Gică spat full of disgust the tobacco stuck on his lips. "Do you want a smoke to taste it?"

"No, thanks. I don't want to spoil the flavor of the Kent cigarette."

George adjusted his rear-view mirror so that he could see what was going on behind on the road. The Lada cars followed them close. Two of them overtook the Seismology's car, honking their horns. At the first intersection, they took a turn, heading for Dobrogea region as Gică showed on the map. The freckled guy and one of his comrades remained behind.

"I'm telling you, they're dubious fellows," George muttered, continuing to scrutinize their car through the rear-view mirror. "First, the freckled said they wanted to go to the Delta. Now I see he's changed his mind. I really don't think they're ordinary tourists."

"Maybe it's just their habit to say one thing and do the opposite. Perhaps it would be better to get rid of them, after all. Let's test their driving skills!"

Gică turned on the blue rotative beacon over the car's cabin, started the siren, and stepped on the gas. The car sped off in a dangerous slalom among tractors and carts.

* * *

May 25, 1987, 6:35 AM- local time
US - Space Monitoring Center

The officers in charge were called again for an urgent meeting. General Alan King gave them new details on the *Fishing in the Mountains* operation.

"Gentlemen, things start to get complicated. We discovered that the Soviets have infiltrated several agents in the area, and it seems their mission, like ours, has two purposes. In some ways, we have common interests. They also intend to shut down the Romanian seismic surveillance system, but I don't have information on how they will do it yet. On the other hand, a well-trained commando group will operate where the impact is to take place. One thing is clear, though. Their coordinates coincide with ours. Professor Gordon's calculations are correct. Our agents might bump into the Soviet ones. The *Ilf and Petrov* team must be alerted urgently! What news do you have from them, Captain Power?"

"They've just got the protective equipment from *Hotel Lima 3* and are heading North. We communicate only when strictly necessary. Apparently, the Romanian secret services noticed an intensification of the radio traffic in the area. They have already broadcast some trap radio messages."

"This is not good news. Turn off all terrestrial radio calls. Use only satellite telephony that cannot be intercepted by the Romanian secret services. For short communications use the paging system. Did our agent in Romania manage to annihilate the seismic system?"

"Not yet, but he will soon," Captain Power assured him.

"There's another unforeseen problem," the General informed them. "There is a kind of seismic alarm in Romania. They are on alert. An eccentric guy, a friend of Professor Gordon, apparently, to whom he also left a message on the answering machine, claims that a catastrophic earthquake may soon occur in Vrancea, the most active seismic region in Romania. If this earthquake does occur, we will have the perfect coverage. The potential disaster might help us carry out our operation without obstacles. Otherwise, we'll have to face a prolonged state of alert with unexpected delays and repercussions."

Colonel Mc Stevenson suggested informing the Romanian secret services discreetly about the presence and mission of the Soviet agents on their territory could be beneficial.

"We already know all the license plate numbers of the cars they drive in Romania. It would be a major blow for them.", he said thinking that it is a very good option.

"And a huge mistake on our part, Colonel!", General Alan King contradicted him. "The Soviets would do the same to us. We would expose each other. In this game, both sides know each other's moves. Only our professional discretion helps us give the impression that the opponent is ahead of us. This is what I like to call the *chivalry of espionage*. The outcome of not respecting this basic principle would be a wretched Romanian prison cell shared by our agents and their rivals. We don't wish to reach that point. Let those Communist countries wash their dirty laundry together, like a family." He looked at the digital clock on the wall and add: "According to Gordon's calculations, the impact will occur in approximately three hours! Once the *code module* is captured, it will have to be immediately removed from the Romanian territory. We will receive the support of an Aircraft Carrier in the Mediterranean Sea. I asked for two helicopters to be ready for the final phase of the mission. They will fly at night, at low altitude, under the radar curtain to avoid detection."

"Why don't we use the same *Hotel Lima 3* agent?" Captain Power asked. "He will be able to pick up the package from the same place and take it to the Panamanian ship."

"Negative!" the Commander firmly replied. "There is the high risk. I have information that the boats of the Romanian Border Police are swarming all over the area.

Chapter 8

May 25, 1987, 2:00 PM - local time
Bucharest Air Defense Unit

The Radio Moscow announcement of a satellite that was about to crash into Earth put the Romanian Air Defense on *yellow alert*. Colonel Theodor, the shift Commander of the Bucharest Air Defense Unit, carefully analyzing the reports on the last few hours. The radar stations had not recorded any special events, just the regular airliners traffic. At the shrill sound of the operative phone, he immediately picks up the handset. It was Captain Panait, the shift chief at the local Radar Surveillance Station.

"Comrade Colonel, allow me to report!" he began a little alarmed.

"Go ahead, Captain! I'm listening," the Colonel replied, expecting a routine situation report.

"Unknown target in square 22, comrade Colonel. Azimuth 14, elevation 70. It doesn't respond to any recognition code. It's practically coming to us from Space!"

Colonel Theodor thinking nothing but the worst: the crash of the Soviet satellite on Romanian territory. However, he calmly ordered:

"Keep the antenna on the target and determine its trajectory as accurately as possible. It could be a weather balloon. Get in touch with the Institute of Meteorology and keep me posted."

"If it were a weather balloon, we should have been notified on the regular channel."

"I know, but check and report anyway!"

After a few minutes, the hypothesis fell through. There was no information of any meteorological balloon that would cross the Romanian airspace.

"What should I do, comrade Colonel? May I transmit the data to the Missile Battery?", Panait asked in alarm.

"Not yet! Wait until I get to the Command Post. I'll be there in a few minutes."

The Radar Surveillance Station and the Command Post were camouflaged between two huge mounds of soil. The soldier guarding the access barrier recognized the Commander's car from a distance. He adjusted his outfit and, shouldering his AKM weapon, took the regular salute position.

"It's urgent, soldier! Lift the barrier!" cried the sergeant driver, putting his head out the window.

The soldier, however, remained tense, with his weapon on his shoulder, and began shouting as loud as he could:

"Shift corporal, come at the post number one! Shift corporal, come at the post number one!" He then started hitting with a hammer a piece of metal hanging from a tree branch, making a deafening noise.

The entry formalities took a while and annoying everyone, but that was the rule. The corporal in charge of the sentries' changing had to be present and identify any person or vehicle entering the area.

Colonel Theodor was eager to see the radar echo produced by the detected target.

"It's at a very high altitude," he said.

"Could it be a meteorite entering the atmosphere?" asked one of the officers.

"Impossible! The speed is much slower. It looks more like a controlled fall," said the Commander after looking very closely at the notes on the board. "I'm afraid this target has something to do with the announcement on the radio…"

"Do you mean the Soviet satellite that got out of control?" Captain Panait asked really alarmed.

"Exactly! From the information I have, it's a real monster. It has atomic batteries to power the electronic systems."

"Do you think it could fall on our territory?"

"It might if it stays on the current trajectory…"

Panait knew that it was his responsibility to go through all the steps required by the regulations in such cases, as soon as possible.

"Then I ask for your permission to alert the entire Air Defense System!" the captain became impatient.

"I don't see the point," said the Commander. "It will crash just like a boulder anyway, and, unfortunately, no one knows where."

"Maybe we should launch a ground-to-air missile to destroy it. We would pulverize it in the upper layers of the atmosphere, thus canceling the repercussions of the crash at the soil."

"But the danger of the radioactive contamination of a large area will remain," pointed out Colonel Theodor. "I will report the situation to the upper echelon. Keep one of the antennas on this target only and inform me regularly about its evolution."

The Colonel saluted, hurried out, got into the armored SUV, and sped off back to the Air Defense Command.

**

May 25, 1987, 7:00 AM- local time
US - Space Monitoring Center

Captain Power was walking among the radio traffic controllers' desks sipping from a large cup of coffee. He had given instructions to cut the ground radio communications with the *Panther* agents on the mission. Due to the risk of being intercepted, the only calls considered safe were those made via satellite phone, much more difficult to trace.

The sergeant in charge of telegraphy monitoring came in and presented him with a report sheet.

"I intercepted this encrypted message, Captain. It's in ultra-fast telegraphy. It has been repeated at least three times so far."

Power glanced at the message and flinched.

"Monitor everything transmitted on this frequency, sergeant!" he said without giving any further explanations. After calling General Alan King's office, asking to speak to him confidentially as a matter of urgency, Captain Power ran down the hall, the sheet of paper with the encrypted message in his hand.

"We have a sign from *Rasputin*, General!" he said excitedly, after making sure the office door was closed and the jamming system running.

"That's great news, Captain!" his superior beamed. "Agent *Rasputin* deserves his name. He has nine lives! I thought he was killed."

"I thought so too. He's been silent for too long. Apparently, he's fine. Looking at the message, Power tried to decode certain passages. "It's fantastic!" he exclaimed. "He is back in the *lions cage*, in the Soviet Space Center, in Kazakhstan."

"Interesting…"

"I see he's not only fine but coming back in force. He wants to negotiate the retrieval of the *code module*. He says that he can give it to us without incidents."

"We must be careful," the General frowned. "It could be a trap. A false lead. You know that *Rasputin* is a specialist in the double game. I can't authorize such a negotiation without consulting the State Department first. Let him know on the regular channel that we'll contact him."

"I think he wants to play fair," Power said, not taking his eyes off the message. "Check out these groups of numbers. They are the coordinates of the impact zone. If you compare them to those calculated by Doctor Gordon, you'll see they're almost identical!"

"Of course, he realizes we've already estimated the coordinates by now," Alan King said. "*Rasputin* is the best disinformation agent I've ever heard of. Doesn't it seem strange to you that he managed to send a message from the Soviet Space Center area where they use the most sophisticated means of tracking and monitoring? I believe *Rasputin* is a symbol, a legend, or a ghost. I wonder if he really exists."

"I think he's very much real, and could be one of the most important people in the Soviet secret services," Power countered convincingly.

"I'm afraid there are actually dozens of agents behind this code name, agents commanded by the diabolical mind of a KGB General. *Rasputin* has mailboxes all over the world, but none of our people have yet been able to meet him. Two of our agents, who tried to contact him, died in suspicious circumstances. He's been working for us for so long, and all we know about him is that he gets his payment in Switzerland, from a dumpster on the outskirts of Geneva. *Rasputin* appears and disappears…"

"It's true, General," Power acknowledged, "but all the information he's provided us so far has been correct. He never misled us. My opinion is we should not miss this opportunity," he insisted. "If you allow me, I can start negotiations immediately."

"All right, I authorize you," the General said skeptically. "In the meantime, I'll try to get more information on another channel."

* * *

May 25, 1987, 15 :00 AM - local time
Bucharest – Măgurele Faculty of Physics

Professor Dumitriu's prediction caused a real "*earthquake*" that spread rapidly through the offices, on the telephone lines, the corridors, the buses, and even on the streets. He was called to the local Party Bureau of the Faculty of Physics and reprimanded. Under the threat of being fired, he was requested to formally retract his prediction of a potentially devastating earthquake in Romania. A commission was to be set up to investigate the situation and propose sanctions.

The top Communist Party leadership was closely interested in the case. The rumor of a possible destructive earthquake was considered a deliberate diversion of hostile elements, just before the National Party Conference began. Dumitriu did not let himself be intimidated, but he promised to remain silent about his prediction and continued his Academic courses as if nothing had happened.

The amphitheater was almost full. The Professor drew the atmospheric layers on the board using colored chalk and explained the structure and composition of each one in detail. To his delight, he also noticed a few students from other groups. The rumor of the earthquake prediction and the radio news about the crash of the Soviet military satellite had drawn them like a magnet to his lecture. At the end, he spared a few minutes to answer questions, but the remaining time proved insufficient. The students made numerous comments on the military satellites, being particularly interested in the international agreements governing the launch and use of such equipment.

"The technical progress of the Humanity also has its disadvantages," the Professor said at last. "Unfortunately, the main achievements of mankind are geared toward military purposes. Many of the satellites launched on Earth orbit carry military devices and hang like a true *Sword of Damocles* over our heads."

"Do you think the Soviet drifting satellite is a danger for us?" someone asked. "Could we know approximately where it will collapse?"

"Of course, the Soviets have the data about the initial velocity and the entry angle into the atmosphere. They have probably already estimated where the impact will occur. What is certain, the remnants of this satellite will reach the Earth. This type of military device has a special armored shields against the laser weapons, that provides good thermal protection during free fall."

Although the class was over, the conversation would have lasted longer if his assistant had not opened the amphitheater door, speaking in a slightly impatient tone:

"Professor! A comrade colonel on the phone. It's urgent!"

"What else do they want from me?!" Dumitriu replied nervously. "I said all I had to say! From a scientific point of view, I support my statement."

"I don't think he's the same colonel, Professor."

The students looked at each other in amazement and watched Professor Dumitriu as he grabbed his handbag with a gesture of disapproval and headed to the door. He stopped on the threshold and swiveled around, putting a hand to his forehead as if he had forgotten something. The students said an admiring *Wow!* in a chorus.

"It wouldn't have any charm if you don't remember something in the doorway, Professor!" said a cheerful voice from the room.

He shook his head and smiled sadly.

"I have nothing more to add for today. We'll see what tomorrow brings. Class dismissed!"

Dumitriu found the telephone receiver on the desk and put it to his ear.

"This is Professor Dumitriu, I'm listening," he said, his voice a little tense.

"What are you doing, *scholar*? I've been aging here on the phone, waiting for you to answer."

The Professor immediately recognized the voice and speaking manner of his former high school classmate, Colonel Theodor.

"My respects, *Marshal*!" he burst out refreshed. "Did you hear about my earthquake predictions too?"

"Yes, but that's not why I'm calling you! I have a problem and I want to ask your opinion. It's urgent! I've already sent a car to pick you up."

"All right, I'm coming!"

* * *

May 25, 1987, 8:00 AM - local time
US - Space Monitoring Center

The Telecommunications Room was a hive of activity at that time. Captain Power was trying to sort out the information he received from the *red zone*. The two *Panther* crews had somehow entered a shadow cone, acting inertly. On top of everything, there was *Rasputin,* a new element that could simplify or make everything worse, compromising the whole operation.

After General Alan King, who was more suspicious by nature, had reluctantly authorized the contact with *Rasputin*, Captain Power and the alleged agent exchanged recognition messages. *Rasputin* was no longer in Kazakhstan. The operators located him somewhere in the south of Ukraine, quite close to where the impact was to take place. For Power, things were clear. *Rasputin* hadn't lied; he was involved in recovering the *code module* and wanted to make an honest negotiation. The captain asked for the offer and, after decoding it, he presented it to his Commander.

"*Rasputin* is in trouble again, General!" reported Power. "He wants to take advantage of the operation in Romania and flee the Soviet Union. He finds himself in a precarious position and wants to vanish quickly. He proposes to meet with our agents at the impact site. He wants to hand them the *code module* and be taken over by the services of the American Embassy in Bucharest. He wants to leave Romania with an American passport and enter our identity change program."

"It's a touching story," General Alan King said ironically. "A KGB officer wishes to serve the United States because he no longer wants his pension in rubles, but dollars. I didn't believe him to be so naive. Apparently, *Rasputin* confuses communist Romania with Central Park, which he could cross on a leisure walk. He's a fool if he thinks our Embassy in Bucharest will take such risks for his sake without having to bribe the Romanian secret services."

"He's aware of that. That's why he plans to hand over all the Soviet agents involved in the operation to the Romanian Securitate."

"Big deal! I repeat it over and over: in Communist countries, the dirty laundry is washed in the family. *Rasputin* would better expose some of the KGB agents who are probably swarming through my department," said the clearly irritated Commander. "And you, Captain, should order your idiot agent, Gilbert, to surrender voluntarily to the Romanian authorities. He's nothing but a pain in the butt! Can you believe this?! To let his pager get stolen by gypsies. He's a moron!" he raged. "How the hell did you recruit this Bedouin? Once his mission is over, dismiss him without delay. I don't want to hear from him ever again! And I no longer accept such people in our services, even if they are from allied countries."

"Yes, Sir! I will do it!" Captain Power assured him.

His superior was right. He still could not get over the embarrassing moment when he had to ask at the American Embassy in Bucharest to equip the agent in Romania with another pager after some gypsies had stolen the previous one in unclear circumstances. As a result, the codes of all their agents in the Communist countries had to be changed.

Clearly, General Alan King did not like *Rasputin*'s proposal, because of its many subversive elements that could compromise the image of the United States. Captain Power's insistence did nothing but was beginning to annoy him. So, the General thought it was time to end the discussion.

"Go back to your people!" Alan King ordered. "As for *Rasputin*, I think it's the Foreign Department's issue. I will, however, report the whole situation to the State Department. Meanwhile, I'll continue the operation *Fishing in the Mountains*. Once I receive other orders, I will obey them. Personally, I don't trust *Rasputin*'s offer."

* * *

1987, May 25, 2:30 PM - local time
The military airport of the southern Ukrainian SSR

Colonel Igor Zapojnikov established his command post in one of the abandoned buildings of the military airfield from where he was trying to coordinate his people on the mission in Romania with maximum efficiency. At set intervals, he took off with a helicopter that made a fixed point at a few hundred meters altitude, to maintain radio communications in good conditions.

The agents had reported enough problems. The Romanian customs officials had been reluctant and didn't want to allow such a large amount of gasoline to pass through. Finally, several bottles of vodka and a few other gifts smoothed out the negotiations. But that wasn't all. In the absence of traffic signs, the agents lost their way and wasted precious time. Compared to the original plan, they were behind schedule. And then, on top of everything, there was the hostile attitude of the military commander of the airfield. Although he had precise orders to make available all the necessary logistics to Igor Zapojnikov, he invoked various regulations and procedures to delay things.

Igor's intruder status made those around him wary so he felt somewhat isolated. His several attempts to contact General Pucinski in Kazakhstan had been futile. The Soviet Space Center's operational communications system appeared to be shut down. There was something going on, but he couldn't do anything but make assumptions and be suspicious while carrying out his mission.

Before entering the final phase of the operation, Igor had to be sure the field crews were back on the right track and had no problems. He took his communication equipment and asked the pilot to get up in the air. They were preparing to take off when the Control Tower banned the flight.

"What's going on?", Zapojnikov asked in surprise. "I need to contact my people in a few minutes!"

"A military prosecutor wants to ask you some questions," the Control Tower informed him in a menacing tone. "Get off the helicopter, otherwise we will attack the aircraft!"

Igor knew too well that a meeting with a military prosecutor directly on the track, during this very important mission to recover the *code module*, could not be auspicious. He took off his headphones, unbuckled his seat belt, opened the helicopter's sliding door and descended.

The aircraft was immediately flanked by a black ministerial Volga with smoked windows and a military truck full of soldiers armed with Kalashnikov assault rifles, who rapidly surrounded the aircraft. A lieutenant from the KGB forces got out of the cabin and pulled his pistol from its holster, pointing it at Zapojnikov, who involuntarily took a step back. For a few moments, Igor was perplexed, but he immediately understood that he was about to be caught in a KGB race. He knew very well the style of action and the "*ceremony*" of arresting senior officers who became undesirable.

"What the hell is going on here, Lieutenant?" he thundered. "I'm on a mission ordered by the Supreme Soviet!"

The military prosecutor, an old officer with thick glasses, stepped out of the Volga car and asked in an authoritative voice:

"Are you the citizen named Igor Vasilievich Zapojnikov?"

"Yes, I am," answered Igor calmly. The prosecutor shook his head somewhat regretfully, unfolded a piece of paper, and read out loud:

"Citizen Igor Vasilievich Zapojnikov, on behalf of the Supreme Soviet, you are degraded from the rank of colonel to the rank of soldier, and arrested on charges of high treason! Your rights as well as your rights of defense are guaranteed by the Constitution of the Soviet Union, meaning you have the right to a lawyer." Then, turning to the Lieutenant holding his gun on Colonel Zapojnikov he added: "Comrade Lieutenant, I order you to carry out this arrest warrant!"

Zapojnikov understood that the nightmare was beginning. He received the terrible news with indifference and not a single muscle on his face flinched, as if everything referred to another person, whom he didn't even know. In a few moments, the colonel's rank was torn from his shoulders and someone handcuffed him. He felt the pipe of a Kalashnikov in his ribs, and a soldier with a Mongoloid face pushed him toward the truck, snarling between his teeth:

"Move, you fucking traitor! You're done for!"

* * *

May 25, 1987, 3:30 PM - local time
Bucharest Air Defense Unit

The car that took Professor Dumitriu to the Air Defense Command Unit was speeding with its blue flashing beacon on and the driver used the siren occasionally. As they went through the gate of the military unit, the Professor realized something special was happening. Many trucks full of soldiers were going out and the guard posts had been reinforced. Colonel Theodor was waiting for him on the plateau in front of the building.

"Welcome to the Professor who is the best specialist in Globe Physics!" he grinned, shaking his hand.

Dumitriu recognized the usual hint of irony in his friend's words.

"Okay, okay... What happened here?"

"We detected a dubious target over the territory of our country. I think it's the satellite..."

"Are you serious?"

"I like telling jokes, but now it's not the time for that. We've been watching it for almost half an hour. It's basically in a free fall at an angle of 70 degrees."

In the Command Room, several young officers were focused on maps and drawings. The Professor was introduced to them and a brief discussion followed. The Brigade General was expected to arrive at any moment.

"The crash on our territory seems imminent," said Colonel Theodor, after returning from the adjoining room, where the data coming directly from the radar station was noted on a special transparent board. "The question is: where will it happen? It's no secret that this satellite contains a significant quantity of radioactive substances that can contaminate an entire area. That's why I asked you to come, comrade Professor. Do you think you could help us estimate the coordinates of the impact zone?"

"I'm afraid it's not that simple," Dumitriu shook his head. "I have a colleague abroad who's dedicated most of his career to studying the trajectory of celestial bodies entering the atmosphere. The computing programs are complex and include lots of parameters. In any case, I will try to do my best using the existing data. The problem is that the angle at which the target approaches doesn't allow too good a resolution so I need a powerful computer."

"The computer Felix of our Air Defense Unit is at your disposal, comrade Professor," said Theodor. Turning to the group of young officers who were still examining the maps, he ordered: "Lieutenant Barbu, take Professor Dumitriu to our Computing Center!"

* * *

1987, May 25
USSR - Journey to a secret destination

Zapojnikov felt like he no longer existed. At the end of the runway, a couple of soldiers took him out of the truck and pushed him up the stairs of a twin-engine plane preparing to take off. Inside, two officers from KGB forces handcuffed him to one of the seats. A civilian in a beige sweatshirt soon boarded the plane and gave some brief orders to the two officers before entering the cockpit.

The plane gained speed, raised its nose to the sky in the deafening roar of the engines and began to climb hard. Flying through the clouds, without wanting to, Igor remembered his childhood the days when he was sitting in front of his parents' house near Smolensk, looking at the sky and wanting to float on the white and fluffy clouds like cotton wool. Arriving high above the layer of clouds, he felt as if he was free, although the handcuffs tied him to the chair. He tries to order his thoughts and look for the reasons for his arrest. He did not understand why he, an officer, who had put all his energy and skill into the service of the Soviet Union, was accused of high treason.

He began to systematically recall everything he had done since the moment he left home almost 24 hours ago. There were a lot of things that each had a certain meaning, above all being the contradictory discussions with the mysterious civilian with smoke glasses and his threats. The fact that Irina introduced him as General Vladimir Ivanovich Petrovsky, her father, seemed like a typical KGB story.

There was, however, one very serious thing that had happened immediately after he received the order from Moscow to go on the operational mission in Romania. Igor had intercepted an encrypted message sent from the very inside of the Soviet Space Center. He tried to decode it but failed. However, he recognized *Rasputin*'s coding style and warned his commander. He wrote down his suspicion in a notebook and, without any comment, gave it to General Pucinski to read before leaving the Space Center. Now Igor wondered if he had not made a huge mistake by this. He probably triggered a real *"witch hunt"*.

The officers dealing with data protection spoke fearfully about *Rasputin*. They believed to be a high-ranking person with access to top-secret documents. He always watched everyone from the shadows, making his presence felt only in certain moments by contacting his Base abroad and transmitting information.

As all the Soviet secret services wanted to catch *Rasputin*, perhaps now Colonel Zapojnikov, the head of Counterintelligence on Soviet Space Center became one of the main suspects. That was the only way he could explain why his bosses in Moscow had unexpectedly forbidden him to leave Soviet territory. They needed a *"scapegoat"*. Maybe they'll say: *"I've finally found Rasputin! Arrest him!"*. He was aware that there would be no escape from such a situation.

Igor thought of Tania and their girls who would endure the persecution and humiliation of being treated as the daughters of a traitor. But no! Such a misfortune could not happen to him. He couldn't wait to deny any accusation against him and felt strong enough to defend himself with or without a lawyer.

It was difficult to determine which way they were heading. The plane took all sorts of turns to the right and left as if it was slipping through a canyon. Outside, the haze was intensifying, and Igor couldn't see much. When the plane came out of the clouds, he caught sight of a vast expanse of forest below. One of the KGB officers escorting him approached his seat and blindfolded him without saying a word.

The plane began to descend, rapidly like on a forced landing. Igor felt a strong pressure on the eardrums and hard contact with the runway. After the aircraft braked and stopped, he was quickly transferred to a car, still blindfolded and handcuffed. He could feel a lot of potholes on the road they were on. Apparently, they were crossing a forest, for the driver opened a window, and Igor heard trills of the birds and feel the wet earth smell. When the short drive ended, strong, energetic arms grabbed him and lead him somewhere, inside of a building where he was forced to sit on a chair. Everyone was silent. Footsteps echoed down a corridor, and soon somebody ordered:

"Take off his blindfold!"

Igor immediately recognized the voice.

Released from the blindfold, he was blinded by the spotlight directed at him. It took him a while to adjust his vision and get a better look at General Petrovski, who was standing a few feet away, grinning like a devil.

"You may go, comrades!" he told to the others. "I want to be alone with… our guest."

Igor was not surprised. He was convinced that General Petrovski was the puppet master who sought to destroy him, using Irina as his *mole*.

After the officers left the room, Petrovski rattled a bunch of keys, and once he found the right one, he uncuffed Zapojnikov and casually gave him a cigarette. Petrovski lit his own cigar, turned off the upsetting spotlight, and looked out the window.

"It's so quiet here," he said. "Would you like to spend a vacation in this place, away from the hustle and bustle of Moscow?

* * *

May 25, 1987, 4:30 PM - local time
Bucharest Air Defense Unit

Accompanied by Lieutenant Barbu, Professor Dumitriu returned to the Command Room with a printed list. He had made some rough calculations based on a few pieces of data and concluded that the impact could occur in the South-Eastern part of Romania.

"The results aren't 100 percent accurate, but that's all we have for now," he explained cautiously.

"This will not do," Colonel Theodor retorted, shaking his head disapprovingly. "We need precise information! The satellite's nuclear devices will fall on the ground and contaminate a wide area! I've already alerted our Decontamination Unit and the Institute of Atomic Physics promised to send their dosimetry specialists, but the teams must have precise coordinates as soon as possible. I don't want to grope for radioactive traces until some mayor announces that something bad happened in his village because the cows grazing in the meadow are dying."

"But you have the radar stations…"

"The resolution of the radar echo will be ineffective due to the high speed of the target in the last part of the trajectory."

"In this case, I believe the specialists from the Seismological Institute might be of real help," the Professor said. "The impact will likely produce a deep crater, generating seismic waves strong enough to be detected by their stations."

"Do you think they have the ability to locate such events?" asked with great interest the Brigade General, who listened to their discussion.

"Absolutely! Their real-time earthquake detection network and location software are among the most advanced in the World!"

"Then the Seismological Institute remains our only solution," the General decided. "Put me on the *short line phone* with the Director, quickly!"

* * *

May 25, 1987, 4:35 PM - local time
Institute of Seismology

Ion Gonea the Director of the Seismological Institute was agitated. The alarming, interminable, sometimes embarrassing discussions prompted him to instruct the chiefs of the collectives and laboratories that all employees should receive clear orders to combat the rumor of an upcoming devastating earthquake. The phones rang incessantly because of this. The population started to panic. Although he asked his secretary to stop forwarding him the calls and tell everyone he was not in the office, the Director couldn't prevent the *short line phone* from ringing. Its shrill sound made him frown. He was already fed up with explaining the difference between the magnitude and intensity of an earthquake, and the difference between the Richter and Mercalli degrees, to a dignitary or someone from the higher leadership of the Party. He picked up the receiver and barely articulated:

"Director Ion Gonea on the phone, I'm listening to you…"

The Brigade General left him speechless:

"Comrade Director, from now on, the seismic surveillance service of the national territory is at the disposal of the Ministry of Defense! You must consider yourself on *Red Alert* and take all the necessary measures. An operative group of officers will soon arrive at your Institute to establish a direct link with our echelon. I ask you, give them all your support!"

"I, I don't understand… I don't understand," the Director mumbled. "Professor Dumitriu gave a false alarm. We sent a press release. There will be no earthquake!"

"Forget about the earthquake, comrade Director! This is a totally different situation. The Seismic stations will have to determine the place where the Soviet satellite will crash!"

"What satellite? What… Which one?" the Director grew more and more puzzled.

"Didn't you hear the news taken by Agerpres from Radio Moscow?"

"No, I didn't listen to the radio! You know, Professor Dumitriu and I… the Council… a case of indiscipline in…"

"You'll get all the details of the problem soon!" the General assured him and hung up.

The Director got up from his desk in a daze. He knew very well the instructions for such special cases because he had just recently been trained at the Party Branch. He looked at the large red button embedded in the wall behind his desk. He never pressed it. It was still sealed. He hesitated for a moment, then tore open the seal and pushed the button. The sirens start to resounded in all the laboratories. The Director turned on the amplification station and spoke into the microphone, his hoarse of emotion voice:

"Attention, please! Attention, please! Director Ion Gonea is speaking. Starting from now we are in *Red seismic alert.* This is not an exercise! I repeat: this is not an exercise! This is a real situation! I ask all of you to act according the *Indicative Seism*! I repeat: *Red seismic alert*! Act according to the *Indicative 'Seism*!"

Chapter 9

1987, May 25, 4:45 PM - local time
Urziceni - Bucharest National Road

The *Seismology Intervention* vehicle engaged in a risky overtaking.

"Slow down, my friend! Slow down! I want to get home, not to the hospital!" George shouted, grabbing the handle above the glove box.

"Everything is under control!" the driver assured him euphorically. "If you wish, I will turn you over to your wife tonight on a signed and stamped report. I will ask her to check on you and find that I brought you in good condition." He laughed and looked in the rearview mirror. The car of the Soviet *tourists* remained behind the heavy trucks he had just overtaken. "Soon they'll lose our track," Gică said content.

"If you keep it that way, we might lose our wheels," George growled. "Can't you hear the car's joints cracking?"

"This car has still a long way to go. Its time hasn't come yet," the driver nodded in a euphoric state of optimism. He sped through the narrow aisle between two intersecting tractors, repeating the same dangerous maneuver.

"Man… you're not feeling well today!" George shook his head disconcerted. "You have bad brain cooling!"

It was the ironic diagnosis George often used when someone did crazy things. He thought it would be best to leave Gică alone so that he could focus on driving, and find something to do. Thus, he began to adjust the radiotelephone on board. The muffled sound of a voice came through the noisy background of the speaker.

"I think someone's trying to reach us again," he said without enthusiasm and turned up the volume. He wasn't wrong. The Seismology Command was calling them, but they couldn't get in touch. George could hear only fragments of words and noticed that they were at the edge of a grove that attenuated radio waves. "I think we'd better stop somewhere on a higher plateau so I can establish the radio connection," he added.

"If I stop now, they'll catch up on us and I'll have to start the race again," Gică replied with a frown. "Try to manage it while we're on the move."

A little nervous, George pressed the broadcast button and shouted into the microphone:

"Yes, *Vrancea One*! This is *Vrancea Two*! I hear you very badly. Break, break!"

They were crossing a bridge over the railway. Thanks to the altitude, George could receive the call.

"Pull over! I can hear them better up here!" George exclaimed pressing his foot to the floor as if he stepped on an invisible brake.

"Are you out of your mind? Don't you know it's not allowed to stop the car on the bridge?"

"But tripling is?" George countered.

The Seismology Command kept calling desperately, and they had to stop in the first parking lot. The two Soviet *tourists* hurried past them, honking, and waving friendly.

The reception was much better and George finally established the radio connection. Engineer Florian Ionică, informed them about the satellite's imminent crash. In spite of the *Red Seismic Alert* that urged him to act according to a certain protocol named *Indicative Seism*, George wished nothing more than to return home.

"I understand the gravity of the situation, boss, but we've completed our mission here, so we can return to Institute. I'm sure you need us there. Over!"

"No, we don't! That's exactly what I'm trying to tell you. Stay in the area!", said engineer Ionică categorically. "As you know, an intervention crew close to the epicentral area is mandatory in such situations. If necessary, prompt action must be taken to rectify potential faults. I'm afraid we'll have problems in Pietrosu again. Storms are no joke! Over!"

"Please, understand, boss! We have wandered around all day in the mountains and we're simply exhausted! Over!"

"We're on *Red Seismic Alert*, don't you understand? It's madness here! Everyone calls and asks either about the satellite or about the earthquake. I'll give you a day off if you just to stay in the area! Return to Pietrosu right now! That's the *Achilles heel* of our seismic network, you know it better than anyone else! I asked those at the Forest District to remove the rocks and the trees from the road and I hope they will solve the problem soon."

The driver swore between his teeth, growing annoyed as he listened to the conversation. The idea of returning to Pietrosu made his blood boil. At one point, as the discussion kept going, an authoritative voice boomed into the speaker:

"Why are you still talking to them, comrade? An order is an order! It must be executed!"

Hearing that voice in the background, George understood it belonged to a big shot from the Party or Securitate. He resignedly pressed the broadcast button, and answered in the most disciplined manner possible:

"Roger, *Vrancea One*! We are going back to Pietrosu. Over!" He placed the microphone in the holder and with a bitter smile on his face, he said to his colleague: "Well, my friend, this is our job… Now, let's swear as loud as we can because no one can hear us."

"That won't help," Gică reply, "but cigarettes and food will."

"We could find some cigarettes, but I don't know about the food. Where do you think we are, in America? We're lucky if we can get a loaf of bread."

"We'll show them the delegation papers and they'll have to give us something to eat."

"They don't give a damn about our delegation papers!" George snorted. "Haven't you seen how the food sellers in the provincial towns treat us? As if we were beggars: '*Get out of here, I won't give you anything! You are from Bucharest, from Bucharest to eat.*' He shakes his head bitterly and adds: "It's clearly about the food. How about gas?"

"Luckily, I took the extra canister before I left," said the angry driver. "This can only happen in Romania: we cannot find *gas at the gas station* and *bread at the bakery*. We have to carry the gas canisters in the car. On these damned roads, we can blow up any time!"

"Complaining is a waste of time when they don't even have gas for the ambulances and people are only allowed twenty liters a month. This is actually a good thing for awakening our socialist consciousness", George explains wryly. "We can't consume more than we produce. The accumulation rate must increase, as the General Secretary of the Party requested…"

"Come on, give me a break!" Gică cut him off annoyed. "Everything is a mess, that's what it is! This paranoiac Ceauşescu is twisting us around his little finger. And I wonder how much longer it will last. I don't care who hears me, I am fed up with all the nonsense in this country!"

He turned the car irritated and set off in search of a loaf of bread and a pack of cigarettes.

* * *

May 25, 1987, 5:35 PM - local time
Institute of Seismology

The pens of seismographs drew small oscillations on paper. The *swarm* of earthquakes had ceased. The seismic noise returned to normal. The recording room was full. Anti-aircraft officers, seismologists, and operators watched the seismographs spinning undisturbed in the quiet hum of the electric motors. Everyone was waiting for the unwanted event to happen; they were waiting for the Earth to receive the impact of that dangerous body coming from Space.

Outside, in front of the building, a radio relay had been installed in a military vehicle to maintain the connection with the intervention teams. From time to time, at equal intervals, a liaison officer reported: *"Nothing special!"* These two words sounded like a clock ticking that dilates time far beyond people's perceptual power.

A few miles away, on a plateau, three helicopters and the emergency crews were waiting tensely, ready to fly toward the impact site. The military had prepared their gas masks, gloves, and radiation protection equipment. A few were testing their dosimeters. The radioactive background was normal.

Triggered by the vibrations of the Earth, the seismic recorders' alarm released a sinister sound, like a wail. Everyone in the room shuddered. The seismographs started to show rare but increasingly strong oscillations. The officers grew impatient. Mircea Achim, who was explaining to them how the seismic equipment worked, said that it was a distant earthquake, a teleseism. The computer estimated the epicenter at about four thousand kilometers to the East. They examined the World's map. Somewhere in Asia, the energy of the Earth erupted violently. After a few simple calculations, the seismologists estimated the magnitude of over 7 degrees on the Richter scale.

"There could be victims!" said Mircea. "It is an unpleasant thing to look at how an earthquake is recorded and to think that, at the same time, somewhere, people are dying and you cannot do anything about it."

Most of those present gathered around the long-period seismic station, a special device built to record distant earthquakes. They watched in silence how the pens of the seismograph moved slowly, as if the Earth were a tired being taking sluggish deep breaths.

May 25, 1987, 5:40 PM - local time
Brădet village, Buzău County

Gică stopped the car in front of a country pub and went in to buy a pack of cigarettes. Inside one could cut the tobacco smoke with a knife. Most customers were drinking cheap brandy and talking about their affairs. Some leaned against the counter waiting to be served. Gică got in front, slipped a crumpled bill to the bartender, and asked for a pack of Snagov cigarettes.

"Hey, boss, you must stay in line here!" a hoarse voice came from behind.

"I'm in a hurry!" Gică sought to apologize and George came to his aid, saying from the doorway:

"Please, understand, we're on a mission!" He pointed through the open door to the car with the spinning blue light. One of the customers narrowed his eyes blurred by the drink. Upon reading the sign on the car door, he exclaimed:

"Hey, these are guys from Seismology!"

A young man in jeans, who was apparently one of the notable people in the village, asked:

"What's going on, sir? Will it be a strong earthquake tonight? That's what everyone was talking about on the bus..."

A tense silence fell in the pub. The bartender, who poured the customers' drinks into glasses with the carefulness of an attentive pharmacist, said gravely:

"I just talked on the phone with my godfather from Focșani. There's no joke about it. People have started carrying things out of their homes. Those who live in apartments go out in the field and sleep in their cars."

George felt obliged to intervene:

"That's only a rumor. Rumor spreading is unfortunately the only thing that works perfectly in our country. The earthquakes cannot yet be predicted!"

"Then what do you do if you're seismologists?" a naughty one asked. "Burning daylight?"

"We make sure all earthquakes are recorded so that we can study them."

"How can that be of help to the people who lose their houses and their lives if you cannot warn them before the disaster happens?" the young man in jeans asked.

George clarified:

"That's the only way we can figure out how to build the houses in different regions of the country."

"They know, but they don't want to say it! They keep it a secret like they do in the army," said an old man with a red nose, who was drinking a pint of beer. "I remember the earthquake from 1940. To me, it seemed stronger than the one from '77. I took my children in my arms and went outside. The dogs howled, the hens struggled in the coops, the cattle lowing was deafening and the Earth wobbled like a cart going on a plowed land. That was the time when Ion Găloiu's house fell into pieces."

"Well, it was the same in '77," said another, who reeked of manure. "Lights flickered in the sky, and thunder rumbled as if it was *the End of the World…*"

George thought it was time to leave. He greeted them and turned on his heel, but several voices held him back:

"Wait, boss, where are you going? You didn't tell us about the earthquake. Will it be this night or not?"

"We don't know anything. What do you think? Would I still be here talking to you if I knew for sure? I live in a block of flats. I have a wife, I have children… Your houses are on the ground. You don't live on the tenth floor and you wouldn't feel the concrete slabs shaking under your feet! That's life, folks! We can't escape the earthquakes," George said, heading to the door. "We have to go back to work."

"Are you going to Bucharest?" asked a guy with interest, a plastic bag in his hand.

"Not yet, we have work on Pietrosu Hill," replied Gică.

"They're going to the seismic antennas," said a forester, who had been listening to the discussion while sipping his brandy from a small glass quietly. He addressed George politely: "The road has been cleared, boss. I just got back from there with a bulldozer. Your colleague with a white ARO car came to us at the Forest District and asked me to help her. She couldn't drive up to the seismic antennas because of the rocks blocking the way. It's because of the rains, you know…"

"A colleague of mine?" George asked surprised, then noticed the forester smoking a Kent cigarette. He approached him and asked, his voice no more than a whisper: "Was she blonde? Was there a dark-haired guy with her?"

"Yes. He looked like an Arab to me and could barely speak Romanian. She said he was a foreign researcher who came to study the earthquakes here in Vrancea. He seemed like a nice lad. He gave me a pack of cigarettes."

"And what did they do? Did they go up the mountain after all?"

"Yes… They said they were going to the seismic station… to fix some devices. The lady told me she didn't know the way, that she hadn't been there for a long time, so I showed them how to get there…"

George was stunned. He wanted to explain to the man that the foreigners had lied so that they could get help from the Forest District, but it was pointless now.

"Please tell me, is it possible to get beyond Pietrosu Hill to the Roman camp in Valea Mare?"

"No way! The waters broke the bridge over Gurgui stream this spring. I don't know who the hell is going to fix it. The mayor says he has no money."

The driver was losing his patience and turned on the car's siren to compel George to end the discussion. The villagers came out of their gates and stared frightened. Gică laughed and shouted to his colleague, who was finally leaving the pub:

"What took you so long, man? Come on! Do you want to pick you up from the pub with emergency siren?"

George got into the car quickly and told Gică what he had learned from the forester about the blonde woman and her companion.

"We could still find them in Pietrosu. They can't get to the other side. The bridge over the Gurgui stream is broken. We have to go after them!"

"Are you out of your mind? Leave them alone! Perhaps, after meeting us, they thought they could be more convincing as *seismologists* when asking for help at the Forest District."

"There is something wrong with them. They asked the forester how to get to our seismic station."

"So what? It's their business! Why should we chase them? Can't you see it's getting dark?"

George looked at the sky. The sun was looking for shelter somewhere in the valleys, and the shadows of the evening came out from behind the rocks, stretching over the village.

* * *

May 25, 1987, 6:30 PM - local time
The seismic radio relay on Pietrosu Hill

The blonde woman and the foreigner left the car at the edge of the forest, sheltered by a clump of greenery. She was peering around like a fox ready to pounce on the prey. There was no one in the area. It was quiet. Only the sound of bells coming from a sheep flock could be heard in the distance. The cabin of the seismic equipment was on a rock spur, a kind of small bastion surrounded by a barbed wire fence, above which rose the pillars with their antennas.

"We're late, hurry up!" she urged her companion, who was still working on a telescopic fishing rod.

He connected a cable that came out of a small shoulder bag for photo flashes and said:

"Be careful! Ready! I'm trying the fishing rod!" He touched the top of the fishing rod to the wet grass, pressed a button, and produced a bluish spark.

"It works!" exclaimed the woman. She turned on a small radio scanner receiver that automatically found the frequency of the transmitters. The radio subcarriers of the telemetered seismic stations sounded like a field full of crickets through the receiver speaker. They removed the lock from the gate, by a hammer, entered the barbed wire enclosure of the seismic equipment cabin, looking in all directions to make sure there was no one around, and began the operation. The dark-haired guy touched each of the antennas with the tip of the telescopic rod, producing sparks, thus destroying the radio equipment in the same way as the lightning.

"Well done!" she encouraged him as the sounds of the device in her hand grew fainter. "Come on, finish them all!"

Once the scanner receiver fell silent, she said with satisfaction:

"All right, all the *crickets* are dead! Report mission accomplished and let's go!"

After they dismantled the set-up used for shutting down the seismic network radio equipment, the man took out his satellite phone with large gestures, like a true hero, and climbed a bush-free mound. He looked South, pointed the antenna, and contacted his boss. Their conversation was short and encrypted. At the end of the call, he turned to the blonde woman and said in dismay:

"What the hell… my boss is angry and I don't even understand why. He said the operation has not ended yet and ordered me to stay put until he pages me. Where the hell should we stay? We're in the middle of nowhere and the night is coming."

"We have no choice then," the woman said firmly. "Let's move the car further into the woods, so we cannot be seen from the road, and wait for the signal. Where is the pager?"

He searched his pockets with a kind of despair and finally took out the nickel-plated lighter. She almost snatched it from his hand and hissed:

"Give it to me! You almost lost it."

"The woman in Romania thinks she's smart. It's different in my country," he grumbled. "She is submissive, she doesn't scold the man. She cooks food and takes care of the children…"

"Yusuf, I heard that in some Arab countries women are still traded for camels," she said with a wry smile.

"That's a lie! burst out the man. Currently, such transactions no longer take place. It was happening a long time ago in the nomadic tribes…"

"I hope that, if I marry you, I won't end up being traded for a camel," she added, feigning concern.

"Come on, Ileana, be serious!"

He took her hand, kissed it and said:

"I love you very much and I want to spend the rest of my life with you in the States. We make a very good team, don't you think? You understand my work and you've been a tremendous help in my missions. My bosses know that. You are resourceful and brave and know how to twist the Securitate guys on your finger. Now, for instance, I couldn't have managed to complete this mission without you."

"You were lucky because my uncle, who lent me the car, doesn't need it for a while. Miliția withheld his driver's license for two months for red-light running."

"However, I know very few things about you, Ileana," he continued, on soft voice, almost a tender whisper. "I'd like to meet your family, your parents… We've known each other for so long and all I know about you is that you're a student at the Faculty of Electronics. Still, you're barely present at courses."

"What's the point of wasting my time when I can find all the books, I need at the faculty library? Look, I promise that you'll meet my parents soon. They want to meet you too."

They returned to the car and Yusuf drove to a side road in the forest. He parked in a small clearing from where he could see the sky while Ileana put the pager-lighter in the windshield to make sure they would receive the message sent by satellite. While they waited, Yusuf talked to her about his plan to settle in America.

* * *

May 25, 1987, 6:35 PM - local time
Institute of Seismology

In the Seismology Command room, time seemed to slow down. With their eyes fixed on the seismic recorders, the operators and seismologists analyzed every vibration and every noise that might have any meaning. The head of the Technical Service walked from one console to another to make sure that the entire territory of the country was monitored and that any movement of the Earth was recorded. From time to time, he checked the control panel that indicated the operating parameters of the seismic stations. One of the officers observed how particularly interesting it was to watch the movement of a vehicle from hundreds of kilometers away.

"I believe such a system would be very effective in guarding military objectives, too," he said.

"It's effective, yes, but not quite cheap," replied engineer Apolzan. "In any case, it can be very useful, especially for the border police. If your superiors would be interested, we could make an offer of collaboration."

Engineer Apolzan went on to describe the system of seismic sensors that could be planted on the borderline at certain distances and monitored from checkpoints.

"In this way, the places used by smugglers and illegal border crossers could be quickly located.", he said as conclusion.

"No, shit!", engineer Florian Ionică muttered as he eavesdropped to the nonsense his colleague was saying. "The Romanian borders are lined with barbed wire fences, anyway. We're living in a damn huge jail…"

In front of the long-period seismic station, the seismologists were still commenting on the recording of teleseism from Asia. They had requested additional information from the press agency, but no telex arrived from the area. Meanwhile, the Strasbourg Observatory issued a statement estimating the magnitude at 7 degrees on the Richter scale. Some seismologists with experience in teleseisms estimated that the magnitude could be even greater, and a real dispute broke out.

The officer who was in radio contact with the Army intervention teams kept the radiotelephone close to his ear all the time, in case of a possible call. At about 10-minute intervals, he made the radio connection and reported the same "*Nothing Special*" which turned into a routine. From a military standpoint, there was nothing out of order, but from the seismologists' point of view it was a highly important thing. A catastrophic event was being recorded on the seismograms just before their eyes.

Suddenly, the warning lights of the emergency systems flashed and a shrill sound made everyone look at the central panel, where the sections of the telemetered seismic network were drawn on a map.

"No way! We have problems in Pietrosu again!" exclaimed the head of the Technical Service Department. "The most sensitive part of the network is out of service. Call *Vrancea Two* team right now! I ordered them to stay in the area."

* * *

May 25, 1987, 6:20 PM - local time
Forest road for climbing Pietrosu Hill

The car was struggling to go up through the boulders on the road. The sun had set somewhere behind the mountains, and the evening mist hovered over the valleys. Upon gaining altitude, the two passengers could feel the pressure on their eardrums. The driver lit a cigarette a little unnerved.

"George, what we're doing right now it's simply nonsense. We should have remained on a plateau at the base of the mountain, waiting for instructions, not wander aimlessly. What does the *blonde woodpecker* have to do with our seismic stations? They're looking for shards of broken pots, bones, artifacts, and whatever the hell archaeologists look for…"

"If those guys are archeologists, then I am the president of the United States! I should have challenged them to an expert discussion on artifacts. I didn't like her companion at all. But he distracted us with those damned cigarettes," said George reproachfully. "The world isn't fair, is it?" he continued resignedly. "God gave some people blonde women, Kent cigarettes, good shiny cars, nickel-plated lighters, and perfumes, all the *capitalist decay*, and to others shabby cars, unfiltered cigarettes, annoying wives, whiny children and bad roads…"

The driver frowned, barely listening to his colleague's rattle.

"Now, why do you really want to go after them?" Gică asked conspiratorially. "Do you want to see the *blonde woodpecker* again? To be honest, I'd like to have some fun with she, even for a night…"

"Out of question!" George cut him off. "I believe there's something strange about their electronic lighter. I remember seeing a similar one in a movie. A cop from the West had an identical one, but it was actually a pager. There was this scene where the device beeped in his hand and he ran to the first public phone to call the office. I don't remember the name of the movie, though… Anyway, what I'm trying to say is that those guys might be spies or something. And I think it all has to do with that satellite."

"Well, you're definitely crazy! I think you watch too many movies."

They both laughed.

"Here's the thing," Gică proposed firmly when they reached the same fountain and made the usual stop. "It gets dark in half an hour. I say we stay here and pick some mushrooms from the meadow. Then, you call the Base and ask about that damned satellite. I don't want to remain in the mountains all night and share my mushrooms with *Grandpa Martin*."

George nodded. After filling the car radiator with water, they turned up the volume on the radiotelephone and ventured on the rain-soaked grass of the meadow, picking the scattered whitish round heads of the mushrooms. In less than ten minutes, the shrill sound of the radio call echoed in the peaceful valley. George ran back to the car and picked up the receiver, panting:

"This is *Vrancea Two*… Go ahead!"

Florian Ionică sounded panicked. The radio relay on Pietrosu Hill had stopped working again, and they had to fix it as soon as possible.

"I have a special request, chief. Please, check the seismogram for any footsteps or car noise recorded around the seismic station from here in Pietrosu, just before the breakdown. Over!" pleaded George, rather suspiciously.

"Affirmative, *Vrancea Two*. I repeat: Affirmative! Footsteps around the seismic stations have been recorded. Are they yours? Over!"

"Negative! It wasn't us! We're going up there right now. Stay tuned. Over!"

George was convinced that the shutdown of the seismic equipment in Pietrosu was related to the crash of the Soviet satellite.

"Gică, let's go! We have a real emergency!", he shouted to the driver who was very concerned about gathering mushrooms.

"What the hell happened? Have the barbarians invaded again?", Gică asks angrily, coming quickly to the car, sweat dripping down his face.

"I think so. The barbarians have invaded us again. This time they messed with our seismic stations!"

"What the hell? Why?"

"Because the stations can detect where that damn satellite will crash. I'm not that crazy after all!"

Gică's jaw dropped as he understood.

Without wasting any more time, he got in the driver's seat and turned on the engine.

***

RED ALERT FOR ROMANIA

May 25, 1987, 6:40 PM - local time
Bucharest-Măgurele
Somewhere near the Institute of Seismology

The Soviet *tourists* stopped on the ring road of Bucharest, simulating a flat tire issue. The road was empty, only a car or two passed by from time to time. The freckled man looked around with a pair of binoculars, then studied an unfolded map on the car hood. His companion pretended to be working on a wheel.

"The target has been spotted!" the freckled man announced victoriously. "I can see the antenna tower!"

He peered at the map again, checking the route they had to take. They were close, only a few miles away, but they had to go through a village. He folded the map, put the binoculars back in the leather case, picked up a screwdriver, and began to unscrew the lid of the car door. He pulled out a tin box with buttons and a small motorcycle battery. He connected some wires to the box with precise quick movements, while the other man replaced the registration plates of the car with Romanian ones.

"Take down the gas canisters from the trunk and hide them somewhere inside. Romanians are not used to this. We don't need to draw attention," said the freckled man, walking around the car and inspecting it before moving on to the last stage of the mission.

When everything was ready, they set off. They crossed the village, and came out on a country track in a field, close to the antenna tower. It was late. The sun was setting beyond the edge of the forest. The freckled man, who appeared to be the boss, looked at his watch and set out the details of the action:

"You stay by the car, pretend you're fixing something, and I'll do my job. If I don't come back in an hour, it means something unforeseen has happened. From then on, everyone will manage on their own. We are less than sixty kilometers away from the Bulgarian border."

He holstered the pistol under his arm, put the tin box and the battery into the bag on his shoulder, and headed to the tower, using a path that bordered a vegetable garden. He jumped over a fence, sneaked into the bushes, and reached the base of the tower. Several military cars were parked a few steps away, in the courtyard of the Institute of Seismology, where there was a commotion.

The Soviet agent took the device out of the bag and programmed it to jam the receivers of the telemetered seismic stations. He covered everything with grass and branches, then, crawling on his elbows and knees, reached the fence and jumped back over it. But he went in the wrong direction for he soon found himself somewhere in the middle of a garlic field. He looked around, turned left, and headed to the car, walking slowly so as not to attract attention.

On the other side of the field, the guard of the garlic plantation came out of his shed and shouted:

"Hey! Who are you? Don't step on the garlic! Get away from there!"

The foreigner ignored him and kept walking as if nothing happened.

"Hey, you! Wait!" the guard cried again and sicced the dogs on him.

Several shabby-looking shepherd dogs rushed after the intruder, barking. The freckled man started to run but tripped and fell. He stood up and spat the clay and the garlic leaves that got into his mouth. He continued to run as fast as he could. The pack of dogs got closer now. The guard was behind them, stirring his club menacingly above his head. The freckled man almost got to his car when the fastest dog grabbed his leg. Luckily, his comrade, seeing the scene, waited for him with the door open and the engine running. The car started, splashing mud on all sides, as the guard kept shouting and swearing:

"Damn you, bastards! Go to work, not stealing!"

On the back seat, the freckled man opened a bottle of vodka and washed his ankle bruised by the dog's teeth.

"To hell this whole mission!" he growled.

"We have just received a crypted order from the Centre," his attendant informed. "They said: *Abandon Option A, pursue Option B.*"

"This sound very good.", the other cheered up, forgetting about the dog's bite. "Stop outside the village, change the license plates, and go straight to the border. There is nothing left to do here."

* * *

May 25, 1987, 7:00 PM - local time
Institute of Seismology

In the Seismic Recorder Room, the head of Technical Service suggested that a possible diversionary group could have shut down the seismic devices on Pietrosu, in order to thwart the operative detection of the place where the satellite was to crash.

"We should not let our imagination run wild. I'm sure it's merely a simple breakdown no one is responsible for," said engineer Apolzan.

"But the seismograph captured the motion of footsteps around the station. *Vrancea Two* said it wasn't them," Ionică contradicted him.

"Maybe some gypsy kids or villagers messed around with it. It's not the first time we've been in trouble because of them. There were situations when the children smashed the solar panels with stones."

"We've put all sorts of warnings on the fence of stations, but in vain: *Attention, radiation! High voltage, do not touch!* It's as if anything you say is dangerous arouses curiosity and becomes an attraction point." Ionică said.

"I was in Japan," a senior seismologist intervened. "I saw expensive seismic equipment left in the field, with a simple label on it reading *Japan Seismological Service*. No one dared to touch it. Out of curiosity, I asked my Japanese colleagues: *Aren't you afraid that someone might take the equipment?* They looked at me baffled and replied: *Why? It says very clearly that there are our devices.* What they really meant was that the equipment didn't necessarily belong only to *Seismological Service* but to all Japanese people, who have a real cult for seismology. I immediately thought of how much useless theory is done in our country on account of public wealth, and wondered when we, Romanians, would reach the same level of consciousness."

"Come on, sir, let's be serious! We can't find food for children and gas for the cars and you compare our nation to the Japanese one?" murmured Ionică.

The seismologist didn't seem to hear the others.

"And what a communication system they have...," he said lost in his memories of Japan.

"We have a great communication system too," added Ionică wryly. "We climb to the top of the hills to hear each other. Not to mention that sometimes, the radiofrequency band they have assigned us is full of noises."

As if triggered by these last Ionică's words, the reception system's alarm pierced their ears. The emergency lights flickered, and the pens of all seismic recorders oscillated uncontrollably, spewing ink. In the radiotelephone that kept in touch with the field crew *Vrancea Two*, there was an annoying noise and many thought this was caused by the fall of the satellite.

"Shit! This has never happened before!" exclaimed Apolzan, afraid that the entire seismic network collapsed because of the loud noises coming through the reception channels.

"It's a very violent broadband jam!" noted engineer Ionică, keeping his calm. "Can you still hear the colleagues outside?" he asked the officer who was in radio contact with the Army car from the courtyard of the Institute.

The officer put the radiotelephone to his ear nervously but flinched and removed it quickly, disturbed by the noise coming from the reception channel.

"I can barely hear them! What the hell is going on here?" he asked confused after trying to call them a couple of times.

"I think there's a multi-channel jamming station installed nearby. It crippled all our radio connections. It will be difficult to locate it because it's too close and might inhibit any type of goniometer," said Ionică professionally. "In any case, we urgently need a goniometer. We must try to locate the jamming source!"

***

May 25, 1987, 8:00 PM - local time
The seismic radio relay on Pietrosu Hill

It was dark when George and Gică reached the top of Pietrosu again. They parked the car away from the seismic cab so that the headlights could illuminate the antennas poles. George unlocked with a simple jerk the small Chinese padlock on the barbed-wire fence gate. The keys had long been lost. First, he examined the antennas cables. He didn't find anything suspicious. Then he went into the booth to check the transmitters.

"Oh, my God! Everything is burned here!", he exclaimed in utter astonishment. "Those bastards screwed us over!"

Puzzled, the driver looked in the booth over George's shoulder. There had been no storm that afternoon, so one couldn't put the blame on the lightning. But he still couldn't believe that the blonde woman and her friend did that.

"The bridge to Valea Mare is broken and the only way back is the road we came on. We couldn't have missed them, so they must be still around. Please, stop the engine!" George said, lowering his voice.

They listened intently for a while. It was quiet, everything seemed calm. Only the wind hissed through the pine branches. The stars shone in the sky and seemed so close that you were tempted to climb the top of the mountain and reach out to touch them.

"I think they went to hell," the driver said between his teeth, breaking the silence.

George took new transmitters out from the toolbox and set to work. After installing them, he made a final overhaul, locked the barrack and he changed the rusty and weak Chinese padlock on the gate of the seismic relay enclosure, with a strong American steel padlock. He turned on a flashlight and inspected the surroundings of the seismic station. George thought he saw a shadow moving and approached the spot but found nothing. Returning to the car, he called the Seismology Command who confirmed that all stations were back in order.

"Something strange happened here, sir," George reported and continued to describe the state in which they had found the equipment.

"We've had our problems, too," engineer Ionică replied. "Someone planted a jamming device close to the tower. Fortunately, we found it in time. Please, be careful out there! I spoke to the County Miliția Office from Buzău. A crew is probably on its way to you. It might get dangerous. We seem to be the target of some diversionary actions. Stay close to the radio relay. Over!"

"We want to get away from here as soon as possible, boss," George pleaded. "If we are in danger, we have no means to defend ourselves. We need to get to the nearest village at least. We'll return here with the Miliția crew and wait until the crash of the satellite if necessary. Please approve! Over!"

"Request approved, *Vrancea Two*! Stay tuned! Over!"

"Thanks, boss! We'll remain on the same reception channel. Over!"

Relieved, George turned to Gică, who was still admiring the starry sky, and said worriedly:

"Let's go, my friend! It smells like gunpowder in here." A few moments later he added in heavily accented English: *"Come on, boy, we've got a job!"*

He really liked this line from the cartoon *Tom and Jerry*. It filled him with energy, suggesting a state of dynamism, and he used it whenever he got the chance, especially in gloomy situations.

"Yeah, a very special job, like queuing at the grocery store," said Gică getting in the driver's seat without enthusiasm.

They set out for the stone-covered road. On the slope at the edge of the forest, the car picked up speed and the driver pressed the brake pedal in vain. Gică felt a shiver run down his spine. Believing that air got in the brake system pipe, he pressed it several times but it was no use. The car didn't slow down.

"What's going on?" George asked panicked.

The driver pulled the handbrake on, desperately. Nothing! The car started downhill like a sled on a chute. Gică tried to reduce the speed by changing the gear to use the engine brake, but the maneuver was in vain. The car didn't listen to him anymore and it was gaining speed. He managed to keep the car on the road at the first curve, but at the second one, the car went straight through the parapet and fell into the ravine.

Chapter 10

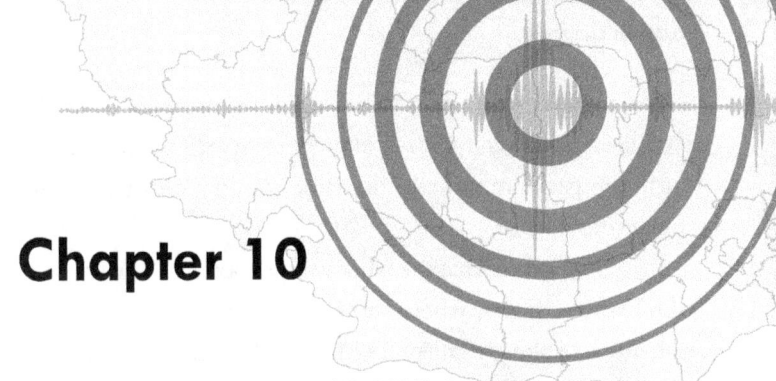

May 25, 1987, 9:00 AM - local time
US- Space Monitoring Center

Professor Gordon had fallen asleep in the armchair. When he woke up, he had the impression that he was in some kind of tomb. He wondered what would happen if, by mistake, they forgot about him completely. He inventoried the soft drinks in the mini-bar and estimated that all these would be enough for him but only for a few days. He wondered if the young man Sorin Crainic from Bucharest, who had been stuck under the rubble of the March 4 '77 earthquake, did the same. Isolated in the basement of a bar, he survived for eleven days and was saved by chance. The Media had been in uproar at the time. He imagined himself in a similar situation and how the journalists would be witness to his removal from the bunker. He could see himself dehydrated, lying on a stretcher, dozens of flashes lightening his body.

Time was moving insanely slowly. The satellite most certainly crashed long ago, he thought. The Professor didn't understand why he was still a prisoner. Maybe the recovery of the *code module* was not over yet or something unexpected happened. He wondered if he had the ability to anticipate the things. The fact that, during the helicopter flight, the symposium on earthquake prediction in Romania had unreeled before his eyes like a movie and, shortly after, he estimated the coordinates of the impact site to be in the same country, didn't seem like mere coincidence.

He tried to imagine what was happening there, close to the Danube Delta, where, according to all probabilities, the satellite had already fallen. The image of the map displayed on the monitor at the end of the calculations remained stuck in his mind. Before the guards had escorted him out of the workroom, he took one last look at the screen, as a farewell to that special place he'd grown to love over the years.

Perhaps charred pieces of the satellite were already scattered on the ground and a cloud of radioactive dust carried by the wind was spreading quickly over the arid ridges of the old Mountains of Dobrogea, contaminating everything in its path. Perhaps large flocks of birds, frightened by the explosion of the impact, had taken flight, carrying the radioactive powder on their wings. That place, which he knew well and which always triggered for him a kind of metaphysical immersion in the geological past of the Earth, would be enclosed with barbed wire. Access would be prohibited and the decontamination teams would roam around for a long time.

He imagined General Alan King congratulating his subordinates, inviting them to a glass of whisky, and Captain Power boasting that his men had once again behaved exemplary. Congratulations, promotions, bonuses, vacations in Bahamas, while, in the opposing camp, others held meetings, gave explanations, and proposed sanctions. There were no winners. Earth, the home of alike, had been irresponsibly contaminated.

Neither General, nor the Communist authorities cared about that geological reservation. Its beauty could be appreciated, as in the case of works of art, only by connoisseurs.

Either minutes or hours passed until Professor Gordon saw the General entering the door of the apartment and wondered if it was reality or just a lucid dream. Alan King looked grim, if not disappointed, and Gordon understood that something didn't go as planned.

"That's it, Doctor Gordon, it's over. You can leave. Thank you for your effort," the General said in a tired and upset voice.

The Professor left the bunker escorted by the same guards and got into the same convertible Jeep. The military man who was driving seemed more polite this time. He turned on the radio and asked him if he was okay with some music.

The helicopter was waiting for him on the plateau. The sliding door was open and the pilot motioned for him to board. Gordon sat next to the pilot, put on his headphones, and heard the permission to take off. The aircraft rose above the rocks surrounding the plateau and, tilting forward slightly, rushed over the sea.

They were flying at low altitude. Gordon could see the crest of the waves rising and curling until the white foam disappeared in the blue water. He tried to make some conversation with the pilot, but he got only curt answers. When the Professor wanted to know what happened with the satellite, the pilot simply said that he had no information about it. Gordon was frustrated. No one wanted to talk about the satellite. Something was going on.

* * *

Adrian Grigore

May 25, 1987
KGB conspiratorial location

Igor Zapojnikov was still writing the statement he had been asked for when General Petroski, who circled him, cigarette in his mouth, said abruptly:

"I think you wrote enough, comrade Zapojnikov. Now it's time for you to find out why you are really here. Everything that has happened to you lately is part of a top-secret plan approved by the Supreme Soviet. I wouldn't go into details, although each one matters. Let's call it a trial one has to pass before having the great honor of being entrusted with a special mission on enemy territory by the people of the Soviet Union. Your file has been well investigated, and your evolution and behavior were carefully assessed. Congratulations!"

Igor stared at him stunned.

"I don't understand. Then why they removed my military ranks? And why was I arrested? I need some explanations."

The civilian smiled understandingly.

"Of course. Fortunately, I am authorized to give you all the explanations. You had to be arrested on the grounds of that military unit in Ukraine according to the script. We had to perform the entire show for two reasons: to remove you from the official scene and to uncover a whole network of NATO agents who infiltrated our structures. Because of your arrest, they started making reports, got in touch with their bases, and thus exposed themselves."

Zapojnikov wasn't completely satisfied with the answer.

"Still, I don't understand! The loss of my military ranks was official, ordered by a military prosecutor. According to the law, I am a mere soldier now, I am soldier Zapojnikov and that seems ridiculous to me."

"No, comrade Colonel. The loss of your military ranks was just part of the play. It was fake. You haven't lost your status as a senior officer of the Soviet Union, not even for a moment. Your Colonel insignia is in the wardrobe, in the apartment upstairs assigned to you in this conspiratorial residence. However, you will change into civilian clothes, because from now on, you will have a different identity and you will work undercover on the enemy territory, as already I told you."

Igor looked with great mistrust at the civilian, who continued in a subversive tone:

"You are already a lucky Soviet citizen, of Jewish descent. You inherited a considerable fortune in America from an uncle without offspring who left you everything. The lawyer responsible for fulfilling the will has contacted the American Embassy in Moscow, which, with the help of the Soviet authorities, identified you. Starting from this moment, your name is Leibovich Alexei. You are 45 years old; you are single, you live in Moscow and you work as a civil servant. The American lawyer will come to Moscow in exactly a week to meet you. You do not need any plastic surgery because you look exactly like the subject in the lawyer's photos, we already sent him. You will receive the emigration approval and you will have to go to America as soon as possible."

"And what will happen with Zapojnikov, the Counterintelligence officer?" Igor asked calmly. "What will happen to his family, to his daughters most importantly?"

"Zapojnikov was arrested for high treason... He is a notorious spy. Officially, he'll spend the rest of his life in prison. The agency for which he worked already wants to get him back and offer another *heavy piece* instead. There will be negotiations, and in the end, his daughters will receive the approval to emigrate in exchange for the release of a Soviet agent who has been captured on the enemy territory."

"Why only my daughters?" Igor asked, feeling that something was wrong.

"Because your wife has already left you, comrade Colonel. The news of your arrest found her in the arms of a painter, a lover about whom we warned you about, by the way... She will file for divorce and in twenty-four hours will receive the court decision. The law is on her side given the fact that... her husband is a traitor and a dangerous spy."

Igor accepted the information resignedly. However, something was bubbling up inside him, like the defensive instinct of a cornered beast. He thought he would feel much better if he pounced on General Petrovski and strangled him. He would free himself of all the anger and frustration. He asked incredulously:

"How can I be sure that my daughters will not be persecuted and receive permission to emigrate?"

Instead of answering, General Petrovski went to a safe in the room, opened it, and took out a thick red folder. He gave it to Igor, saying:

"Here you will find everything you need to know."

Igor felt breathless when he read the large words printed on the file: *Operation Rasputin - Top Secret*.

"I know you can handle English," continued the civilian, carefully studying his reaction. "Although you must improve it during the upcoming short training period. I found you a good teacher." He turned to the door and called out in English:

"Please, come in!"

As the door opened slowly, Igor thought he was hallucinating. Irina, his secretary, entered the room smiling, an English textbook under her arm. She was no longer wearing her Lieutenant's uniform but a short summer dress.

* * *

May 25, 1987, 10:30 AM - local time
Professor Eduard Gordon's residence

The return flight seemed much longer to Professor Gordon. When they got close to the villa, the pilot made several turns. The high and rocky cliff favored the turbulence of the strong wind. After several attempts, the helicopter landed safely. When Gordon saw, through the oval porthole, the bushes in his yard bending as they fought the air currents produced by the propellers, he finally had a sense of security. He was home again.

He didn't go inside the house but took a short walk around the garden instead. After all the hours spent in the bunker, he felt the need to move. The wind blowing from the ocean brought the strong scent of salty air. Somewhere below, the melancholic sound of waves crashing against the rocks made him miss his wife and children who were on holiday for almost a week. He wished he could go with them but he had a lot of work to do. He had woken up early morning with the intention of completing a scouting report, but Captain Power arrived and took him to the Base.

In his office he found that everything was exactly as he had left it; the coffee he hadn't had time to drink and the glass of red orange juice were waiting for him on his desk. His gaze was immediately drawn to the pulsating green light of the answering machine.

The first message was from his wife, Janet, telling him that she and the children were all right, having a wonderful time up there in the mountain resort. The second one was from Professor Dumitriu.

"In that part of the World no trouble comes alone," Gordon thought out loud as usual. Upon listening to the message, he believed that his Romanian friend was exaggerating. A prediction based on some summary data was pretty much like a tarot reading. He remembered George Purcaru, another Romanian seismologist who lived in Frankfurt. During a congress, he had told him that accurate earthquake prediction is not possible. There are three precise components that must be considered in a prediction*: the place, the time,* and *the magnitude* of the seismic event. The professor smiled to himself saying:

"That's kind of philosophy, but who knows?"

He logged into the computer network and first, full of curiosity, looked for news about the Soviet satellite. He was completely relieved when he found out that he had been diverted at the last moment into the Soviet territorial waters of the Black Sea. Of course, General Allan King had every reason to be upset.

Then he requested information from the US Geological Survey in Denver, Colorado, on the most important seismic events in the World from the past twenty-four hours. He was surprised by the devastating earthquake in Asia and wondered if Dumitriu's prediction did not refer to this event.

He decided to call him. It took him a while, for the telephone connection was difficult. Finally, he was put on the line and the Professor's wife answered him. He understood that Dumitriu was at the Institute of Seismology and, from what she said quite shyly in her poor English, the Professor would be coming home late because he was participating in an important meeting. Gordon thanked her, sent his greetings to the family, and hung up. He knew he couldn't find out more over the phone. The Romanian political police could cut off the telephone connection at any time. It was obvious that something was going on at the Institute.

Without hesitating, he looked for the number of the Seismological Institute in Bucharest in the phone memory, programmed the call until the connection could be made and went to the minibar in the living room to make himself a cocktail.

* * *

May 25, 1987, 9:30 AM - local time
US- Space Monitoring Center

General Alan King couldn't accept the outcome. He had engaged all the forces of the Space Monitoring Centre in an action without resolution, in a job that went wrong. It was both a personal and a professional failure that was causing him serious problems with the State Department and the Foreign Services. Before officially announcing the end of the *Fishing in the Mountains* operation, he summoned Colonel Mc Stevenson and Captain Power.

"Gentlemen, it looks like we're going to come out of this a bit crumpled," he said, without losing his sense of humor. "That damned satellite is somewhere, on the bottom of the Black Sea, and the *code module* is lying among benthos, instead of being in our hands. It is hard to understand by what devilish work the

Soviets were able to activate a rescue rocket at the last moment and divert the satellite to the sea, from its original seemingly clear trajectory. I think it was a deliberate action! They probably wanted to test our operational capacity in Eastern Europe."

"I believe the same thing, sir," said Captain Power. "We managed to intercept the messages sent by the Soviets to the crews infiltrated in Romania. Strangely, they were ordered to cease operation almost thirty minutes before the operators got back control of the satellite and activated the *rescue rocket*. It was all a trap! They wanted to test our reaction."

"The things are not quite clear," Colonel Mc Stevenson put in. "The operation was coordinated from a military base in Southern Ukraine by Colonel Zapojnikov, an important counterintelligence officer working for the Soviet Space Center. What we know is that he was arrested on the airport runway while the operation was in full progress. It is believed that he was trying to flee by flying off in a helicopter. He could be agent *Rasputin* because, after his arrest, the messages from *Rasputin* stopped abruptly."

"I'm not entirely convinced about this. Anyway, the arrest of this alleged *Rasputin* triggered a real tragedy for those in our foreign services. They accuse us that, although we used the *valuable information, Rasputin* gave us in recent years, we neither accepted his offer nor helped him in time, passing the problem to them. Let's be serious! Most of that so-called *valuable information* were things we already knew or could discover ourselves by reading between the lines of the articles in Pravda."

"Some voices in the foreign services want the negotiations with the Soviets to start immediately," Mc Stevenson informed a little embarrassed. "They want to get *Rasputin* in exchange for the Soviet agent who was caught on the Orlando airport with the stolen documents from Cape Canaveral."

"That's their problem. I don't want to be involved in this bluff," General Alan King raised his hands defensively. "As for me, I consider I have done my duty to the US and it's time to order the end of this operation."

He activated the operational communications circuit and his voice resounded throughout the entire underground base:

"Attention, please! Attention, please! *Number One* is addressing all of you! Operation *Fishing in the Mountains* is over! I repeat: Operation *Fishing in the Mountains* is over!"

Captain Power had a deep frown on his face. For him, the job was not over. He had to withdraw his *Panther* crews and be sure the agents were not exposed. The General added fuel to the fire:

"Be careful with your *Panthers*. There is still a state of alert in Romania. Let that idiot Gilbert wander through the mountains, maybe he'll get smarter! However, his girlfriend seems to have real potential. I think it's time to bring her here for some training. I want all her data."

"All we know till now is that her name is Ileana Popescu and she is a student at the Faculty of Electronics in Bucharest. She hates Communism because it destroyed her family. Her parents and grandfather fought in the mountains as partisans against the establishment of the Communist regime in Romania, and they were killed by the Securitate. Apparently, agent Gilbert is in love with her and wants to marry her."

"It sounds good," the General muttered to himself.

* * *

Adrian Grigore

May 25, 1987, 9:00 PM - local time
Institute of Seismology

There was an uproar in the Seismic Surveillance Room. Some seismologists supported the hypothesis that the satellite crashed during the time when the seismic stations were being jammed. According to Professor Dumitriu's calculations, the satellite should already be on the ground. He suggested that Colonel Theodor convey this information to the upper echelon of the Romanian Army. On the other hand, the helicopters with the radiation measurement and decontamination teams have been ordered to perform a reconnaissance flight over the area where the seismic network computer detected an event. It turned out to be the explosion of a propane loading station and the nearest fire brigade units were alerted.

Several radio communications specialists retrieved the jamming transmitter found near the antenna tower and they were now analyzing it. Undoubtedly, the device was made in the Soviet Union, even if all its electronic components were of American origin. The acid battery was the main clue. They concluded that the device had been set to function for almost an hour, during which the impact to take place. But that hour had long passed and everyone wondered if the state of alert was still necessary, even though no one could do something about it.

The quarreling ceased when Professor Gordon called and asked to speak with Dumitriu. He listened, like conscientiously schoolboy, as his American fellow chided him in a friendly tone for his earthquake forecasts.

"Leave that away!" Dumitriu burst impatiently. "We have bigger problems here. We are on *Red Alert*. A dangerous object from Space is about to crash on our territory."

"You don't have to be secretive; I know all about the Soviet satellite. According to my calculations, the satellite should have crashed somewhere in the Hercinic Mountains of Dobrogea region. But you are lucky. It seems the Soviets managed to activate a correction engine that changed its trajectory at the last moment. The satellite fell into the Black Sea."

"Are you sure about that?" Dumitriu's face lit up.

"One hundred percent sure. They made an official announcement here. Right now, CNN is commenting on the event."

Dumitriu covered the telephone receiver with his hand and turned to his colleagues:

"It's over, my friends! The satellite fell into the Black Sea!"

In the office next door, engineer Ionică had just listened to the news broadcast by Radio Free Europe, in the headphones of a high-performance *Kushman* scanner on his desk. As this was strictly forbidden, he came into the Seismological Command Room, with a mysterious small, and told everyone that Agerpres, the official news agency of Socialist Romania, had just announced that Soviet satellite had fallen into the Black Sea. A few minutes later, this news was confirmed on the phone by Colonel Morar the Securitate officer in charge with Seismological Institute, and everyone cheered.

Happy about this, the Director Ion Gonea made the official announcement that the *Seismic Red Alert* has ended.

"It's a pity, comrades, that Decree 400 forbids us to drink inside of Institute. We really deserve a cognac after so many hours of strain…" he said frustrated at the thought of those times when it was no problem to have a drink during working hours.

The Director spotted Dumitriu in the midst of the Antiaircraft officers. He had just finished talking to the American Professor and everyone was looking at him as if he was some kind of movie star.

"Comrade Professor, I believe this was, in fact, the *earthquake* you predicted this morning," the Director said with a smile and stretched out his hand conciliatory.

"Indeed, it could be as bad as an earthquake! Honestly, this morning I had the strong feeling that something special would happen today," said the Professor shaking hands with the Director.

Colonel Theodor thanked the seismologists for their cooperation, and the military group left. In front of the building, the researchers continued chatting for a while. Engineer Ionică was about to join a discussion when he became aware that he hadn't heard from *Vrancea Two* crew in a while. Returning to the Command Room, he asked the duty operator to contact them.

"They are probably in a shielded radio waves area," the operator said after a few failed calls. "I will try later!"

Ionică looked at the seismogram of the Pietrosu Station.

"They were there until recently. Footsteps have been recorded around the seismic equipment cabin. They are probably on the road somewhere in the forest and can't hear you. When they pick up the call, tell them the alert is over. They can come back."

He looked at his watch. It was quite late and he hurried to leave. He wished his colleagues in charge of the permanent seismic vigil a peaceful night, and at the threshold he shouted:

"I have free seats in the car! Anyone interested in traveling to the city?"

Only the echo from the corridor answered him, because everyone had already left.

* * *

May 25, 1987, 9:00 PM - local time
Pietrosu Hill

The car had rolled down the steep into the stream bed and burst into flames. Clinging to a tree trunk, George stared in horror at the remnants of the Seismic Network's emergency response lab: a pile of twisted iron pieces and burning tires releasing a heavy, choking cloud of smoke up into the sky. He coughed a few times and peered around, but his vision was blurry.

He had sheer luck. After breaking the parapet, the car had stopped on the crest of a rock and swung a few times before falling into the abyss. That's when he opened the door and jumped out. He hoped Gică had done the same.

George called out to him several times but got no response. When he tried to get down, he almost slipped on the detritus. The fire illuminated the slope intermittently. He heard a groan and saw the driver a little further down, lying between two boulders. George crawled to him and grabbed his hands to lift him up. Gică's scratched face twisted with pain. His leg was broken and he couldn't move. He was breathing hard and felt so thirsty he would have drunk water even from a dirty puddle.

George looked around desperately, barely keeping his balance on the slope. Getting help seemed impossible. He wished he was dreaming or for a film director to suddenly come out of a bush and say: "*Cut!*" It was night already and the flames of the burning car were their only source of light. He needed to find a solution quickly. He remembered there was a path down in the valley, leading to the grotto of Father Ambrose. The monk knew how to heal both spiritual and physical wounds. The woodcutters and shepherds living in the mountains relied on him when they had accidents. George had to find a way to get his friend to him.

Gică was slowly recovering from the shock but felt the pain more sharply. He looked at the car in confusion, his eyes clouded with smoke.

"I don't understand what happened," he mumbled. "Maybe a sharp rock cut the brake circuit pipe, but I don't see how that could have been possible. I should have checked the brakes before I left… Instead, I looked at the stars like a fool!"

"Someone did this to us, I'm sure. Someone messed with the brakes when you were looking at the stars."

"What? What are you saying? How do you know that?", winced the driver, momentarily forgetting the pain of his broken leg.

"I was in the cabin of the seismic devices. I heard noises outside, like someone was check the car. I asked for a screwdriver, but no one answered me and immediately there was silence. I initially thought it was you."

"But it wasn't me!" said Gică, rightly astonished. "I didn't check the car this time…" he added with a belated regret.

"Yeah, clearly you didn't. It was someone else, we know that now. Come on, we must get to Father Ambrose. Can you stand up?"

His friend grimaced in pain as he tried to move his broken leg and shook his head helplessly:

"No, I can't. You should go to the road and wait for the Miliția crew. The chief said they would come to our aid."

George looked up the slope, where the car broke through the parapet. The last section of the slant was vertical like a wall. The climb would have been impossible, so they decided to go down in the valley.

A ball of fire shot up with a bang from the burning car. The gas canister in the trunk had exploded. The men watched the scene aghast for a few moments until they finally started walking. George stepped carefully on the stones. Gică leaned heavily against him, dragging his leg. They covered their faces as they went past the huge threatening fire that could spread any minute now. A thread of burning gasoline ran downhill through the trees. Small flames danced in the bushes, casting dozens of flickering shadows.

A voice suddenly pierced the roar of the fire.

"Attention, *Vrancea Two*! Attention, *Vrancea Two*! Do you copy?" The radio was still working, but the call was soon muffled and the two men couldn't hear anything but the crackling of the fire.

Soon, the driver was at the end of his strength. His fractured leg had swollen like a stump and he could barely move. He needed to get to the hospital as soon as possible. The nearest village was still far away, at the foot of the mountain. George couldn't drag his friend all the way there. Then an idea ran through his mind. If he went back to the seismic station, he could send a Morse warning message to his colleagues in the Institute, tasked with seismic surveillance during the night. He could deliver the message by knocking near the geophone, but to get up there he had to climb the steep slope first. He helped Gică sit on the ground and lean against a log before starting the climbing.

At first, the muscles resisted the effort but gradually he got into a rhythm, all his survival instincts awakening. Adrenaline rushed through his body so he didn't feel any pain from the bleeding scratches covering his hands and face.

The seismic cabin was only a few hundred meters away, toward the top of the mountain. Near the ridge, George believed he saw a glimmer of light. He wasn't mistaken. It was the beam of a flashlight illuminating the masts of the antennas. Someone was walking around the seismic station.

His first instinct was to run away. Most certainly he was about to bump into the person who tried to kill them. Then his anger took over and crept through the thickets at the edge of the forest and around the spur of rock until he reached the bushy slope behind the seismic station. From there he could see two silhouettes he recognized almost instantly: the blonde woman and her foreign companion. George watched them as they cut the barbed wire fence with a pair of pliers to get inside. Certainly, the American lock that he had put on the gate of the seismic station's enclosure when he left, could not be removed too easily.

The woman was speaking in English. He was urging his partner to hurry up. Something was bothering her. He didn't like the fact that the seismic relay had been switched back on so quickly and the *"crickets"* - the radio subcarriers of the seismic stations - were once again being heard in the scanner he was holding.

Soon there was a shrill beep and George remembered the strange lighter. He had not been mistaken: that was a pager. He saw it shining in the blonde's hand, who said:

"Done, Yusuf! Your boss orders the end of the mission. Let's get the hell out of here!"

Her companion let out an exclamation and began to pick up some things scattered on the grass into a bag. The woman helped him, pointing the flashlight at the ground. George didn't miss the chance. Their car was very close to him, parked on the slope, with the door open. He quickly took a few steps to the vehicle and jumped into the driver's seat. He released the handbrake and started downhill with the engine off. The two realized what was happening only when the car was at a certain distance. They ran after the car shouting. Then George changed his mind. He wanted revenge. He started the engine, turned on the headlights and swiveled the car round. He hoped to scare the imposters and put them on the run. Just then, something pierced the windshield, passing by his ear. They were shooting at him.

* * *

May 25, 1987- Late in the night
Brădet village, Buzău county

Sub-officer Zamfir, the head of the Miliția Post in Brădet, woke up to the banging on the gate. The neighbors' dogs were barking full of anger. Zamfir slowly opened the window and asked in a hoarse voice:

"Who's there?"

"It's me, Pandelică, the night watchman! The Sergeant sent me for you. He said it's urgent!"

"What happened, did the Tatars invade us again?"

"It's bad, chief. Come on, I'll tell you on the way to the Post. I can't say it out loud."

Zamfir closed the window muttering annoyed. He dressed quickly and went out. On the way to the Post the watchman told him a nonsensical and very confusing story.

"Chief, a comrade from Seismology came by car! The bastards fired at him with a gun but missed. There are holes in the windshield! I saw them with my own eyes! He says he left his colleague down, in the valley, with a broken leg. Their car exploded! He says he couldn't go after the wounded colleague because they were chasing and shooting him!"

"Who was chasing and shooting him, Pandelică?" the sub-officer asked with patience as if he were addressing a child.

"I don't know, chif! He's full of scratches!"

"Who, Pandelică?"

"The comrade from Seismology, didn't I tell you that? The poor guy told us the rascals cut off their vehicle's brake pipe when they weren't paying attention. The driver could no longer stop the car and they fell over the parapet!"

"Damn it, Pandelică! I don't understand anything of what you're saying!"

"Well, it's a complicated matter, chief. That's why the Sergeant sent me to fetch you."

An ARO all-terrain vehicle with the lights on was parked in front of the Miliția Post. The deputy, Sergeant Dobrică, carefully examined the car. Next to him, a young man gave explanations, gesticulating.

"What happened, Dobrică?" Zamfir asked sullenly as he approached them.

"Comrade Commander, this is a stolen car! I asked the Registration Service and they don't have a car with this number on record. Look, they put fake number plates. The comrade says he didn't steal the car."

"If he didn't steal it, then why the hell is the car here?"

"He says he took it from Pietrosu, from someone who damaged the seismic station."

"Then it means he stole it! Who is he?"

"He says he's from the Seismological Institute."

George stretched out his hand to Zamfir to introduce himself, but he remained with the hand outstretched.

"Let's go inside and have a little chat," said the Sub-officer, peering incredulously at the disheveled man with torn clothes in front of him.

Zamfir showed him into a small office and sat down at a desk framed by two metal lockers.

"Take a seat, comrade…" He gestured to a wooden chair that have a broken foot.

George was still agitated and hardly felt like sitting down. Zamfir lighted a cigarette, took a few puffs, and said in an authoritative voice:

"I want to see your driver's license, car registration, and ID, comrade."

"I don't have them anymore. All my documents were in the car that burned. Please, comrade, my friend is still out there, up in the mountains. He needs urgent medical care! Please, help me take him to the hospital, then we'll settle the rest of the matters."

"So, you say you work at the Seismological Institute?" Zamfir continued unaffected. "What are you doing here, in Pietrosu?"

"We had to do some breakdown maintenance for seismic equipment. You can verify that. Please call the Seismology Command! I'll give you the number," George said trying to be calm.

"Let's take it slow so that I can understand what this is all about."

"Don't you understand that a man must be saved?"

"I understand, that's why I want to clear things up first."

"I don't think he's lying, boss," the Sergeant intervened from the threshold. "I received a call earlier this evening from the County Miliția Inspectorate. There was a bad connection and I couldn't hear them well, but they said something about some comrades from Seismology who were at the seismic station in Pietrosu and need help from us."

"Why didn't you say so from the start, Dobrică?" Zamfir snapped.

"Well, I wanted to, but..."

"Forget it! Send for the forester and get some men. We must go up to Pietrosu!"

"Yes, comrade Commander" The Sergeant raised the hand to his temple, then turned to the watchman: "Did you hear what the boss said? Quickly, carry out the order!"

The Chief of the Miliția turned the telephone crank vigorously. It was an old-fashioned machine with a magneto that had to be turned by crank to call the switchboard operator.

"Hello, operator, hello!"

Because no one answered, he turned the crank again, cursing between his teeth. When he finally heard the operator's voice in the receiver, he raged:

"Hello, comrade! I am Sub-officer Zamfir, head of the Miliția Post in Brădet. Put me through with the Ambulance Service!"

After waiting for a few minutes, he almost shouted into the phone:

"Hello, I need an ambulance! Can you hear me? I am the head of the Miliția Post in Brădet! We have a wounded man up in the mountains!"

He listened for a moment then turned to George:

"Is your friend bleeding?"

"I don't think so, He has a broken leg."

"Just a broken leg?" Zamfir frowned. "Hm, that won't work." He shouted into the telephone again: "He's badly hurt, comrade! He fell into a ravine."

The reply came categorically, and the Miliția chief hung up the phone with a shrug.

"They're out of gas. They have finished their fuel quota for this month. They wouldn't have come to this dump anyway. They said we should take him to the hospital."

The Sergeant came in panting:

"I brought the forester. He's still a bit drunk, but he recognized the car! He says a blonde woman came in it at the Forestry District. She asked them to clear the road of the fallen rocks at Duruitoarea."

The forester stumbled into the office and leaned against one of the lockers.

"Yes, Chief, there was a blonde lady from Seismology… She was with a guy… he was a bit sunburned… They couldn't pass…"

George recognized the man from the village pub and jumped up.

"She doesn't work at the Seismology! She lied!"

"But my boss from the county called me and said I had to help two comrades from Seismology."

"Yes, you were supposed to help me and my colleague! Not the blonde woman and her guy! They are imposters! They damaged the seismic station and tried to kill us!"

The forester looked at him confusedly, swaying and struggling to keep his eyes open.

"Comrades, let's take it easy!" Zamfir urges them and adds scratching his head: "Comrade Ghiță, are you saying that this car, which is now outside, was at Forestry District today?"

"Yes, chief."

"Who was in the car?"

"Didn't I tell you, chief? A blonde woman. Very attractive, chief," he winked.

"Was there anyone else with her?"

"Yes, chief, she was with the sunburned guy, chief, I told you. He looked as if his mother had forgotten him on the fire at birth and roasted him more than she should have," the forester chuckled. "He didn't speak Romanian well… He said he was a foreign seismologist and came to study our earthquakes because in his country they are not so strong…"

"Good. Sit down, Dobrică, and write down everything comrade Ghiță says." Then to the forester: "Tell us what happened, Uncle Ghiță."

"Well, the young lady came to us and asked for our help politely. She said they wanted to get there, to the antennas, and the road was blocked by rocks. I went with them because I had a bulldozer near the Bear Cave refuge. You know, rocks keep falling when it rains a lot."

"Okay, okay, we know that. Keep going."

"I did my job and they wanted to pay me, but I didn't want to take money from them, especially since it had been an order from my boss. Someone from Bucharest had called and told him to clean up the road."

"Who called?"

"I don't know that, chief, … I don't know…" the forester stammered, barely keeping his balance.

"Okay, let's leave it at that, we'll find out soon enough. What happened next?"

"The brown stranger gave me a pack of cigarettes."

The drunken forester took the *Kent* pack out of his pocket, grinning triumphantly. Zamfir cleared his throat.

"Well done, Uncle Ghiță! You smoke *Kent* and I smoke *Snagov*! Life is fair, isn't it? Do you know what the law says? The gifts from foreigners are confiscated!"

"Please, chief, I don't receive presents from foreigners every day," Ghiță said giving a cigarette to each person in the office. "I worked for them; may I be damned! If it were up to me, I'd have taken three hundred for the work I did! My brandy was also coming out but the boss called me…"

"Come on, Uncle Ghiță, stop whining! Anyway, you get enough brandy from other parts. We know everything that's going on because we're the Miliția and that's why the State pays us for… You'd better tell us what the blonde woman and her friend did!"

"I explained to the lady how to get to the antennas, she didn't know the way, you see, and they went up Pietrosu!"

"Well done, Uncle Ghiță, you sent her to the right place," George cut of ironically. "She had told me that they wanted to go to the Roman fort in Valea Mare," he explained to Zamfir. "They fooled us all."

"These spies have a lot of training," said Zamfir, shaking his head. "I know it from the time when I was a soldier and fought against the bandits hidden in the mountains. They were waiting for the Americans to overthrow our popular democratic regime. But as you can see, the Americans didn't come and never will… At that time, we used to have a lot of fun at the popular demonstrations on May 1st and August 23rd. Some of us used to shout: *Where are the Americans?* And others answered in chorus: *They hid like rats!*" Zamfir burst into a strained laugh, but no one thought it amusing.

Three tractors stopped in front of the Miliția Post and the watchman appeared at the door wrapped in a sheepskin, a heavy club in his hand.

"I came with the boys, chief! They say a big fire was seen tonight on Pietrosu!"

"Well done, Pandelică!", Zamfir nodded. Then he ordered his deputy: "Comrade Sergeant, take two AKM automatic assault rifles and four magazines of war ammunition from the armrack. We're going to Pietrosu."

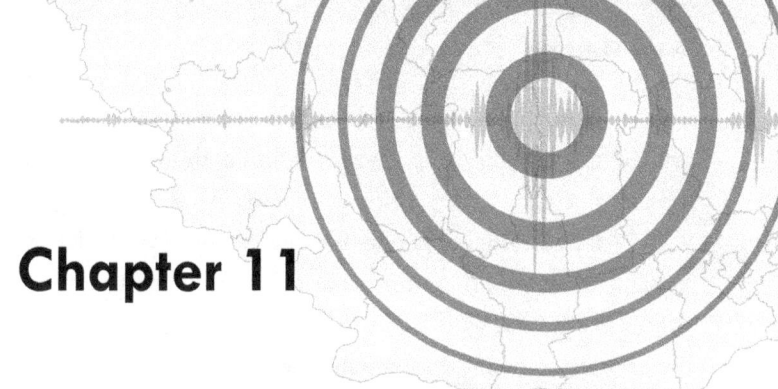

Chapter 11

The night between May 25 – 26, 1987
Pietrosu Hill and Brădet village

The taillights disappeared into the darkness after the first bend in the road. The man and the woman remained alone at the top of the mountain. Ileana was nervous. She still had the Beretta revolver in her hand after firing three shots without the slightest hesitation at the car stolen by George.

"How the hell did that happen!?" she burst out exasperated. "What are we going to do now, wise guy?"

"I don't understand how he managed to get so close to us without being seen," said her flustered companion. "Anyway, how come you carry a gun, Ileana? Here in Romania, it is forbidden for ordinary citizens to carry fire guns or any kind of weapons for that matter. It is the reason why I was not given a pistol."

"It's a family heirloom I keep in secret. I have this Beretta from my grandfather who fought in the mountains against Communism, waiting in vain for the Americans to come and save us from the Russians."

Yusuf accepted the explanation with some reluctance.

"What are you going to tell your uncle about the car?" he asked worriedly. "It's a brand-new car."

"I can handle it, no problem!" Ileana said. "I will report the theft to the Miliția and they will find both the car and the person who stole it. The problem is what we do now, in the night."

"I have a satellite phone. We can ask one of your relatives or acquaintances in Bucharest for help. You must know someone who has a car and who might come to pick us up. By the time we get to the foot of the mountain, they could be already there."

"Are you crazy!? All phone calls are tracked. Do you want the Securitate to locate and arrest us? I have another plan: we will go down the mountain and get to the nearest train station. It is about ten km from here. We will return to Bucharest on the first train."

"Right," Yusuf said. He took the bag in which he had the devices used to disable the seismic relay, put it on his shoulder, and started forward.

On the road near the fountain, they came across three tractors going up to Pietrosu, but remained hidden in the shadows. It was past midnight when they reached the village of Brădet. They were tired and muddy. The village was quiet, the streets dark and deserted, and only a few dogs were barking. They had to cross the village and reach the road leading to the railway station.

When they arrived to the Miliția Post, they stopped really surprised. A man wrapped in a sheepskin coat, with a large club in his hand, was guarding their white ARO car. Ileana pointed the flashlight to it and, as she looked more closely, she noticed a hole in the windshield and a broken headlight.

"We are lucky!" Yusuf said and approached the car wanting to try the doors to see if they were locked or not.

"Hey, chief! It's not allowed!" shouted the night watchman, raising his club. "This is a stolen car!"

"Comrade, this is my car!" Ileana said flatly. "It was stolen from me up on Pietrosu a few hours ago. We've just come from there on foot."

"I don't know, miss. I'm just doing my job and my boss said not to let anyone near the car until he returns."

"Where did your boss go? I want to talk to him."

"He went up to Pietrosu with the tractors to bring a comrade from Seismology who fell into the ravine with his car. He said that someone fired a gun at the car, that's why it has a hole in the windshield and a broken headlight."

"Of course, first they're driving drunk, make an accident then steal our car and destroy it," Ileana snapped.

She grabbed the handle firmly and finding it locked, she rummaged through her backpack.

"Look, comrade, I have the spare keys here," she added, opening the door. "You can tell this to your boss when he will come back. I don't steal like others… I just take back what's mine."

"Miss, please, don't cause me problems!" the watchman begged her. "Stay here and wait until the head of the Miliția Post comes back, and if he gives you the permission, you can take back your car. Maybe you'll have to write a statement…"

"What statement, comrade?" said Ileana impatiently, opening the car and getting behind the wheel. "Those bastards who stole and destroyed my brand-new car need to give statements. It will cost me a fortune to fix the headlight and the windshield!"

She started the engine while Yusuf got in the right seat.

"Should we give him a pack of Kent?" he asked.

"No cigarettes! No cigarettes!" shouted the watchman and grabbed the steering wheel with his strong right hand. "Get out of the car! Get out of the car!"

Ileana took out a pepper spray and spattered it on the man's face. The watchman released the steering wheel screaming in pain, and covered his face with both hands.

"Go to hell, you wretched peasant!" she growled.

"Thieves, thieves! Help me! The thieves!" the unfortunate watchman shouted desperately, blinded by the irritating substance.

The neighbors' dogs barked agitated. The people woke up and came out at the gates as the car started with a squeal of wheels and quickly disappeared along the road.

* * *

May 25, 1987, evening
Bucharest

General Pleşca had been busy all day preparing for the trip to Zaire. His Supreme Commander had summoned him to give him a series of instructions, but he had been waiting in the anteroom of *Cabinet One* for more than an hour, a sign that Ceauşescu was not in a good mood.

The General had asked Major Alexe to keep him informed on the status of the Soviet satellite. Alexe had reported to him that six Soviet agents had passed through the Giurgiuleşti customs early in the morning which may be connected to the fact that the satellite could fall on the Romanian territory. The Securitate agent from the Vama Veche border sent an informative note on two suspicious Bulgarian tourists who had entered Romania.

In the evening, when the General was informed on the operational circuit that the satellite had fallen into the Black Sea, his first thought was to order Bebe Gold to stop the action. They were in contact through encrypted terrestrial radio relays so they could talk freely. Bebe reported to him that the Israeli agents had already been notified by the satellite phone that they must withdraw. The loss of a significant amount of currency made the General regret that the satellite had not fallen in the Dobrogea Mountains.

"Any unwanted guests?" he asked more out of curiosity.

"Yes, Boss, they were. I treated everyone the same, without discrimination: broken windshields, slashed tires, broken hands, broken heads... a real hospitality... I don't think they'll ever set foot here again".

"Well done, Bebe! Well done, my boy! Don't let them think that Romania is a village without dogs."

"I serve my country, Boss!" answered Bebe happy that his mission was fully appreciated.

The General had no news from Ileana and this somewhat worried him. He knew, however, that she was resourceful and trusted her to have everything under control.

* * *

May 26, 1987, 2:00 AM - local time
National road to Bucharest.

Ileana was driving tense, her hands tight on the wheel. The right headlight had been shattered by the bullet so she couldn't see much ahead. Yusuf offered to take her place.

"My dear, if you're tired, let me drive," he said in a sweet voice.

"No way," Ileana said firmly. "A Miliția crew can stop us at any time because of those damned broken lights. In case it happens, you should have two or three packs of Kent within reach. I will handle the rest…"

"You never cease to amaze me, Ileana. I don't know how I would have carried out my mission without you. You have a Beretta pistol, pepper spray, a hunting knife… This is what a commando agent would keep in his backpack, not a young lady student."

"I learned how to defend myself in case of need. The World is full of dangers."

"That's true," said Yusuf.

"As I told you before, I come from a family of warriors who fought against the establishment of Bolshevik Communism in Romania."

"Please, tell me more. I want to learn about your family history," he said.

Ileana was silent for a moment, and then she began in a low voice:

"After the Soviet troops occupied Romania and established the Communist regime, my family retreated into the mountains, alongside other insurgents. My grandfather, who had been an officer in the Royal Romanian Army, organized a group of partisans. They communicated with the *Free World* by radio. Regularly, the Americans supplied them with weapons, ammunition, and food, which they parachuted at night in places marked with lit fires. I was born in the cave where my father and mother were sheltering. I grew up there until the age of four. I remember how my parents would light the fire in the mouth of the cave to cook the food, careful not to make too much smoke that could be seen from afar."

"No kid deserves such a childhood. What did you play with in that cave?"

"My mother made me rag dolls from old clothing, and my father carved wooden toys. I have a few memories from that time. I still remember how, on a Christmas night, my grandfather came with a bag full of apples, gingerbread, and chocolate. I was very happy and I recited a short poem to him about the Nativity that my mother had taught me." Ileana stopped abruptly as if she didn't know what else to say, but she took a deep breath and continued:

"The Securitate forces hunted us at every step. I remember how they attacked us one day. There were many soldiers. The bullets were whistling everywhere, ricocheting off the rocks. My father, my grandfather, and other fighters were firing their weapons trying to defend themselves. I was crying and my mother took me in her arms and hid me at the bottom of the cave. The rest is blurry in my mind. That's when both of my parents died fighting. My grandfather and several other men escaped but were soon captured, following a betrayal. They were executed without any trial".

"What happened to you?"

"I was captured by the Securitate and taken to an orphanage from where I was adopted."

"Do your foster parents know about your past?" Yusuf asked greatly impressed by Ileana's story.

"I think so, but we have never talked about it. I feel they love me as their own child. They spoiled me, granting all my wishes, but I confess I have one great desire left."

"What desire?"

"To leave this country as soon as possible. I am suffocating here. I want to breathe and feel the freedom I once had in the mountains as a child. I want to get away from the omnipresent surveillance of the bloody Securitate."

"I'll help you do it, Ileana, don't worry," said Yusuf firmly.

"I hate Communism with all my heart. It killed my parents, alienated me from the rest of the family, and humiliated me!"

"Once we get married, I will take you to the States. As I told you, I have American citizenship and it will be easier for you to become an American citizen as my wife."

Ileana drove in silence for a while. The road was almost deserted. Rarely a vehicle came from the opposite direction. Yusuf kept wondering how Ileana inherited the Beretta pistol from her grandfather if he was killed by the Securitate when she was only four years old. As if reading his mind, the young woman continued her story:

"A few years ago, I went to the village at the foot of the Făgăraș Mountains, where my parents lived before, they took refuge in the cave. I was curious if I could find any relatives alive. People were still afraid to talk about the partisans. The Securitate had tortured many villagers who supposedly helped the insurgents. I was directed to an old priest who knew the whole story of my family. He took me to the village cemetery and showed me three graves covered by weeds and guarded by old wooden crosses. He told me that they had been secretly buried there at night. First my parents, then a week later my grandfather. The night before he was caught, he visited the priest, whom he trusted. He probably had a feeling that his end was coming. He confessed and received the Last Eucharist, according to the order of our Christian faith. Then he entrusted to the priest a copper tin box in which there was this Beretta revolver and several cartridges. He asked the priest to bury the box in his grave and to dig it up and give it to me when I came of age. He wanted me to continue his fight. I found the box. The gun and cartridges were in good condition because they had been covered with a thick layer of tallow. Since then, I've been carrying the revolver in my bag whenever I went on a dangerous mission."

"It's an amazing story," said Yusuf. "But what would happen to you if someone discovered it?"

"I don't want to think about it. The Securitate would beat me until I told them where I got the gun from and if I had another one hidden. Then they would put me in jail for illegal gun possession."

"I still don't understand why you risk so much," he wondered.

"As I told you before, I'm a fighter like everyone in my family. Tonight, for example, if I had not scared the guy who stole our car by shooting at him, maybe he would have been the one to attack us."

"I shouldn't have cut their brakes. I could have killed them…"

"This is the risk of your job, Yusuf. You're an undercover agent on enemy territory. You're trained to kill people. I am a student trained only to defend myself, if necessary."

In the distance, Ileana saw the reflective sash of a Miliția officer who signaled them with a flashlight to pull over.

"Give me the cigarettes and don't say a word. Pretend to be asleep," she said calmly.

Ileana pulled off the road, got out of the car, and showed the officer her documents and a certain ID. They exchanged a few words and she slipped two packs of cigarettes into his pocket. The officer greeted her politely and the woman got back on the driver's seat.

"We're good to go," she said triumphantly.

"Impressive," Yusuf said blinking.

"Kent cigarettes work wonders in Romania. They are like a strong currency."

* * *

May 26, 1987, 6:00 AM - local time
Bucharest.

The General waited in vain until late at night for a sign from Ileana. In the morning, she called him.

"I'm back, Boss. Mission complete," she said with a dull tired voice.

"How was it, daddy's girl? Did you do a good job?"

"Everything went according to the plan, but we had an unpleasant incident. A guy from Seismology stole our car and we had to walk several kilometers to Brădet."

"The bastard! How did he dare to steal our car!? Well, as a *reward*, I won't approve his colleagues' travels abroad for Congresses and Symposiums for a while."

"Don't worry about the car, Boss. I managed to get it back. It was parked in front of the Miliția Post in Brădet. It has a broken headlight and a bullet hole in the windshield. I shot at it to scare off the guy."

"You had an eventful evening, my girl. Are you okay?"

"Yes, Boss, I'm fine, but I have a big request."

"Anything, my girl!"

"I need to lose my trace. The Miliția in Brădet took too many statements."

"Don't worry, consider it done. You drop off the car at the garage. Engineer Paraschiv will take care of it. You can rest and go back to your studies."

"There's something else, Boss. The *Fox* keeps insisting on meeting my family…"

"We'll take care of this, too, dear. I will be away for a few days, but when I return to Bucharest, you can invite him to our *Storks' Nest* to meet a real Romanian family…"

"Thank you, Boss! Have a good trip and come back safely!"

* * *

May 26, 1987, 9:00 AM - local time
Miliția Post-Brădet

The rescue team made a stretcher out of branches and got the wounded man out of the ravine. Upon getting Gică to the village with the tractor, Sub-officer Zamfir called the Ambulance Service again, but the answer remained the same: they couldn't come because they were out of gas. So, Zamfir had no other choice but to take Gică to the hospital in his own car. Then he spent the rest of the night taking statements from everyone involved in the incident. The sun was rising when he was writing his own report. He wanted to send all the necessary paperwork to his superiors, as soon as possible. It was a shooting incident with unknown perpetrators and that was quite serious. A criminal investigation was mandatory.

Zamfir was alone in the Miliţia Post when the door opened and a tall man appeared in the doorway, a leather bag in his hand. He wore a short haircut, sunglasses, and a light-colored sweatshirt.

"I'm Major Dulca from the State Securitate," he said bluntly, without any other greeting, and briefly showed his service card.

The Sub-officer introduced himself and explained that he was just finishing the report on the recent incident.

"Why so late, comrade?" Major Dulca asked clearly irritated.

"The investigation took me almost all night…"

"Foreign agents were involved in this incident. Hence it becomes the responsibility of the State Securitate. Why didn't you report the case directly to us? Why did I have to come all the way here myself?"

"With all due respect, comrade Major, I reported everything to my superiors from the County Miliţia," answered Zamfir without being intimidated.

"Starting this moment, the Securitate takes over the entire investigation!" Major Dulca said. "I want you to hand over all the witness statements and your report on this case at once."

"I understand, but, in this situation, what should I send to my superiors? They're waiting for these reports…"

"You will give them exactly what they deserve, which is nothing! Why didn't they send an operative intervention crew?

Why did they let you search the mountains at night with a posse of tractor drivers and night watchmen? To play *Cowboys and Indians* like silly children? Good thing the saboteurs didn't shoot any of you!"

"I think we handled the situation well. First, we rescued that comrade from Seismology and then we searched through the forest for those who fired the gun but, unfortunately, we didn't find them."

"Of course, you didn't. You were looking for them in the forest and they were here, getting back their car and going about their business, thus depriving us of the most important piece of evidence: the bullet-riddled car. I want to see all the statements you took. I am primarily interested in those given by the Seismology employees."

Zamfir took out several sheets of paper from a drawer and flipped through them.

"I have here only the statement of Costinescu George, the electronics technician. I don't have the driver's statement yet because he could barely speak, but I'm going to visit him at the hospital today."

"There's no need, we will take care of it."

Major Dulca read George's statement and asked:

"Where is this comrade Costinescu George?"

"He left for Bucharest by train."

"You should have detained him. He is an important pawn in the investigation."

"I had no legal right to detain him, comrade. He is a victim, not the aggressor."

"That is for us to decide. He says here that he handed over to you the keys to the car he had stolen. I want the car keys as well."

Major Dulca opened the briefcase with the intention of putting the papers inside when Zamfir said:

"Excuse me, comrade Major, but we will have to make a Handover Minutes first and a list of all the documents you will pick up from here."

"There is no need for that. I repeat: starting from this moment, the Securitate takes over this case. Your job is done. Do you understand?"

"But you can't do it without the Minutes! It's against the rules!" Zamfir insisted. "I want to report the situation to my superiors." He grabbed the handset and started turning the crank to call the operator. Major Dulca put his hand over the telephone.

"There is no point in stirring the waters. If your bosses ask about statements or reports, tell them they were taken by the Securitate on the orders of comrade General Virgil Pleşca. I think you know who he is."

"Yes, I do! He is the head of the State Securitate Department. Nevertheless, I want you to show me a proof, a paper or something, that you were sent here by comrade General Virgil Pleşca.", said the head of the Miliţia Post firmly.

"I will convey your request to the comrade General.", Major Dulca replied with a disdainful grin on her face. "Meanwhile, I want you to put everything on the table, any paper or evidence related to this case", he adds downright menacingly. "Forget about last night! Take care of the local affairs. Catch the hen thieves and those who steal from the public property of our socialist society. Otherwise, you could be transferred to a God-forgotten village at any time."

Sub-officer Zamfir finally realized the gravity of the situation. That man could cause him great problems. With a heavy heart, he gave him all the papers related to the case as well as the keys to the car.

* * *

May 31, 1987, morning
Buzău Municipal Hospital

It was a beautiful morning. The sun was shining brightly in the clear sky, sending its scorching rays through the large window of the hospital room. Gică got up from the bed leaning against the crutch. The leg was still giving him trouble. He needed fresh air so he opened the window. Somewhere, in the park in front of the hospital, the happy voices of children filled the air. In the distance, Pietrosu Hill loomed over the blossoming vaults of chestnut trees. He had lost his identity there, in the ravine, as all his documents had been destroyed in the burning car. Now he could be anyone, he could have any name and it wouldn't have mattered if he was called *Popescu* or *Ionescu*; which only made matters worse when they brought him to the hospital and he couldn't identify himself in any way. Fortunately, one of the doctors ditched the paperwork and sent him straight to the surgery room for an emergency intervention: he had a double fracture. Even if they put a rod in his tibia, the doctor told him he would heal quickly.

The door opened and George rushed in waving a piece of paper.

"You are no longer an anonymous citizen!", he says laughed. "Look, I managed to get you a temporary ID. Don't let your wife think you are a foreign agent infiltrated into the family."

"By the way, two young guys with blue eyes from Securitate visited me here in the hospital and asked me various questions about the *blonde woodpecker* and her companion. Something like: how I met them, what I talked to them about, if I could recognize them from the photos, who I suspect they are and all kinds of details. They then asked me to write a statement that they dictated to me, reasoning that this is easier for me. I asked them if they caught the two spies who wanted to kill us, but they pretended not to hear my question."

"Well, that's how they are from birth, very secretive," joked George. "They summoned me too, and I had to meet them in a large building, with some long poorly lit corridors where officers in blue uniforms and many civilians dressed almost the same, with gray suits and red ties, were hurrying by. I also saw some sad *guests*, handcuffed, with swollen eyes and bleeding lips, who were just taken out of the interrogation rooms in the basement, and escorted by some non-commissioned officers. That led me to do my best and to answer all their questions and write my statement as clearly as possible. They were particularly interested in how I stole the agents' car. They seemed satisfied with my cooperation and said they would call me again if it were necessary. I was very happy that they didn't *invite* me *to visit* the basement."

"I do hope the rumors are true," Gică said with a kind of satisfaction. "I heard a nurse say that some spies have been arrested."

"Arrested? By whom? By their own colleagues? Keep in your mind wat I say: even the Western spies operate in our country with the Securitate permission. You will be shocked when I will tell you where I saw the *blonde woodpecker*!"

"Where, man?" asked the driver overcome with childish curiosity.

Although they were alone, George looked cautiously around and spoke almost in a whisper:

"She was there in that big building with long corridors... She was dressed in a blue Securitate officer uniform."

"No way! Are you sure it was her?" Gică asked really perplexed.

"I recognized her right away."

"Damn, that's too much. I don't understand what is happening in this country anymore...", Gică said in astonishment and remained in his thoughts.

"Politics, my friend, politics... The games are tough and dangerous, but the network is well organized. They are a big gang, some on one side, some on the other side of the *fence,* and they know each other well, because they meet at receptions, on the golf course or at the tennis court. Sometimes, ignorant people like us fall in the middle, and they have a lot of fun on this topic."

"We could have lost our lives because of their games!", Gică got angry.

"Our lives mean nothing to them."

"What a tangled business...," murmured the driver as for himself.

"For thousands of years, everything has been foggy in this country full of conflicts of interest. The Moldavian chronicler

Grigore Ureche was right when he wrote: *a country in the midst of all evil."*

"It's very true and actual on our days. Looks like all the bad things in the World have turned upon us: droughts, floods, earthquakes... On top of everything, Communism is eating us alive."

"How dare you, comrade?! Don't you enjoy it?" began George making, like usually, *a joke at the expense of the trouble*, as an old Romanian proverb says. "You must be proud to have the historical chance to complete the construction of Socialism and to move to the most advanced form of social structure in the World, the Communism that is the *golden dream of mankind*! The General Secretary explained so many times that each of us is a small cog in the great mechanism of building Communism."

"Come on! Please, stop! I am tired of these ridiculous words that belong to the *wooden language* of Communist propaganda."

George laughed bitterly and added:

"To better understand the situation, we, the normal citizens, are unfortunately the anthill on which they are conducting this murderous experiment..."

"Okay, leave it at that. Tell me, better, what else happened at the Institute." Gică urged him, eager to change the subject of the discussion, so as not to get angrier again.

George took a seat on a chair near the Gică's bed and said:

"Well... the usual drill. I think Professor Dumitriu is going to finally give up on earthquake prediction, at least for a while... It seems that this time the scandal reached Ceaușescu's ears. The Professor was forced to *self-criticize*, and deny everything, saying that the articles he published don't have enough scientific basis. You know how it is... Perhaps it would be better for people like

Dumitriu to write two articles: one predicting the earthquake and one where it can be argued that there will not be any earthquake. The articles should be published in two different magazines and, depending on the circumstances, the most convenient article would be promoted."

"Well, that's how he gets the Nobel Prize," laughed the driver.

Finally, George thought it was time to move on to the good news that helps with keeping the sanity and say:

"I spoke on the phone earlier with the surgeon who operated on you and he told me that you will be discharged today."

"Are you sure?", Gică asked incredulously. "He keeps telling me that for a few days now. I don't believe him anymore."

"Today is the day! That's why I came here. Besides, I have another big surprise for you!"

"What surprise?", the driver asks in amazement, trying to guess what big surprise it was about.

"Just wait and see! The surprise must first be kept secret…"

George and Gică were going out the hospital gate in less than an hour. The driver was leaning on crutches, and his colleague was waiting patiently for him. At one point, Gică lifted his head and caught sight of a new, blue ARO SUV, fully equipped with antennas, loudspeakers, and blue rotative beacon. On the front doors was printed the emblem: *Seismology - Interventions*, in large, red letters.

"Yes, a real surprise…" he stammered.

"You see, my friend, we had to go through hell so our bosses could remember we existed. We were supposed to have a new car months ago, but the investment plan had been slowed down by our Communist bureaucracy. Because we lost the old car, they had to do the paperwork faster."

Helped, the driver settled in the seat to the right of the steering wheel, where he didn't really like to sit. George got behind the wheel and, honking briefly to greet the onlookers from the hospital windows, sped off down the avenue lined with blossoming chestnut trees.

Once they reached the national highway, he radioed Seismological Command:

"Attention, *Vrancea One*! Attention *Vrancea One*! The crew *Vrancea Two* is on the move again. Communicate any breakdowns."

* * *

May 31, 1987, evening
"Stork's Nest" Securitate conspiracy house

Stork's Nest had been specially prepared for agent Gilbert's visit. As *mother* and host, comrade Maria hung on the walls several family pictures with Ileana from when she was a child, and prepared a special dinner, with caviar, turkey steak, champagne, chocolate cake and tropical fruits. She had the supplies sent over from the Party farm and for the Ministry of the Interior's special store, because on the socialist market there were only chicken heads and claws as well as pig hooves, which the Romanians called "*sneakers*".

General Virgil Pleşca, *the father*, sat in an armchair smoking a cigar and reading a newspaper. He was wearing a red silk robe.

Ileana picked up her boyfriend from the student hostel, using one of the Securitate's special taxi cars, driven by a Sub-officer dressed in civilian clothes whose mission was to guard the young couple. After the General had been basically kidnapped by Israelite Agent Amin a week before, Pleșca wanted to make sure that was a one-time incident.

Ileana rang the doorbell in a certain way that did not escape to agent Gilbert. *Father* greeted them lightheartedly and invited them inside. Ileana made the introductions:

"This is my friend, Yusuf Haid. He studies History," she said cheerfully. "They are my parents, Maria and Constantin Popescu. My mother is a housewife and my father is an engineer."

They shook hands and Yusuf gave Maria a spectacular rose bouquet and a box of Cuban cigars to Constantin.

"For you, *Mister Popescu*. Ileana told me you prefer cigars."

"That's right. Thank you, Yusuf! You shouldn't have bothered," said the other.

They all sat around the table and Maria offered them drinks.

"Yusuf, I don't know if your religion allows you to drink alcohol… I understand that you are Palestinian…"

"I am a Palestinian Orthodox Christian, as you Romanians" Yusuf said with a smile.

"Perfect! In this case, you're most invited to try a traditional drink from Transylvania. It's a double-distilled plum brandy. It's called *palinka*."

"Oh, I know… I like it very much!"

The *father* poured the drink from a rush-braided bottle into four small clay cups. Urging everyone to drink, he proposed a toast:

"My dear children, it is a great joy to see you here together. To love and youth!"

They clinked the cups and Yusuf demonstratively threw back the shot, hoping to impress *Mister Popescu*.

He then shook his head saying:

"It's great! It's better than any whisky!

"Of course, it is one of a kind!" *Mister Popescu* added laughing, and filled the Palestinian's cup again.

During dinner, they talked about trivial subjects: the weather, football, and tennis. Although General Virgil Pleşca knew everything about Yusuf, *Mister Popescu* didn't. So, when they got to the cake and champagne, he asked the young man about his family in his usual interrogatory manner:

"Yusuf, I understand you are an American citizen. Is it true?"

"Yes, I am."

"And you come from Palestine. Which part?"

"My parents lived right in the Gaza Strip. They had to leave because of the insecure situation there."

"When did your family immigrate to the United States?"

"Ten years ago. They applied for a visa in the United States and received a positive response."

"That's curious… I know the Americans are friends with Israel and they don't really welcome Palestinian immigrants."

"My parents are doctors and their profession weighed a lot in the process of their immigration."

"What kind of doctors?"

"My father is a surgeon and my mother is a dentist."

"Where does your family live now?"

"In Florida, in Titusville, quite close to Orlando."

"Do you have any siblings?"

"Yes, two younger brothers and a younger sister."

"How come you ended up studying history in Romania? Foreign students usually come here to study medicine, agricultural sciences, civil and industrial construction," *Mister Popescu* kept asking.

"I've been passionate about history since I was a child. I'm mostly interested in the history of my people. My bachelor thesis I will present at the end of this Academic year focuses on the material and spiritual traces left by the Palestinians who were soldiers in the Roman legions stationed in Dacia. Many of them settled in Dacia upon finishing their military service."

Mister Popescu nodded thoughtfully.

"As far as I know, the 13th Gemina Roman Legion was made up of Palestinian Jews and stationed in Oltenia. Perhaps that's why the people there are quicker and trickier by nature," he chuckled. "Have you been around the counties of Oltenia?"

"Yes, I went there for some archeological investigations."

"Did you learn any tricks from the locals?"

"I learned a few things… In fact, I think that Romanians, in general, although they are very cunning, are open-minded and friendly. I'm sorry I'll be leaving soon."

"Why don't you stay in Romania then?" *Mister Popescu* grinned.

"I have to return to the States. I have career plans there at Brown University," Yusuf answered in a serious tone. "I want to take Ileana with me. I don't know if she told you… We want to get married and I want to ask for your consent."

"Yes… she said something about that," said *Mister Popescu*, a little confused. "We have nothing against your marriage, especially if the religion matter won't be a problem…"

"I assure you she will be happy with me. Ileana will obtain US citizenship quickly by marrying me. You will be able to visit us, we will visit you here…"

"However, as a father, my question is what will she do about her studies? She will graduate from the Faculty of Electronics in two years."

"Don't worry, Dad, I can continue my studies there," Ileana said. "I just have to pass a couple of equivalent exams."

Mister Popescu raised the glass of champagne and said:

"Well, children, if that's the case, you have our blessing. We wish you much health and happiness!"

Ileana hugged and kissed her *parents* on both cheeks and Yusuf did the same. Then he took a small box covered in blue velvet out of his pocket and knelt before Ileana. Opening the lid, he revealed a stunning ruby ring.

"My dear Ileana, with your parents as witnesses, I ask you here and now: do you want to be my wife?"

"Yes, I do!" she replied excitedly letting Yusuf put the ring on her finger.

The young people kissed under the happy gaze of their *parents*.

Chapter 12

April 1990
Vantaa Airport Helsinki, Finland

After a smooth, without turbulence flight, George got off the plane and headed to the passport control point. It was the first time he entered in a non-socialist country. He had little emotion. The *Socialist Republic of Romania* logo imprinted on his green passport immediately piqued the interest of the officer behind the counter who peered at George and asked him the purpose and duration of his visit to Finland. George repeated the answer he had prepared for this moment:

"I work at the Institute of Seismology in Bucharest and I've come to Finland for a one-month training at the Vibrometric Oy in Helsinki."

The officer nodded and put the entry stamp on his passport. After passing this first obstacle, George stepped into the Finnish territory without needing a visa. It was comforting for him to know that the Romanians were finally part of the civilized World. Still, uneasiness overcame him when he reached the conveyor belt to pick up his luggage. He had a bottle of Vrancea brandy in the suitcase. He knew that access with alcohol in Finland is quite restrictive.

He headed toward the green corridor where it was written *"Nothing to declare"*. In the arrival's hall, his friend Călin, the Director of Vibrometric Oy, was waiting for him. They shook hands and went outside to the parking lot. Călin had a brand-new BMW, with leather seats and a cell phone. George had never traveled in such a car before, so when Călin asked him if he wanted to call home, it only added to an overwhelming surreal feeling amplified by the landscape outside the window. The wide, multi-lane, well-marked, clean roads crossed pine forests and towns with beautiful and well-kept houses. To him, it looked like a fairyland. George picked up the phone and dialed the number. Far away, in Romania, his wife and child were waiting to hear that he had arrived safely in Helsinki.

* * *

July 1990
France

Gică was driving a new red Renault Magnum truck on the highway between Strasbourg and Besancon. He had been working for a few months at a Romanian-French transport company, after leaving the Institute of Seismology. Although he was sorry to part with his colleagues, he needed to travel and see the World, his life-long dream. He traveled all over Europe, ate at self-service restaurants, and slept in parking lots, where he met many Romanian drivers. He enjoyed talking to them through the CB radio on his truck board as it reminded him of the old days in Romania.

He couldn't quite remember where he had put the bag with the documents after leaving the customs. He pulled off the freeway into the first parking lot and searched desperately in the truck. A prostitute in a mini-skirt came to his truck and knocked on the door. After chasing her off, he continued his search, still cursing. He had been in a hurry and could have forgotten the documents in the customs area. But he would have had to travel back more than 150 km to retrieve them. It wouldn't have been a problem if his truck had not been monitored by the Outreach GPS system. Any deviation from the route meant a monetary penalty. Gică stared for a while at the GPS antenna installed on the truck's cab. Then he came up with an idea. If he shielded it, the satellite connection would have been lost.

Without losing any more time, he left the parking lot and kept driving until the first footbridge. He stopped under it, leaving the hazard lights on, took a tin bucket, and fixed it over the antenna with insulating tape. When he was done, he turned the truck around and went back to the customs office, where he found his documents.

On the road back, he stopped again under the same footbridge, took off the bucket covering the antenna, and continued his way, remembering a wise Romanian saying: "*Those who leave in a hurry meet with the delay.*"

* * *

July 25, 1991
Tampa, Florida, USA

The much-awaited day for Ileana to take the oath and become an American citizen had finally come. She had been living in the United States for almost four years since her immigration. As an undercover officer, Ileana was codenamed *Chrysanthemum*. The original plan was to remain *canned*, without any connection with the Securitate Headquarter in Bucharest, or with the Romanian Embassy, and to be *activated* by receiving a white chrysanthemum from a liaison, but only after she became an American citizen.

The Revolution in Romania in December 1989, however, had led to the official abolition of the Securitate structures. The Romanian Intelligence Service, the new secret service that had taken its place, advertised the fact that it was totally separated from the Securitate. However, most of its employees were former political police officers.

Ileana was confused about her future as an undercover agent. When she left Romania, she received a series of instructions and a lot of advice from her adoptive father, General Pleşca, with whom she kept in touch once a month by phone. She called him at *Storks' Nest* during the evenings he was playing poker and made small talk in slang.

Her mission was to infiltrate a high-tech field of activity, which she managed successfully upon graduating the *Electrical and Computer Engineering - University of Miami* and started working for a company that designed and built satellites for NASA programs. She considered herself a professionally fulfilled woman. Unfortunately, the marriage with Yusuf Haid did not go well. He was the jealous type and tried to restrict her freedom. As a former secret agent, having been dismissed for reasons of incompetence, Yusuf found consolation in alcohol. Hence both his university career and marriage fell apart. He and Ileana split amicably, but the deal was to remain officially married until she got her US citizenship. She passed successfully the required tests: American history, administrative science, written and spoken English.

The naturalization ceremony took place in a large room of the *City Hall*, on the walls of which were the paintings of the Founding Fathers of the United States. A large oval table with upholstered chairs, a desk, and a large American flag filled the room. At the desk were seated the officials from the Government, a lady, and two gentlemen. The candidates were standing behind their chairs, waiting for the ceremony to begin. The Covenant was written in large letters in front of each of them. Ileana waited excitedly. To her right was a gentleman with a large mustache, most likely Russian, and to the left a Hispanic lady.

They sang the National Anthem first, following the lyrics displayed on a giant prompter. Then they all took the oath in choir, repeating after one of the Government's men:

I hereby declare, on oath… that I absolutely and entirely renounce and abjure… all allegiance and fidelity to any foreign prince… potentate, state, or sovereignty… of whom or which I have heretofore been a subject or citizen…

While reciting the oath, Ileana noticed the man on her right. He was silent, his face expressionless. Ileana couldn't help thinking he was probably a Soviet agent but she didn't have time to process this idea for she had to focus on the ceremony. Soon, each candidate was invited to sign into a register. The lady from the Government handed them the certificate of citizenship, a folder with documents, and a small flag. Thus, Ileana learned that the gentleman on her right was called Alexei Leibovich which intensified her suspicions. At the end of the ceremony, everyone was smiling happily and taking pictures, except for Mister Leibovich who left the hall in a hurry as soon as he received the certificate and the other papers. Ileana didn't linger either.

When she got to her dark blue Jeep Cherokee, Ileana found a beautiful white chrysanthemum on the driver's seat and a note in Romanian saying: "*Congratulations! Look in the glove box.*" The woman opened the compartment and took out an envelope with $10,000 in cash and another envelope with the words: "*To be destroyed after reading",* written in capital letters. Inside she found the instructions for her first mission on American land. She had to obtain the documentation for the correction engines of the reconnaissance satellite she was working on. The delivery was to be made in a month in a restaurant in Orlando.

All the way from Tampa to Cocoa Beach where she lived, Ileana kept thinking about how to get out of this situation. The risk was high, especially since she came from an ex-Communist country. More than likely, she was closely monitored. Nevertheless, Ileana thought it odd that they were interested in American space technology. The only beneficiary could be the Soviet Union, but the relationship between the Romanian and Soviet secret services was not good. She stopped at a gas station to fill up the tank and to drink a coffee. As if by chance, Alexei Leibovich followed her in, ordered a coffee, and asked her permission to sit at the same table.

"How do you feel as an American citizen, Mister Leibovich?" Ileana asked, trying to start a conversation.

"Pretty well, thank you, ma'am. I see you remember my name from the ceremony… I'm sorry, I didn't get yours."

"Ileana Popescu Haid. Nice to meet you!"

They shook hands.

"Are you Romanian?"

"Yes, I am."

"I am a Jew from the Soviet Union. I received an inheritance here from a rich uncle and I managed to emigrate. How did you leave Romania? I know Ceaușescu's regime was very strict when it came to emigration."

"I married an American citizen. I also had to bribe someone at the Passport Service in Bucharest," she grinned meaningfully.

"Starting today, I have both Soviet and American citizenship," Leibovich said proudly, ignoring her answer. "I can say that I am a citizen of two big and powerful states. Did you also keep your Romanian citizenship?"

"Yes, I did."

"It's important to maintain good relations with the mother country. Moreover, we, the people from Eastern Europe, must be loyal to our homeland. Sooner or later, loyalty will make the difference between life and death. In the Middle Ages, the loyalty oath was respected with sanctity, and its violation led to the loss of wealth and even life."

"The oath I took today had great meaning to me," Ileana said, remembering that Mister Leibovich had been silent the whole time, while the other candidates were taking the oath in chorus. "For me, it was a special, impressive, and unforgettable moment."

"Yes, I must admit that the Americans know how to make a show out of anything, however insignificant the event may be. They know how to skillfully manipulate ordinary citizens. But we are not so easily impressed, are we? For we are used to it."

Ileana understood to whom she was talking to. Leibovich was the one who left her the white chrysanthemum, the money, and the instructions. Something was not right. Her identity had most probably been sold to the Soviets who wanted to use her as their agent in the United States. She had to contact her adoptive father, General Pleșca, as soon as possible.

"I founded an association for the Eastern Europe emigrants," continued Leibovich. "We campaign for the rights of those who arrive here from the former socialist countries. If you are interested you can join us."

"Yes, I'd like to," said Ileana without hesitating.

Leibovich contentedly stroked his mustache and took a business card from his wallet.

"Here are the contact details of the *Friends of America Association*. I am the president," he said proud.

Ileana smiled and, in turn, gave him her business card on which only her name and phone number were printed.

* * *

July 25, 1991 - evening
Snagov, Romania

Few people knew that the venerable bearded old man who lived in that charming little house on the shore of Lake Snagov was the former Securitate General Virgil Pleșca. He greeted his neighbors respectfully, who were either post-Revolution upstarts or former senior officers of the Securitate. Everyone addressed him as *Your Excellency* and he was often visited by his former aide-de-camp, Colonel Alexe Marian, who worked in the newly established Romanian Intelligence Service. The General had been dismissed immediately after the Revolution of December 1989, but he had not yet lost his influence in the World of espionage.

He offered his advice to the new Romanian secret services from the shadows, in exchange for substantial payment. Many of his former subordinates, who were also retired, insisted that the General entered politics like them. They had asked him to join the *Romanian Patriots Party*, a political organization made up mostly of former Securitate and Miliția employees. Although they were not officially in power, the members of this party had great influence. They controlled a good part of the Romanian economy and influenced the most important political decisions of the new Government.

Colonel Săftoiu, who was part of the Executive Political Bureau of the Romanian Patriots Party, visited the General one evening under the pretext of a poker game. But the real purpose of his visit was to ask General Pleșca to accept the very important position of Executive Chairman of his newly established party.

"Thank you, dear comrade, for thinking of me, but I'm not interested in politics anymore.", General Pleșca answered him firmly. "My life-long experience with the communists has been more than enough for me. If I were to enter politics again, my new vision would not match yours anyway. Romania took on the wrong path right from the start. The Ceaușescu's were shot like dogs, right on Christmas Day, following a Bolshevik-type mock trial that horrified the civilized World. And President Iliescu's strategy of bringing thousands of miners to Bucharest to beat up his political opponents seems like the action of an African dictator in a horror movie. This recklessness will cost us a lot. We will never get anywhere like that. The best solution for Romania would have been to restore the constitutional monarchy and bring back King Mihai to the throne of the country. The King's connections worldwide are excellent, and his impartiality toward the large number of political parties, which have sprung up like mushrooms after the rain, would have been guaranteed."

"However, Your Excellency, the monarchy seems to me an old-fashioned regime. We are a democratic republic…," said Săftoiu surprised by the words of the former head of the Securitate.

"Democratic republic, my ass! The Republic was created by force on December 30, 1947, with Russian tanks on the flank, threats, blackmail, and guns under the coat. Do your history homework, Săftoiu! Ceauşescu ruled us like a pharaoh, so Romania was not a democratic republic during his time. Now, President Iliescu is following in his footsteps. What kind of democratic republic are we if the Minister of the Interior chases the former King of the country on the highway, and forcefully escorts him back to the airport, even though Mihai Hohenzollern's British passport was in order. They suspected he returned to take back his throne?! The man wanted to go to the Curtea de Argeş Monastery to light a candle at the graves of his ancestors who made *Great Romania*. Why didn't they let him? I tell you why! Out of fear! They shit their pants when they hear the King's name. I don't have to remind you that none of them, Iliescu included, hold the power legitimately. They took it through a *coup d'état* masked by the Revolution. During the last elections, they stole the votes, manipulated, and twisted the minds of the Romanians with Bolshevik propaganda worse than the one in 1946. They scared the peasants by telling them that the landlords would return to take their lands if they didn't vote for Iliescu. They scared the workers by saying that the owners of the factories would return and fire them, reducing them to beggary. They brainwashed the poor people so much that they started to shout on the streets: *We work, we don't think!* Indeed, they don't! To tarnish the image of the monarchy, they are currently making a big propaganda in the media, by broadcasting some supposed *emperors* and *kings* of the gypsies who seem to have all gathered in Romania. In Sibiu, the Gypsies have both a *king* and an *emperor*, who built palaces with turrets, side by side. What the hell! I just saw on the news that the former Minister of the Interior, that humiliated our King on the National Highway, was taking a ride in a *royal carriage* through the streets of Sibiu, together with two *Roma* minors, *the prince and princess*, who had just gotten married in defiance of Romanian laws regarding the protection of minors. The minister was their godfather. To be honest, I was so angry that I wanted to break the TV. They have made our country a mockery of the World. It took Baroness Emma Nicholson to take a tough line to get *Roma* children back to their families and to school. What kind of country is this one, Săftoiu? It's all going to hell!"

The General heated up more than usual and felt the need to calm down. He poured some whisky into his glass and lit a cigar. Colonel Săftoiu listened to him completely nonplussed. It was the first time he heard the General speak so vehemently.

"Your Excellency, this is exactly the reason you should get back into politics, alongside your former comrades…," he dared.

"I don't have time, Colonel… My time is running out… I'm ill. Liver cirrhosis. The doctors gave me only a few more months to live…"

The colonel received this sad news in dismay.

"I'm very sorry to hear that, Your Excellency…"

"Don't be. I get what I deserve. Ceaușescu was right when he kept warning me that I would die like an idiot because of drinking."

"Liver transplants are possible nowadays…"

"No," the General waved his hand dismissively and somewhat tired. "It's already too late for me…"

They finished the poker game in silence and Săftoiu left, sadness imprinted on his face. The General went for a walk in the garden, on an alley lined with rose bushes which he tended with great passion. A cool evening breeze brought him the sounds of the pond creatures from the nearby lake. He was waiting for Ileana to call him so he had the wireless terminal in his pocket. The sound of her voice uplifted him.

"Dad, today I became an American citizen, with all the rights and duties…," she said cheerfully. "I took the oath!"

"Congratulations, my darling girl. I wish you good health and all my best."

"I found a beautiful white chrysanthemum and two envelopes with *greeting cards* in my car. Do you know about this?"

"No, I don't know anything, my dear," said the General in surprise. "They are not from **us.**"

"Then it is as I suspected. Some strange guy from the ceremony, Alexei Leibovich. He's after me like a hungry dog."

"Be careful, Ileana. Soon, I won't be able to do anything for you anymore… I'm not well…"

Silence fell between them. The General could hear his daughter taking a sharp breath. She was strong, that's how he had raised her.

"How long?" came her question.

"Just a couple of months."

"I'm coming to see you. I'll get on the first plane."

"Good. Since you are starting a new life there, my advice is to confess to *Father Fabian* from the *Armenian Church,* as soon as possible."

The general's coded message was very clear to Ileana. In their slang, "*Father Fabian*" was the FBI, and the "*Armenian Church*" was the United States Embassy. She urgently needed to go to the American Embassy in Bucharest and reveal to the FBI office that she was a former Securitate agent who had infiltrated American territory before the Revolution.

"I understand, I will do so!", she said very determinedly.

After ending the phone conversation, the General became even more restless. The thing he feared had happened. The Soviets got their hands on the list of undercover Romanian agents in the United States, along with all the details of their activation. He turned on the jamming device, for he suspected his garden was bugged, and called Colonel Alexe, asking him to come over urgently. It was already midnight when the former adjutant entered the gate.

"What the hell is going on, Alexe?" the General asked as he opened the front door. "How did the Soviets get the list of our agents in the United States? Ileana called me and said she's been activated by a Russian guy named Alexei Leibovich. What do you know about this?"

"Absolutely nothing, Your Excellency," Alexe said surprised. "Perhaps it was an information leakage…"

"Who is in charge of the former Securitate archives?"

"Mister Colonel Petrescu."

"The bloody idiot from Counterintelligence who used to report our Poker games to Ceaușescu?! How did he end up in charge of the archive" the General raged.

"That was *the recommendation* received by our director from the President's office."

"Right, well… Now, when the Soviet Union is about to fall apart and is giving her last breath, our President came up with the foolish idea of signing a treaty of friendship and mutual assistance between Romania and the USSR. To curry favor with Gorbachev, he most likely ordered Petrescu to give the KGB the list of our undercover agents, whom the Soviets could blackmail and use after we raised and trained them! Do you know how this is called, Alexe? High treason! You can transmit to Colonel Petrescu what I said!"

"Colonel Petrescu is difficult to approach and is very influential," said Alexe with a kind of resignation.

"Of course, he's influential if he handles the Securitate files of all politicians! It's only a matter of time until the political world in our country will be shaken by blackmail and slander."

"We, as an intelligence service, try to distance ourselves from political disputes…"

"No shit! You can't do anything as long as your chiefs obey political orders. It's their business, I don't care about it anymore, but it's Ileana I'm concerned about. She's in danger, I felt it in her voice. If she refuses to work for the Soviets, she could get killed or, at best, handed over to the American authorities, in exchange for some KGB agent. In her case, there is no question of negotiating an expulsion. She's an American citizen now. She swore allegiance to the United States and she will endure the rigors of the American laws. She may be imprisoned for the rest of her life."

"Your Excellency, do you think I can be of any help in this whole matter?"

"Yes, Alexe, that's why I called you. Please, get all your *antennas* up and learn everything you can about this Soviet citizen named Alexei Leibovich, as soon as possible. He immigrated to the United States about four years ago and he received American citizenship today."

"I'll do everything I can, Your Excellency. You can count on me," Colonel Alexe firmly assured him.

"Get in touch with the source *Ivan*", urged the General. "Tell him he'll get a generous bonus from me if he helps us. You know, he's crazy, he's a double-edged sword, and if he's stimulated, he can provide us with valuable information."

The discussion between the General and Alexe ended late at night.

* * *

July 26, 1991-morning
Snagov

Early in the morning, the General received a phone call.

"Long live, Boss! It's Bebe. I apologize for calling you so early in the morning."

"I'm glad to hear your voice, my boy!" the General answered in surprise. "I've been awake for some time, anyway. That's how it is at this age. You can't sleep for more than a few hours per night. Tell me how you are doing. I haven't heard from you for some time now..."

"You know... I'm also a small capitalist now, like many others. I have a company of bodyguards and detectives."

"Well done, Bebe! How is it going?"

"Pretty good, Boss! I have a lot of work, thank God! There are many rich people who want security and protection and many jealous dudes who suspect their wives or mistresses of cheating on them. They pay us a fortune to follow their women to the hairdresser, the manicurist, at the shops, or wherever the hell they go."

"Bebe, tell me how I can help you. Why did you call me?"

"Boss, I want to offer you the services of my company. Marian Alexe called me last night and said you have some problems. I think I can help you. Right now, I'm here in front of your gate."

"From where are you calling me?" asked the General with a frown and peered out the window. "I don't have any phone booth in the front of my gate…"

"I just installed a cell phone in my brand-new BMW, Boss. Wanna come for a ride with me? We'd better talk inside my car, anyway."

NMT cell phones in the 450 MHz band had been recently introduced in Romania and it was a real luxury and a sign of prosperity to own such a device.

The General quickly dressed in a tracksuit and went out. He could barely recognize Bebe, who was waiting next to a new dark blue BMW. He had a short haircut, was dressed in a smart light-colored suit, and wore fancy sunglasses. He looked like a real businessman. His greasy jeans, unshaven beard, and flowing locks, which he had worn while working for the Securitate, were gone. The two men shook hands and hugged each other like two old friends. Bebe opened the door for his former boss who got on the passenger seat. Glancing at the mobile phone installed on board, the General urged him:

"Disconnect it! These damned phones can not only be listened to easily but also locate you where you are."

The General was right. Most cell phone owners were unaware that this new technology made it much easier to intercept and locate conversations.

"Don't worry, Boss, I know the lesson," Bebe said proudly. "I've already disconnected it. I just have to turn on the multichannel jamming device now." He pressed a button hidden under the steering wheel and the radio station was suddenly interrupted by an annoying hum.

"Now, Boss, we can talk freely, like in the old days, when I had my old Dacia car…"

"I should also install a *toy* like this one in my car, to be safe from prying ears," said the General with interest.

"Got it, Boss, I'll get you one! It costs a thousand dollars, but it's worth it!"

"Put me on top of the waiting list."

Bebe started the car and turned into an alley that led to the forest.

"Let's get straight to the point, Boss!" he began. "I understand you are interested in a guy named Alexei Leibovich, a Soviet citizen who immigrated to America a few years ago and who has just received American citizenship. By his name, he seems to be of Jewish descent…"

"I don't think that's his real name. He is a KGB agent under someone else's identity. That's how the Soviets work. Sometimes they steal the identities of those who receive immigration approval. They can even resort to cosmetic surgery if they need it. In this case, Alexei Leibovich could be a Soviet citizen who applied to immigrate to the United States and now rots in a camp in Siberia, while a Soviet agent who stole his identity and replaced him upon departure from the airport, travels at will around the World and, in the meantime, he becomes an American citizen. I want to know everything about this agent."

"I understand, Boss. You will have his file in two weeks at most."

"Are you going to break into the KGB archive?" the General asked half-joking, half-skeptical.

"Don't worry, Boss. Everything in this World is sold and bought. I work with honest merchants. One of them, who was an elite fighter in Afghanistan, is now a secret files dealer."

"I see that, since Gorbachev's *glasnost* and *perestroika*, the downfall of the secret services began in the Soviet Union as well. As for us, what else can we say? The journalists have started finding the files from the Securitate archives thrown into the landfill. A disgrace!"

"Yes, I heard they discovered some files in the Berevoești ravine," said Bebe Gold regretfully. "They tried to set them on fire, but they didn't burn all the papers. I think there is some unfinished business between Colonel Petrescu, who is now in charge of the Securitate archives, and his former subordinates."

"To hell with everyone! They are nothing but a disgrace to the Securitate…," the General muttered like an angry bear. Changing his tone, he asked directly: "Tell me how much the Leibovich file will cost me."

"You'll get a microfilm and a printed version only on demand. This is how we work now."

"I want both the microfilm and the printed version…"

"The whole deal costs you $20,000 payable in cash, in two installments: half at the beginning, half at the end. Considering our history together, I'll give you a 10% discount."

"Thank you, Bebe," said the General and shook the other's hand. "Let's go back to my house to give you the money."

Chapter 13

July 28, 1991, 5 PM
"Henri Coandă" International
Airport, Bucharest Romania

After a journey of almost 20 hours, Ileana arrived in Bucharest on a KLM flight. The transoceanic flight from Orlando to Amsterdam encountered a lot of turbulence. She hadn't been able to sleep at all and felt tired. All she wanted was to take a shower and sleep, if possible, for 24 hours.

She was returning to Romania after almost four years. If Otopeni Airport once seemed imposing to her, now, after having seen the largest airports in the World, "Henri Coandă" International Airport seemed like a small-town train station to her. Passengers were picked up from the plane's staircase in a ramshackle bus that blew smoke out of its tailpipe like a steam locomotive. At the passport control point, she had to stand in line for almost an hour because only one counter was open, although several planes had landed and travelers crammed in the waiting room.

The officer who checked her passport peered at her suspiciously and pointed out that her passport would expire soon. Then she had to wait for the checked baggage for quite some time because the conveyor belt had broken down. When she finally retrieved her suitcase, noticed that someone had opened it, most likely the porters of the airport.

The customs officers were a bit more kind. They did not ask her to open the luggage for control like it used to be in Ceaușescu's time. They only inquired if she had any guns, drugs, or more than $10,000 in cash. In the arrival's hall, Ileana found herself surrounded by dark-skinned men shouting aggressively: "*Taxi! Taxi! Cheap taxi*!" while others waved placards in English on which it was written "*Advantageous currency exchange.*" She looked around in confusion until she finally caught sight of a respectable gentleman with a grey beard holding a bouquet of white roses. Ileana couldn't believe her eyes. Since she last saw him, the General had grown old, his face was pale, and bruised, and he leaned on a cane with a silver handle.

"Welcome home, my girl!" he said, his voice choked with emotion.

"It's good to see you, Dad!" answered Ileana. She let go of the suitcase to hug and kiss him on both cheeks. "What about you? I don't like the way you look," she said unable to conceal her sadness.

"I'm paying the price for all the wrong I've done to so many people, my dear."

"You shouldn't have come to pick me up. I would have managed. I would have taken a taxi."

"You would have deprived me of the pleasure of waiting for you with flowers from my own garden."

They went to the parking lot. An athletic young man with sunglasses greeted them, took Ileana's luggage, and put it in the trunk of a new black Mercedes. The General introduced him as Cosmin, his driver and *guardian angel* who took great care of him. They got into the car and left for Snagov. After a few kilometers the driver warned the General:

"Your Excellency, we are being tailed. It's a taxi. It neither overtakes us nor lags… Today I took the car to the service for the technical review. I think they put a *cricket* in the passenger compartment and now they sit in range to listen to its *song*."

"Screw them! They are not professionals!" grunted the General. "They use poor quality *crickets* with weak emitters, if they stick so close to us. Turn on the *bells* and speed up the car! We have a Mercedes; they have a wretched Dacia."

The driver turned on the light and acoustic signaling of the car and pressed the pedal to the metal, leaving the taxi far behind.

"Who are those people, Dad? Why don't they leave you alone? You're retired now…," said Ileana annoyed.

"They could be foreign agents, agents from the official intelligence services, journalists, private detectives… It's like a madhouse here, my dear. Everyone watches, listens, records, and photographs everyone, either for blackmail or for the tabloids. My house and garden at Snagov are full of *crickets*. I can't even fart without being recorded. But I don't care anymore…"

"Then the first thing we'll do when we get home is a *general disinsection,*" Ileana decided. "I brought with me a smart *toy* that knows how to find even the most sophisticated systems for intercepting the ambient conversations."

"That's not a bad idea, Ileana! In this way, we will also be able to talk quietly without having an audience."

* * *

August 8, 1991, 8 PM – local time
Snagov

The two weeks had not yet ended when Bebe Gold called General Pleșca and invited him again for a short drive through Snagov forest. After switching on the jamming device, he handed him a thick file on whose cover was written in large Russian letters: *Operation Rasputin - Top Secret.*

"My man could barely procure this damned file, Boss," he said worriedly. "I don't know much Russian, but as far as I understood from the seller, it's about an ultra-secret espionage network deployed on American territory. As long as this file is in your possession, your life is in danger. The country is full of Russian and Moldavian *racketzi* who attack and kill on command. I say you read it and give it back to me. I'll keep it in my company's safe." He took out a pen from his chest pocket and gave it to the General. "The microfilm is in the reservoir. You can wear it in plain sight because it doesn't draw any attention."

"What you say makes me eager to study this file," said General, putting the pen safely in his pocket. "Let's go to my house and I'll give you the rest of the money."

"In a moment, Boss. First, I want to make sure the guy behind isn't following us."

The General looked in the rearview mirror and saw a Jeep with the headlights on.

"Put on your seatbelt, Boss!" Bebe urged him and changed the gear, speeding along the forest track.

He turned onto the national road and, after almost a kilometer, stopped in the parking lot of a gas station. After he was convinced that the Jeep had lost track of them, he returned to the General's house in Snagov.

The front door was open and Pleșca believed Ileana returned from shopping. Cosmin drove her to Bucharest that afternoon. Still, the car was not in the garage. The General called out to her, but no one answered. "Maybe they hadn't returned yet", he thought that in his rush to meet Bebe he probably forgot to lock the door and set the alarm when he left.

He went to the bar in the living room, opened a bottle of Chivas Royal, and poured some whisky into two glasses over ice cubes. He believed it was a good time to celebrate the deal he had just made with Bebe Gold.

"Bebe, boy," said the General, raising the glass. "Good luck! I appreciate very much your efficiency and seriousness in business. Keep up the good work!"

"My motto is: *Our client is our master*," answered Bebe with a sly laugh and took a mouthful of whisky.

The General sat in an armchair, the file in his hand, and started leafing through it impatiently. He spoke Russian fluently after the two years he had spent in Moscow.

"I'll go make some phone calls from my car," Bebe said.

"You can use my phone."

"No, Boss, because I'm talking to some *chicks* who don't answer unless they see my number displayed on their cell phone screen."

Bebe went out whistling merrily, the glass of whisky in his hand, leaving the General alone to read the file. As he got into the car, his cell phone started ringing. Agent Anton, one of the bodyguards employed by his company, was looking for him.

Anton had been ordered to follow Ileana discreetly around town, to make sure she was safe. Just in case, he keeps in touch with the driver Cosmin, by Citizens Band radio.

"Yes, Anton, what happened?" Bebe asked in surprise.

"Boss, we're in trouble! Two masked men have just hijacked the Mercedes that Ileana is in."

"Dammit!", Bebe shot. "Where?"

"On the General Store parking lot in Băneasa. I think they are Timur's men. They suddenly appeared from behind a van with guns in their hands, rushed to the Mercedes and have got into the car, one in front next to the driver and the other in the back next to Ileana. They put the gun to the back of the driver's neck and took over the car."

"Be their tail and report to me where they're going."

"They're heading north. We've just passed by the airport."

"For sure they're coming here in Snagov… Don't lose them! I'll block their way at the entrance of the forest."

Bebe hung up and dialed the phone number of his company's dispatcher. He ordered the secretary:

"Get the free guys and send them to Snagov, urgently. I'm waiting for them here. They need guns and bulletproof vests. Put me in touch with Timur immediately!"

Timur was the founder and manager of a rival company. His employees were mostly Moldavian and Ukrainian *racketzi*, veterans of the Soviet-Afghan war. Bebe had made a very clear deal with Timur. They had divided their territories of influence and pledged, under their word of honor, not to interfere in each other's affairs. Now the whole business seemed like a serious breach of the deal. Once he heard Timur's voice on the loudspeaker, Bebe raged:

"What the hell is going on, boss? Your people jumped the *fence* into my *backyard*!?"

"What you're saying, Bebe? I don't understand…," replied the other.

"General Pleşca's daughter and her driver were kidnapped from a parking lot by your *racketzi*! That's what happened!"

"I don't know anything about this! Those are not my people!"

"Then, who the hell are they?" Bebe retorted impatiently.

"They could be KGB agents. Maybe your General got himself into something…"

"Whoever they are, I'm going to beat the shit out of them," Bebe fumed.

"Be careful… you know they're well trained… Do you want me to send you help?"

"No, thank you, boss, my people and I can handle this. I'm sorry for disturbing your evening."

Bebe started the engine, driving along the alley leading to the forest. He had to create an ambush and the right place for that would be the first bend at the entrance to the forest.

He called Anton again and learned that, as he suspected, the Mercedes in which Ileana and Cosmin were sequestered was heading to Snagov and soon will arrive in the place where he was waiting for they. It was very clear to him that the kidnappers wanted to negotiate with the General.

He stopped the car in the middle of the road, put on his bulletproof vest and made sure his Colt pistol was loaded. He took from the glove compartment two more magazines with cartridges for his gun, turned on the flashing hazard lights, got out of the car, and hid in the ditch beside the road. He remained waiting, trying to pierce with his gaze the shadows of the evening that were slowly turning into darkness.

* * *

August 8, 1991, 8:30 PM – local time
General Virgil Plesca residence, Snagov

The first pages of the Top-Secret file confirmed the General's suspicion that Alexei Leibovich was the name of a citizen who had received approval to emigrate in America and who was replaced by Colonel Igor Vasilievich Zapojnikov, aka *Agent Rasputin*. Zapojnikov's mission was to establish and coordinate an espionage network in the field of high technology, especially American Space technology. There were many details regarding the organization scheme of the espionage network, the meeting places, the retrieval and transmission of information, the conspiratorial names of the agents, the organizations, and the official structures used as cover.

"Damn, this World is too small!" he grumbled, in surprise, seeing that *the brain* of the entire *Rasputin operation* was the KGB General Vladimir Ivanovich Petrovski, one of his former colleagues at the *Frunze Military Academy* in Moscow. As he kept reading the pages with great interest, Virgil couldn't help thinking how much CIA or FBI would pay for that file. But he didn't want money. He wanted to negotiate with them the immunity of his daughter, so she could live her life in peace.

Suddenly, a hoarse voice, with a pronounced Bessarabian accent, came from the door of the living room:

"The reading is over, General. Hands up!"

Virgil Pleșca rise his gaze from the file, in surprise. Two athletic guys in black overalls, with masks on their faces, stood on the threshold, pointing their guns at him. The General immediately understood who the uninvited guests were. He took off his glasses calmly and said, contempt in his voice:

"Who the hell are you, scoundrels, and how dare you break into my house and threaten me?"

"We are the ones who will send you to hell if you don't give us the file, the microfilm, and all your money in the safe, right away," said the same voice.

"I see you don't have bad taste, guys...," replied the General nonchalantly, trying to buy some time. He hoped that Bebe would come back soon. As if guessing his thoughts, the husky voice added:

"No one will come to save you. Your friend left, and your daughter and the driver are in our hands. Listen to this, if you don't believe me." He took out a walkie-talkie from one of his pockets, and put it to his mouth:

"Radio check! Radio check! I am *Pawn One*."

"Go ahead, *Pawn One*," a distorted voice came through the loudspeaker.

"Put the *princesses* on. Her daddy wants to hear her sweet voice. Over!"

The General realized that Ileana and her kidnappers were somewhere nearby, within no more than a kilometer radius of the house. That's about the range of the walkie-talkie type that the masked man had.

"Here's your precious daughter, General," said cynically this one, approached and gave him the transceiver.

Virgil Pleșca picked up the radio and asked, his voice slightly affected:

"Ileana, can you hear me? Are you alright?"

"Yes, Dad, I hear you. I'm fine, we're both fine, me and Cosmin," came immediate his daughter's reply. "They won't let us go unless you give them what they want."

"Yes, I know, don't worry, dear."

General gave back the radio to the masked man in front of him and said sharply:

"You'll only get what you want when my daughter and the driver walk in through the door."

"You are not in the position to put conditions, General!" replied the first masked man. "Give us what we asked for or you'll never see your daughter again."

It's been a long time since he had found himself in such a difficult situation, but he didn't lose his composure. Without hesitation, the General handed to masked men the *Operation Rasputin* file, calmly saying:

"You won, gentlemen!" He then took the pen out of his pocket and add: "The microfilm is inside this pen."

The two masked men were a bit taken aback by how easily the General gave in.

"I keep the money in a diplomatic bag inside of my safe", continued Virgil Plesca in the same calm voice. "I won't give it to you unless you release my daughter."

"We want to see the money first." the masked man outbid, as if he were playing poker.

Thanks to his job in the Securitate, Virgil Pleșca had become a good psychologist. He quickly realized the vulnerability of the two masked men and followed his plan. He walked slowly toward a gorgeous Luchian's anemones painting and took it off the wall thus revealing the safe's metal door.

The General opened it, typing the code without avoiding the curious gaze of the two who were guarding him closely. A *diplomatic bag,* on which many stickers of cartoon characters were pasted, rested inside, with a gun placed on it and a pair of handcuffs attached to the handle. With a quick movement, one of the masked men grabbed the gun before the General could.

"Be careful, it's loaded and the trigger is drawn," the General said evenly. "Try not to shoot yourself."

"Fear not, General, I know how to handle such *toys*. Now, open the bag and don't try to play any tricks!"

The General put the *diplomatic bag* on a coffee table nearby, unlocked it, and lifted the lid. The beautifully stacked 100-dollar bills, with Franklin's face, had a mesmerizing effect on the two masked men who lowered their guns pointed at Pleşca. General took advantage of this.

"As you see, gentlemen, 50,000 USD waiting for you. I have fulfilled all your requests. Now it's your turn to fulfill mine. Please, release my daughter! Once I see her walk in through that door, I'll give you the money," he said, and before the others had any time to react, he quickly attached the loose handcuff to his right wrist and grabbed the bag, so that he could point at them a *Mickey Mouse* sticker stuck on front side of the *diplomatic bag*.

"I'm waiting, gentlemen…", he said patiently, satisfied with the maneuver he had just performed. "You are two, young, strong, armed men. I am old, alone… and helpless. You have nothing to fear."

Pawn One took out the walkie-talkie and tried to contact the others again, but there was no reply. He tried again and again, but in vain.

"What the hell is going on?" he grumbled.

The General thought that maybe the kidnappers could have taken Ileana to another place, further from the house where no longer radio contact. This changes his plan of action.

Suddenly, Bebe Glod's voice through the loudspeaker:

"Attention, folks! Put down your weapons and come out of the house with your hands up! You are surrounded! You have no chance! Your comrades have been annihilated!"

Pawn One and his colleague had a moment of confusion before aiming their guns at the General again:

"The General is our hostage!" shouted one of them. "Leave a car in front of the gate with the engine running and move away! Otherwise, we'll kill him!"

"Let me talk to him," said the General calmly stretching out his hand to *Pawn One* who gave him the walkie-talkie. "Bebe, what's going on? Are Ileana and Cosmin safe? Come in!"

"Yes, Boss! They are right here in front of the gate. We are coming inside now!"

"No, my boy. Don't do this! I've made a bargain with these fellows. I gave them everything they wanted except for the money in the *diplomatic bag*. Once I'll give it to them, they'll release me. That's the deal. Tell your people to withdraw. I can handle this. Over!"

"Roger, Boss! Go ahead! Over!" said Bebe pleased. He knew all about the General's *diplomatic bag*. The case was specially equipped for the anti-terrorist actions of the Securitate. It had two compartments: one above, in which $50,000 were stacked, and another one below, in which a modified Kalashnikov submachine gun with a 30-round 7.62 caliber magazine was installed. The bullets exploded on impact, causing serious injuries. The weapon was to be used in rooms or on planes against terrorists taking hostages. The muzzle of the barrel was masked by a *Mickey Mouse* sticker, and the trigger was secured by a system of levers under the handle of the case so that it could be fired with a simple push of a button.

The General gave back the transceiver to *Pawn One* who looked rather taken aback by the unexpected turn of events. Taking advantage of their brief lack of attention, Pleşca pulled the trigger under the handle of the case, setting off the inferno. He machine-gunned their legs with a short storm of gunfire. Shrapnel and shards of glass flew everywhere. Caught off guard, the two masked men collapsed on the carpet. They tried to use their pistols, but Bebe and his men stormed in alarmed by the sound of gunshots.

In the middle of the living room, General Pleşca looked at the two agents lying on the floor:

"I'm sorry, they asked for it!' he said with a kind of regret. Then he added to Bebe: "We have to recover the file and the pen from them, then take them to their masters…"

Bebe bent down and checked the two masked man. They had injured legs and were bleeding heavily. They needed urgent medical care. He asked for the medical kit in his car. After dressing their wounds, Bebe ordered his men:

"Put all the gang in their van and take them to the Soviet Embassy. I have no doubt they are all Soviet agents. Leave the car parked in front of the gate with the hazard lights on and the engine running and disappear quickly."

Ileana came in flustered. She ran to the General who was still in the middle of the room with the diplomatic bag handcuffed by his right hand.

"I'm very sorry, Dad!" she said wrapping her arms around him. "If I had the slightest idea about this, I wouldn't have left."

"The stakes are very high, my dear. It looks like we disturbed a sleeping bear. Tomorrow, we will go to the *Armenian Church* together. I will make a call right now to set up a meeting with *Father Fabian*."

* * *

August 23, 1991
Elias Hospital, Bucharest

General Virgil Pleșca was hospitalized in an intensive care unit of the Elias Hospital, where usually, during the Communist regime, only the top Party members, and their family and friends were treated. He felt worse and called the Ambulance. Ileana had postponed her departure to the United States to stay with him. The doctors told them that both his liver and lungs were covered by cancer. The General's days were numbered. Although he was only her adoptive father, Ileana loved him like a true daughter.

After she graduated from the Securitate School and became an officer, she addressed him with *Boss*, because she felt the official subordination relationship even in the family's intimacy. It was only after the Revolution that she started calling him *Daddy* again, as she did as a child. Her entire childhood education revolved around the unconditional attachment to the Communist system. She had learned many poems about the

Communist Party and the achievements of Socialism, which she used to recite at various celebrations to glorify the totalitarian political regime.

Many times, however, Ileana had conflicting feelings, especially after becoming an adult, when she understood that her parents and grandfather fought as partisans in the mountains and were killed by the Securitate. She ended up in an orphanage, and by the will of fate, she was adopted by the family of a Securitate officer. She often wondered, though, if her adoptive father hadn't been the one who killed her natural parents.

Sometimes she was totally confused and didn't know what to do next. During the negotiation that took place at the American Embassy, after the General handed over the microfilm of the *Operation Rasputin* file to the FBI representative in exchange for his daughter's immunity on American territory, Ileana received a very attractive proposal: to join the fight against the drug and human trafficking at the newly established FBI office in Bucharest. Ileana was stunned and asked for some time to think about it, although the General urged her to accept this extraordinary offer at once.

Ileana was sitting next to her father's bed. He had his eyes closed and was breathing hard through an oxygen mask. It was difficult for her to believe that a man so full of energy was now only a few steps away from death. The General opened his eyes, and, grabbing Ileana's hand, said softly:

"My girl, I'm sorry for wasting your time with me… I'm an old fool who's done a lot of wrong things in my life. I don't deserve your care… Please forgive me for what I'm about to confess to you now… and don't hate me… I won't have the chance to tell you again…"

As if gathering his last strength, the General continued:

"You must know, my girl… I was in command of the platoon that killed your real parents back there in the mountains. They were with a group of partisans who had barricaded themselves in a cave. We attacked them when they ran out of ammunition… Your mother took you in her arms and wanted to run away and hide at the bottom of the cave… A soldier threw a grenade behind her. She felt riddled with shrapnel. She protected you with her body… You were miraculously unharmed… Your mother gave her life for you… She was still alive when I found her. With her last strength, she said: *Mister Officer, please, take care of my girl! Her name is Ileana… She is innocent…* Your mother died holding you close to her chest… I hardly got her hands off your body. I took you to an orphanage as required by law at the time, and then my wife, who could not have children, adopted you under her maiden name… Popescu… You looked like an angel… You had blue eyes like the clear sky and golden hair… You were incredibly dear to us and brought happiness into our life… Please, forgive me…"

Ileana burst into tears. She didn't know if she was crying for her dead parents, killed a long time ago in the mountains by the Securitate, or for the one who had ordered their assassination and was now lying on the hospital bed.

"I only have one last wish…," said the General.

"Anything, Dad…", Ileana answered between sobs.

"I want to make my last confession to a priest… while I am still conscious. Before I die, I want to be relieved of the terrible sins I have committed… I want to be buried in the Christian law of my forefathers, though I have greatly offended God throughout my whole life…"

"I understand, Dad. I'll ask them if there is a priest in the hospital who provides religious assistance to the sick..."

By strange coincidence, just when Ileana was about to leave, a young priest came into the room, a small leather bag in his hand.

"God blesses!" he said, somewhat surprised to find Ileana there. Then he gently said: "I've been guided to this room. I usually visit terminally ill patients in the first part of the day."

Surprised by his appearance, Ileana told him that her father wanted to make a confession. The priest asked the young woman to wait outside for a few minutes, and she turned to the General:

"I'll leave you with the priest, Dad. I'll come back when you're done."

Ileana waited in the hall for more than ten minutes when she started getting nervous and went out, into the inner courtyard, to smoke a cigarette. There she noticed a black BMW parked in front of the central pavilion and a man wearing sunglasses talking on the cell phone installed inside the car. Out of reflex, Ileana pulled out the multichannel scanner she always carried in her bag and tried to intercept the conversation by scanning the frequency used by NMT mobile telephony. She managed to hear the end of the conversation which sounded strange:

"Apply the final solution and hand over the tape with the entire recording immediately!"

"Roger, sir!"

Ileana flinched. She realized that the *"priest"* who was with the General was an agent who wanted to record his latest revelations. She put out the cigarette and hurried to her father's room. The door was locked from the inside. Without a second thought, she took a step back and kicked the door open. The "*priest*" startled, a syringe in his hand as he was about to inject a substance into *the infusion bag* hanging close to her father's bed. She rushed to him and snatched the syringe from his hand, shouting:

"You bastard, I will kill you!"

She knocked him flat and punched him in the face several times. Alarmed by the noise, two nurses rushed into the room, looking frightened at the broken door and at the priest lying on the floor with his mouth full of blood.

"Call the Police!" Ileana urged them, meeting their confused looks. "This bastard wanted to kill my father! I believe he already managed to inject poison into *the IV bag!* Please, stop the perfusion!"

One of the nurses quickly replaced the bag and offered to take the suspicious syringe to the laboratory for analysis.

"No, thank you! I'll take it to a specialized laboratory myself," Ileana said. "It is very important evidence!"

She grabbed the fake priest's bag and rummaged inside, taking out a small tape player still recording. Putting it close to the man's mouth, she fumed:

"Who sent you to do this, you fucking bastard?"

"The devil, lady! The devil in person sent me!" he muttered.

The man with sunglasses from the BMW appeared at the threshold, impatiently and Ileana immediately realized that the "*priest*" had a transmitter under his cassock and that all the sounds background in the room had been listened to by this individual. He took out an ID card, and said with an air of superiority:

"I am Police Commissioner Avramescu. This man is an impostor. I have been following him for a long time. He will go with me to the Police Station. Please, hand over that tape with the illegal recording."

"No!" Ileana said flatly. "I will personally hand it over to the Romanian Information Service. It may contain classified information. You know, my father was a Securitate General."

Hearing this, the so-called commissioner lost his momentum.

"Yes, I understand… As you wish, madam, as you wish…," he replied stiffly.

"In any case, I will file a complaint about imposture and attempted murder. And I'm going to have this substance verified in a special laboratory," she said, lifting the syringe. "Now, please, identify this man in the presence of the nurses, as a witness, so that I know who I am filing the complaint about."

The "*commissioner*" helped the "*priest*" get up on his feet and asked him to identify himself half-heartedly.

"What documents do you need? I am a servant of the Lord…," he said, still spitting blood.

To impress the assistance in the room, the "*commissioner*" handcuffed the "*priest*" saying:

"We are going to the Police Station, and we will make sure you tell us everything you know." He took him to the car, and they hurriedly left the hospital yard.

Ileana understood that very dangerous things were happening in Romania. It was like a nightmare. She didn't know who to trust anymore. She turned on the scanner, hoping it would capture another phone conversation from the BMW. Her wait was rewarded shortly when she heard the voice of the man who introduced himself as the police commissioner. He was giving explanations, probably to his boss. From what she understood, the fault for their mission's failure was Ileana, who ruined their plan. No one knew she could fight.

The general was still conscious and understanding what had happened, said in a low voice.

"My dear, my life doesn't matter anymore. I'm dying anyway. But you are young and have a whole future ahead. You can change something; you can do better things than I did. That's why you should accept *Father Fabian*'s proposal. You need someone to protect you, an *umbrella* to shield you from this *heavy rain*. But you must know… once you enter this *game*, there is no way back."

"I know, Dad. You're right. What happened today made me decide. I'm going to accept their proposal. I'll call the FBI office here in Romania right this evening."

Adrian Grigore
2024, August, *Bucharest-Măgurele*

Instead of an Epilogue

Years later,
Fragment from an alternative History of Romania textbook

"In December 1989, a *coup d'état* masked by a strong popular revolt against Ceaușescu's regime took place in Romania. According to the most recent data provided by the Institute for the Investigation of the Crimes of Communism, the events of December 1989 resulted in a total of 5,205 victims, of which 1,116 died and 4,089 were injured. According to several researchers, the victims did not appear because of the repression of the Communist regime until 12 o'clock on December 22, when the Ceaușescu couple fled by helicopter.

To this, it was added the "*incompletely elucidated terrorist phenomenon*" that led to the death of over 1,000 Romanian citizens during the following days. The self-proclaimed leaders of the time, who pretended to be "*the emanations of the revolution*" using national television, sought to manipulate, scare the population with so-called terrorists, and cause chaos to seize power more easily.

The new power maintained a state of uneasiness and a sense of danger so that it could act freely, either by keeping the people in their homes or by making them rush to their aid by risking their own lives. It was nothing more than a well-directed movie based on a carefully written screenplay. However, these manipulations come to light years later.

Evidence is still being sought that communist activist, people from the structures of the former political police, as well as from the Army - acted as terrorists at the behest of the new rulers and various Generals, in order to eliminate the anti-communist radicals or to create the impression of fighting a hidden, powerful enemy alongside the citizens. They used, among other things, flamethrower simulators, agents of influence to spread false information to scare the population, and snipers hidden in buildings who fired into the crowd, selectively killing the most ardent revolutionaries.

Nicolae Ceauşescu and his wife Elena were arrested in Târgovişte and were shot, right on Christmas Day 1989, after a mock criminal trial, carried out according to a Bolshevik ritual. The crime committed on this Holy Day was the first ***red alert signal*** to the Romanian people that their country was on the wrong path.

The neo-communists - the Communist backup echelon and the former officers of the secret services - managed to seize the entire political and economic power of the country shortly.

During that time, many social convulsions, demonstrations, and counter-protests divided the population into hostile groups due to the antagonistic political views. Workers and peasants were instigated against the intelligentsia, parents against children, and children against parents.

Everything culminated with the so-called "***Mineriada***" from June 14-15, 1990 when over ten thousand coal miners from the Jiu Valley were brought to Bucharest to punish the opponents of the neo-communist regime in power. It was a borderline situation that could degenerate into a civil war. Everything was a real nightmare. The miners devastated the University, the Institute of Architecture, and the headquarters of the Opposition, raped and injured innocent citizens. There were over 100 deaths – unofficially, and over 1,000 wounded.

Following this massacre and destruction, President Ion Iliescu thanked the miners among other things: *"for the response of worker solidarity"* and for demonstrating of *"high civic discipline."* This was one of his major political mistakes who isolated Romania for a long time and kept strategic investors away.

Frightened by the excessive aggressiveness of the miners, infiltrated by former Securitate agents, many Romanians sought political asylum in Western countries, in those times of sad remembrance.

"Infested" by the private companies of the politicians and their relatives, the economy of Romania collapsed soon, which led to the impoverishment of the population. The riches of the country had been given as concessions or sold at ridiculous prices by corrupt politicians. In the years that followed, millions of Romanian citizens emigrated in search of a better life. Many valuable researchers, doctors, teachers, engineers, and top specialists also took the path of self-exile. Romania became increasingly indebted and entered a long and painful transition period, thus compromising the standard and the quality of life of its citizens."

www.ingramcontent.com/pod-product-compliance
Lightning Source LLC
Chambersburg PA
CBHW031156131224
18930CB00041B/289